THE MADONNA ROSA

BOOK #6 - THE JUNO LETTERS

SECOND EDITION

L.W. HEWITT

Contents

DEDICATION

The sinking of the *HMT Lancastria* on 17 June 1940 in the Loire estuary near Saint-Nazaire is at once the largest loss of maritime life in England's history and perhaps the least known, overshadowed by the fall of France and the evacuations at Dunkirk. Nearly one-third of all casualties of the British Expeditionary Force came from those who died at Saint-Nazaire - two weeks after Dunkirk.

The Madonna Rosa is dedicated to those who died, those who survived, and those who stood tall and sacrificed in ways great and small to help others.

Sherwood Foresters -the photograph from Chapter 18. Scott Fitch (far right, with gloves) and George Sherrat (tall, standing next to Scott); from the story. (6) The characters as named are fictitious.

DISCLAIMER AND CREDITS

This is a work of fiction. Although the context of the novel is based on known events, license has been taken to fit the story. The characters and situations are creations of the author's imagination. Any resemblance to persons or historical events is strictly circumstantial. Technical information where not attributed is either freely available from public sources or imaginary.

Cover Photo:
© Can Stock Photo Inc.

Back Cover Illustration: Public domain photograph

THE BLOOD ROSE

There is the rose, in which the
divine word became flesh.
- Dante, Divine Comedy, Vol 3, Paradise

February, 1793; Duchy of Brittany

"The king is dead!" The messenger fell to his knees, gasping for breath. "Beheaded in Place de la Concorde!"

Gaspard Persin read the dispatch, then tossed it into the roaring fire. He called for his guard.

"They will come for us. We must hurry."

Panic swept through the old Breton nobility. Angry mobs had stormed the Bastille and forced concessions from the king. When the royals fled the mobs for Austria they were apprehended and dragged back to Paris - forced to accept an abomination they dared call a constitution. Despite the revolution nobles in the countryside still maintained their iron grip over the peasantry.

But this - the execution of the king! An affront against God! Who would be next?

The following morning a train of carriages waited in the courtyard, a misty-gray shroud obscuring the countryside. Dressed in drab clothing, three noble families descended from the ancient House of Montfort loaded their possessions and a small collection of treasures and rolled through the gates, escorted by a small guard and a party of priests. A ship waited for them at Vannes, bound for England. A sizable ransom paid to a wealthy merchant ensured their safe passage. What awaited them in England was anyone's guess.

"Father, why do these people hate us so? Why do we wear these rude clothes and hide like thieves?"

"Do not be afraid, little one. Where we are going, the people understand the rule of a king. The rabble will bring France and Brittany to its knees, and we will return once again. No man can stand before the power of a king. It is God's will."

They hurried as fast as the sturdy draft horses could trot until forced to stop to wait for the ferry at the River La Vilaine.

"I will seek out the ferryman."

A priest entered a cottage at the river crossing but found no one. He walked over to the ferry tied to the river bank and looked around.

THWAP!

An arrow pierced his chest, and he fell forward without a sound into the water, the red blood mixing with the slow meandering river.

"Father? Father?"

One of the drivers dismounted and followed after the priest toward the cottage. He stopped for a moment, unbelieving, as the body of the priest floated down the river.

THWAP!

"Aaugh!" he cried out in pain, an arrow piercing his shoulder. The others looked up at his cry.

"Bandits!" came a cry from one of the carriages.

The men and the priests took whatever cover they could find and desperately tried to arm themselves. Swords drawn, the caravan guard crouched in a protective circle around the women, children, and a handful of servants. With a volley of arrows all but one of the guards fell.

A little servant girl screamed and ran toward the woods, her mother crying after her. The woman fell forward, an arrow through her chest.

"Now!"

The remaining guard heard the call, and looked in horror as a dozen men armed with crude swords swept out from the woods, pouncing on the train. In a moment he faced five men with swords and died with the first blow. The attackers then turned on the others.

Within minutes all was quiet. One of the attackers returned from the woods dragging the small child by the hair and threw her among the dead bodies.

"I will take this one for my slave. She can wash my clothes until she is old enough to bed."

The thieves laughed and joked amongst themselves as they pulled apart the carts.

"Well, what have we here? Look at this!"

One of the men pulled a long courtier's dress from a trunk and paraded it in front of the others.

"Who gets the dress? Your wife … or your mistress?"

The man laughed.

"Neither one! Neither deserves a dress as fine as this! Time to find a new mistress - or better yet, a new wife!"

From the head cart, the leader of the thieves cried out.

"Muskets! Hah!" laughed Emile Rochére. "Thomas, you are lucky you did not get a lead ball shot through your fat stomach! And look - powder and shot."

They continued to divide the spoils when Emile noticed a loose plank in the floor of one of the carts.

"Aah … they have something to hide!"

He pulled back the wooden plank and a collective gasp spread through the band. A bag of gold coins lay hidden beneath. A wrapping of fine cloth held ornate necklaces with jewels worth a lifetime of toil in the fields.

"Who were these generous people? Nobles, or merchants perhaps? There is enough wealth here to feed even that fat ugly wife of yours, Pierre - maybe even for an entire winter!"

The men howled with delight as they apportioned the spoils of the hidden treasure trove equally among them. These men had been peasants of the nobility before the soldiers came two seasons past and confiscated their winter stores. They took to stealing to feed their families.

None knew the value of the items they claimed, only that this winter they were certain to eat.

"And what else do we have here?"

Emile pulled out a small wooden box from the secret trove and placed it on the ground before the men.

"A plain wooden box. So what?"

"Hiding with all these baubles? Let us have a look."

"Perhaps gold, or more jewels?"

"Maybe tobacco?"

"God help me, I hope so!"

Emile pried open the lid and lifted it off. Something lay in the box wrapped in a thick woolen cloth.

"Pull it out, Emile. Let us see."

He lifted the object from the box, unwrapped the wool covering … and fell to his knees.

"Blessed be the saint!"

He bowed his head and crossed himself frantically. Shaken, Emile slowly backed away. When the others saw what he uncovered they too fell to the ground and bowed their heads.

Finally, Emile found the courage to speak.

"Go and bring the priest."

The men sat in fearful silence, a fragrance of wild roses wafting in the gentle breeze.

Chapter 1

HMT Lancastria

War is a series of catastrophes that results in a victory.
- George Clemenceau

Present Day, Paris

"What is this? You think this is your private office?"

Marcel Carré knew if he fussed long enough I would feel compelled to purchase a bottle of wine and share it with him. Le Café Reuban Vert was busy this morning and Marcel had his daughter Monique waiting tables.

"Oh, Papa, leave Monsieur Larry alone."

I knew I could count on Monique to run interference for me and keep the coffee flowing. Once I broke down under Marcel's incessant pressure and started drinking wine my day would be shot.

I had returned to Paris late the previous evening with the stack of folders Sid gave me in England and managed to get some sleep at my hotel before wandering into my favorite café. I placed the files on the table and just stared at them, unsure where to start.

"M. Larry, what did you bring in today?"

Monique sat in the opposite chair and sipped a cup of strong French coffee.

"I have an interesting task, Monique. You may like this one."

"*Vraitment?* How so?"

"My friend Sid - I told you about him - he left me these folders. They are stories he wants me to look at, stories from his past."

"Let me see … ," and she reached for the first folder in the stack. "As your legal counsel - unofficial of course - have you anything in writing giving you permission to have these?"

"No, and I won't be getting that any time soon, I'm afraid. Sid passed away a short time ago. He left these with me just before he died."

She frowned.

"Without proper documentation, you may have some liability issues … especially if you return them to the states when you go home, M. Larry."

When she was not bussing tables at her father's café, the beguiling Monique studied law at the university. Several times before I had relied upon her to help me break an impasse. She was perhaps the smartest person I knew in Paris.

"Then I'll just have to stay."

She gave me a look, and took a quick glance through the top file.

"I will review the legal issues for you, of course … hmm, have you looked through this file?"

"No, I haven't had the time yet. I was going to start today."

She remained unusually quiet for a few minutes as she flipped through the folder and some of the internal documents.

"At some point, if you follow this information with your usual diligence, you will need my assistance. I have finals next week - just keep that in mind."

She smiled and jumped up just as her father stormed out of the kitchen.

"Monique! I have orders up! Unless that lazy American is buying the wine, we have work to do!"

"*Bon chance*, M. Larry. I think you will need it!" and she left the folder closed on the table. I picked it up and looked at the folder tab - it was labeled:

Madonna Rosa

The file consisted of two stacks of documents stapled together. The first stack contained what at first glance appeared to be a page of nonsensical notes. As I read through the gibberish I realized I was looking at some sort of hand-written code. The words themselves had no identifiable meaning. Buried in this riddle were comments he obviously didn't want anyone else to read. I remembered once about a secret he had told me - to never write down anything that could implicate you. Instead, find a key to create your own private code. Beneath the last of these coded notes was a name:

Anisette Durande

Attached to the coded document was a sealed envelope. I carefully sliced open the top being careful to not disturb the contents - perhaps a fragile letter or a brittle dried flower, hidden for years, ready to disintegrate with the slightest breath. Instead, inside was a small round disk, a sort of bleached-red fiber. A small hole in the top of the disc indicated it was meant to be held on a lanyard or keychain. Letters stamped on the face, faded with time, revealed a name:

FITCH, STF, 4978618, C

I assumed this was a military tag, but not the familiar "dog tag" of an American GI. A quick check online confirmed this to be one of two identity discs the British issued to soldiers - one green and octagonal, strung on a standard issue 38-inch cotton cord; the other red, round, connected to the green disk by a small cotton string. This disk belonged to a soldier named "Fitch" with the initials "STF", service number "4978618", and his religion indicated by the "C" for Congregationalist.

"OK, soldier Fitch. Just who the hell are you?"

Fortunately, this question proved all too easy to answer. I typed "British Army service number registry" into my browser. The first link was to the "Forces War Records" website where I could search World War II personnel records based on the name. I typed in what I had - Fitch, S - and browsed through the return list. On page 5 was the record I was after:

> Scott Thomas Fitch, #4978618, Private,
> Record Year 1939,
> 1 Bn Sherwood Foresters (1)

Scott Thomas Fitch of the First Battalion Sherwood Foresters Rifles served in the British Expeditionary Force (BEF) in France. His record began in 1939, and in 1940 his unit fled the German breakout in the chaotic retreat best known for the Miracle of Dunkirk.

I wasn't so surprised to learn Private Scott Fitch had not survived the war, but why his ID tag showed up in the file intrigued me. What was his identity disc - just the red one - doing in Sid's file if his body was unaccounted for? Typically the red disk would have been removed from a body and turned in to military authorities; the green one remained with the body for processing. A body with only the green tag was one already reported.

Scott Fitch was recorded as "Missing in action; presumed dead."

16 June 1940

The lorry driver stopped alongside the road and pulled out a crude map. The soldiers crammed in the back jumped down to stretch their legs.

"Where do you think we are, Georgie?"

"Hell if I know. Ain't been no German planes since this mornin', that's all I give a rip about."

Private George Sherrat, First Battalion Sherwood Foresters Rifles, looked up in the sky, satisfied no German fighters were ready to pounce on them, then opened the fly of his pants. He smiled as he pissed into the ditch.

"Damn, I needed that! Hey, Scotty, there's a sign post over there, knocked down. Take a look."

Scott Fitch, age 22, was a year older than his friend George. Both had joined their home regiment and trained together. Scotty came from a working class family with roots in Sherwood back hundreds of years. George was a loner who claimed he had no family. He and Scotty became friends over bitters in a local pub - different as oil and water.

They shipped off to France all piss and vinegar, ready to whip the Nazis and push them out of the Low Counties - Scotty for love of country, George for the adventure. Now they were fleeing for their lives, cut off from the British Expeditionary Force that withdrew toward the channel at Dunkirk, heading south toward the Brittany coast. In the chaos they had lost most of their gear, including their rifles. They shared a single rucksack, lucky to have even a change of clothes and a coat.

They had been ordered to Brest, but the Germans began bombing the convoys as they coalesced near the port and had damaged the quay severely. They received orders to turn east and head for Saint-Nazaire.

"It says 'PONTCHATEAU' on one side, and 'REDON' on the other."

"Which way is which?"

"How the hell would I know? The sign was knocked down, for Christ's sake!"

"I think we just passed through Redon."

The driver got out of the cab and spread his map across the ground. A subtle fragrance of wild roses hung in the afternoon stillness.

"Damn, I don't know where we are. This map ain't got 'Redon' on it. Seems we should be going south to the coast, but I don't even know if this road is on the map."

As the men gathered around, a young woman appeared from the woods on the far side. Georgie saw her immediately.

"Wow! Look at her!"

She quickly crossed the road carrying what looked like a baby wrapped in a gray woolen blanket in her arms.

"Monsieur, monsieur, please, please!"

"Oh, no, not me! No, mademoiselle, no! We cannot take your baby. Oh, hell, Scotty. Not again. We ain't no damn baby service."

"Monsieur, no, it is not my child. Please."

"Well, it sure as hell ain't mine!" and he pushed her away.

"Ask her the way to Saint-Nazaire!" the driver interrupted.

Scotty reached out and gently touched the woman's arm.

"Mademoiselle, Saint-Nazaire?"

"Pardon, monsieur? Saint-Nazaire?"

She looked back behind her in a panic, irritated.

"Oui. Yes. Where is Saint-Nazaire?"

Exasperated, she quickly pointed down the right junction road.

"Saint-Nazaire. *C'est direction* … Pontchateau, Besné, Saint-Nazaire."

"OK, boys. Got it. Let's go!" called the driver.

"Come on, Scotty."

"No, please, monsieur. I helped you, now you must help me. Take this with you. You must keep this safe. It is very important."

She thrust the bundle in his arms and frantically looked back up the road.

"What is it, Scotty?"

"Don't rightly know, mate." He pulled back the covering. "A statue of some sort."

"Oui, monsieur. La Madonna. Please. You must take it with you. Do not let the Germans have it. Oh, please!"

The beautiful young woman's frantic voice told Scotty this was no ordinary figurine. What was so important about this?

"Many have died today to protect her. It will be lost in darkness forever if you do not help me."

Scotty rewrapped the artifact carefully in the woolen cloth as tears streamed down the woman's cheeks.

"*Merci, merci.* Go with God."

She reached up and kissed him on the cheek. Scotty watched her turn away, then called out, "Mademoiselle, wait. Wait!"

She stopped on the side of the road and he hurried to her. The driver of the lorry blasted his horn for him to get aboard.

"Here. This is who I am," and he took his pocketknife out of his pants pocket and cut off his red-fiber identity disc and handed it to her. "I will keep it safe, and will get it back to you, somehow. I promise. What is your name … your name?"

"Anisette, monsieur. Anisette Durande. Merci, monsieur," and she stuffed the disk in her apron pocket and took off at a run back into the woods. Scotty walked back and joined George, holding the wrapped object in his arms.

"Really? Your ID tag? The red one to boot?"

"I still have the green one."

"Red mens dead, Scotty boy. Well, maybe she'll look us up after the war … she's a betty!"

"For god's sake, Georgie," Scotty chided him. "We're runnin' from the Germans for our lives and you're still thinking about pretty girls."

"Well, we ain't dead yet. Anisette Durande. Scotty boy, that's a name to remember!"

Scotty looked back in the direction she ran.

Anisette Durande.

He stuffed the figurine wrapped in the woolen cloth into George's rucksack just as gunfire erupted in the direction the woman ran. The driver gunned the truck down the road towards Saint-Nazaire just as German planes began to arrive once more in the skies above Brittany.

"Captain Sharp, how many can you hold?"

The young lieutenant approached the captain on the bridge of the *HMT Lancastria*. Captain Sharp looked out on a long line of small transport vessels overflowing with men, women, and children steaming out from Saint-Nazaire to the ship anchored eighteen kilometers offshore.

"About three thousand, at a pinch."

"You'll have to take more, Captain. As many as can fit."

"We have life jackets for only about 2,200, Lieutenant. And a limited number of lifeboats."

"It cannot be helped, Captain. There are thousands waiting back onshore."

"What's going on? Is this capitulation?"

"Good god, Captain! Don't say that!"

Overhead precious few British Hurricane fighters patrolled the slightly overcast skies. German planes had attacked other ships assisting in the evacuation but so far there were no significant casualties. Troops streamed aboard all morning.

"Hell, Scotty. We're jammed in here like cordwood. What a mess."

George wormed his way through the maze of legs, torsos, and packs scattered around the deck. He carried the rucksack with their meager belongings and the beautiful woman's precious Madonna on a strap slung over his shoulder.

"The sergeant wants us to go below decks, George." George had grabbed him and slipped past the soldiers writing down the names of those boarding and avoided getting stuck below.

"Not me, Scotty boy. Let the ol' sarge find me in this mess. I'm stayin' on deck. Hotter n' hell below, you can be sure. An' what happens in a few hours - the smell! Not for me. I'll take the fresh air."

"And German machine guns," warned Scotty. He would stay with his friend George even though he feared strafing Messerschmitts more than his smelly comrades.

"How many more blokes they gonna cram on this here ship? I say we get the hell out o' here."

They worked their way through two sleeping soldiers for a spot near the rail, upwind of the mass of bodies.

"Bet you're never gonna ride a ship as fine as this again, Scotty boy. One of them fancy ocean liners, this one is. Maybe they're gonna serve us tea and crumpets."

"More like bully beef and swill-water, Georgie. This is no pleasure cruise."

"Too bad that betty didn't come with us. Wow, was she a looker or what? And you - gettin' her name and all. I didn't think you had it in you, boy!" He slapped his friend on the back. "What was her name again?"

Scotty looked shyly down, embarrassed by the antics of his friend.

"Her name was Anisette."

"Anisette. That's a pretty name, for a beautiful woman. Be worth lookin' her up after we win this here war, Scotty boy. Take that wooden figure back, and you might just get lucky!"

"Shut up, George."

As they watched, the steady stream of boats trickled to a few. A pilot boat diverted the remaining boats to another ship anchored further inland in the shallow estuary. They were loaded full - too full.

George had been right - at least the breeze coming off the water kept them cool pressed up against the outer railing. George lay napping against the rucksack. Scotty carefully opened the side pouch so not to wake George and removed a small tin box carefully sealed with heavy cloth packing tape - letters from home, cherished slices of a life he now could only dream about.

He removed a blank piece of paper and began to write.

> We drove south to the coast to make port. George thinks its great fun. I am scared.

> I met a remarkable woman. She was beautiful, but terribly frightened. She helped us find Saint-Nazaire.

> Her name was Anisette.

I might never get to mail this.

He wrapped the tape back around the tin box and placed it back in the side pouch.

CHAPTER 2

DESCENT

Must helpless man, in ignorance sedate,
Roll darkling down the torrent of his fate?
- Samuel Johnson

1350 Hours

"Captain, look! Stukas!"

Out of the early afternoon sky the lookout heard the unmistakable whine of a diving Stuka JU87. A squadron of Messerschmitts attacked the British fighter cover allowing the slower dive bombers to nose over and set their sights on the nearby Orient liner, the *Oronsay*. A direct hit shattered the liner's bridge, killing several of the crew. The liner listed to port as its crew frantically worked to keep the ship afloat.

"Raise the *Havelock*, Number One. We need to leave harbor with those planes overhead, but need an escort."

The destroyers *HMS Havelock* and *Highlander* were there to provide protection from German U-boats, but remained oddly silent. Without an escort Captain Sharp knew the *Lancastria* would be a sitting duck. He decided to wait.

1548 Hours

"Damn, Scotty. Them German planes look like fireflies from down here. A hit on deck an' a lot of these boys is gonna die."

As the two soldiers watched the aerial dance above, a squadron of JU87s nosed over and began their dive toward the port waters, the scream from their air brakes building in a frightening crescendo. A single Stuka pulled up and turned straight for the stern of the *Lancastria*. Scotty watched in morbid fascination as four bombs fell from the Stuka's undercarriage and began their agonizingly slow descent, unable to run in the morass of men on the deck. The first smashed *Lancastria* full in the stern, the shudder knocking the men to the deck. Then in sudden succession three more struck, one down the ship's funnel.

The blast blew bodies over the top of him, the wave of dead men shielding him partially from the force of the blast. In an instant there was no sound, no motion. Just silence.

"Clear away the life boats." Chief Officer Harry Grattidge grabbed a megaphone and bellowed frantically from the bridge to the men on deck below, the voice piercing through the void. "Clear away the boats now, your attention please, clear away the boats."

"Scotty! Are you OK, mate?" George shook Scotty by the shoulders.

"Georgie," was all he could say.

"You there ... ," the voice called to him, "loosen that line! Get that boat in the water!"

George cleared the line securing a lifeboat from its cleat and started to lower the boat to the water. Scotty followed him, mechanically, trying to grasp what was happening around him, stunned from the blast.

Men tried to jump to safety from the fires on deck. As they hit the water feet first, the force of the lifejacket jamming upward with the impact broke their necks, their lifeless bodies bobbing like corks in the waves.

Scotty felt Georgie's strong hands grab him by his field jacket and lift him over the ship's gunwale.

"Go! Go!" George cried out as he lowered Scotty by his arms into the lifeboat, now three meters below him. Two soldiers who had slipped down a free rope into the boat grabbed him by the legs to keep him from falling. Scotty grabbed desperately for George's hands.

"George! Come on. Now!"

He tried to reach for George, but he lost his grip. George lunged for him, catching his hand in his identity disc lanyard. It broke off in his hand as Scotty fell away.

George tossed the rucksack overboard as the liner quivered and shook violently, listing suddenly to starboard. George grabbed the gunwale railing as he rose with the dying ship.

"Scotty! Scotty!"

He disappeared as the ship began a slow roll.

The men on the lifeboat ropes let go and the boat dropped the final meter into the sea, almost capsizing. Heavy bunker oil from *Lancastria's* ruptured fuel tanks spread quickly around the sinking liner. German planes continued to attack; one dropped incendiary bombs to ignite the floating viscous ooze.

A pair of fighters screamed in just above sea level, their machine guns raking the heaving deck. Men scrambled in all directions to escape the deadly fire as blood and body parts flew into a thousand pieces around them. One of the men on the oars of the lifeboat exploded into a mist of blood and gore next to Scotty, his body flying out of the lifeboat, disappearing into a black-red mass of oil and blood on the water. Another man grabbed the oar and they frantically pulled away from the listing liner.

Georgie. Georgie, where are you?

He couldn't scream, he couldn't shout. Scotty stared in shock, numb to the carnage around him. Where was Georgie?

"Stop! Help me! Help me!" The shouts carried across the oily waters as the wounded floated, dying. Thousands of helpless men crawled across the doomed liner's overturned hull. Thousands more remained trapped below decks. Hands reached up out of the black ooze grabbing at the lifeboat, threatening to overturn it.

"Ditch your pack, mate. Make room for one more." The voice seemed distant, removed. Someone tried to grab the rucksack he clung to but he simply shoved him away.

A great splash on the starboard side of the lifeboat was followed by a giant blast that lifted the boat in the air, splitting the hull in two. Blown upward by the explosion, Scotty gazed helplessly as he plunged back into the bloody sludge that was once water. Another great flash, then all was quiet, bathed in darkness. He floated in a perfect void, surrounded by a cold enveloping darkness, the haunting strains of "There'll Always Be An England" drifting in and out of his consciousness.

The sea around them filled with small craft and tugs of all kinds fishing the living from the water. The dead were left to float, alone.

18 June 1940

He drifted amidst the steady pulsing of the engines, monotonous, mechanical, rhythmic. When he was winched on board the *SS Oronsay*, covered with bunker oil, bleeding from shrapnel wounds, he was barely conscious, numb from the cold water. His lungs stabbed at him as he tried to breathe. Patches of burned flesh peeled from his chest, face, and arms. The cries of the wounded, the men clinging to flotsam in the water, a chorus - surreal, distant. Now the chaos, the death - all drowned within the unrelenting cadence of the engines.

"We're out of morphine," was all Scotty could hear in the confused blackness around him. Even when they turned him and cleaned when he soiled himself, unable to move, he did not cry out. He just lay and prayed to join his friend George. He could no longer endure the suffocating heat, the foul air below decks, the pounding rhythm.

Georgie. Where are you, Georgie?

He saw his friend George as he clung to the railing of the ship, then disappeared.

"Scotty! Scotty!"

He heard his friend's words over and over as he lay there waiting to die, to dissolve into the void.

But I promised her, Georgie. To return the Madonna. I promised her.

A corpsman hovered close over him.

"This one's still alive. No ID disc."

"What's he saying?" another asked.

He put his ear closer to the soldier's face.

"He's sayin', 'Her name was Anisette.'"

"Who the hell is that?"

"Papa! Papa! *Vite*! Come quickly!"

The young boy ran frantically up the beach waving his hands. His father, sanding the gunwale of a small fishing dory, stood and called out to his boy.

"What is it, Leone? I have work to do!"

"Papa, it is a soldier. In the water. Come quickly!"

His father dropped his sanding block and followed his little boy back down the beach. About eighty meters further he spotted a dark shape in the tidal fringe, rocking slowly back and forth in the waves rolling up the shallow beach.

"*Mon dieu*," he gasped, and crossed himself. "Leone, get your bicycle and fetch the priest. And tell no one else of this, do you understand?"

"Oui, Papa," and the boy ran off toward their cottage and headed for the nearby commune of Pornic.

"Father, we cannot let the Boche or the police see this. They will sweep through the village looking for other soldiers. It is not safe."

Father Pierpont said a prayer over the body of the soldier as the men who gathered to help held handkerchiefs to their faces to ward off the rancid smell.

"He is British. Probably from that ship the Germans sank at Saint-Nazaire. Bodies have been washing up all along the beach. The police demand they be turned over to them at once."

Jean-Pierre Langille spit on the sand.

"That is what I think of these collaborators and their German puppet masters. If the church will not bury him, I will do so myself."

"Jean-Pierre, tend to your fishing - that is God's calling for you. Leave the dead to me. I will give the poor boy a proper burial."

"Father, what if he is not a Catholic?"

"Our Father embraces all his children when they face His judgement, Rouen. He cares not for our earthly conceits. The boy will be buried in the cemetery."

"But the bishop, certainly he will object."

"Yes, but I will deal with the bishop. For now, we must put this poor boy's soul to rest."

"We will have to make a marker, but what name?"

"He will have a tag," one of the men offered, and holding his breath pulled back the field jacket and opened his shirt. A single green identity disc hung from the dead soldier's neck.

"We cannot put his name on the marker, Father. The Boche will find him for sure."

Another man spoke.

"Father, my cousin Vincent … he left by boat to Spain and abandoned his cottage when the Boche took Poland. I have not told anyone. We could say we found him dead in his bed and bury the soldier with his name. No one will have to know, and the bishop will have nothing to say about it."

The priest crossed himself, but slowly nodded.

A horse cart lumbered slowly across the sandy reach to where the men stood. Grabbing his clothing, they hoisted the body aboard the cart and followed it quietly up the beach, forming a slow procession to the church of Saint Giles.

Father Pierpont put the small green disk in his tunic. He prayed on his slow trek back to the church:

> Father, forgive me my deception. I ask you to welcome this boy into your Kingdom. Comfort his family in their grief, and grant him forgiveness and peace.

———ഐഓ———

CHAPTER 3

FIRST BLOOD

At some point we all look up and realize
we are lost in a maze.
- John Green

"You are Captain Ancil Foucault?"

The chief of the French police in Lorient stood at attention before Colonel Helmut Reiniger, temporary commander of the Lorient occupation force.

"Oui, Herr Oberst."

"You served as the Prefect of Police in Lorient?"

"Oui, Herr Oberst."

God how I hate these ass-kissing Frenchmen. We should just have them all shot.

"Captain Foucault, I have asked you here to request your assistance."

That should get this dirty Frenchman's attention.

"How may I serve you, Colonel?"

"Lorient is wholly under the control of the German occupation authority under the terms of the general armistice. As occupied territory of the Third Reich you are obligated to serve the new regime. Do you understand this?"

"Yes, Colonel. I am a policeman, not a soldier. I serve the legal authority."

"Yes, you do, Captain. And that means you serve me. To maintain a sense of stability and order, the occupation command has decided to retain the existing police departments in the major cities. Local officials will be used to augment the occupying powers more effectively. Captain, you will remain in your post."

"Thank you, Herr Oberst. You will find me most appreciative."

That I don't doubt.

"You will attend a meeting this afternoon with my aide who will outline your new responsibilities and the chain of command. I expect you and the men in your command to follow orders of my administration, Captain."

"Of course."

"Very good. Now, a matter of ... shall we say, a more sensitive nature ... ,"

Foucault caught the subtle shift in Reiniger's tone.

This may prove interesting.

"We have a report a particular religious artifact has gone missing from the Morbihan district. The new administration wishes to establish cordial relations with the Catholic authorities in the new territories despite the Reich's position regarding religious worship. To facilitate this, the Church has offered this artifact for the private collection of Reichsführer Himmler - as a show of respect and trust between the Church and the Third Reich."

In other words, you wish to steal this.

"And where is this object now, Colonel?"

"Now, that is a small problem, one I am certain you can help resolve. It appears the artifact ... what was called in my orders the Madonna Rosa ... went missing in the retreat of the British forces. We have detained a young woman who Bretons cooperating with our new authority have identified as a caretaker of sorts of the relic. We believe she is the only one who knows where the relic has been hidden."

The Madonna Rosa? Your tone tells me you have tortured and killed everyone else who knows of this. I smell an opportunity here.

"I expect you to find this artifact, Captain."

"It may be outside of Morbihan District, Herr Oberst."

"Yes, so it may."

The colonel reached for an envelope on his desk and handed it to Captain Foucault.

"These orders will permit you to act in any capacity necessary throughout the occupied territories for the purpose of securing the artifact. You are to report back to my aide on your progress. Once the icon is recovered, I expect you to deliver it personally to my office. Is that understood?"

"Certainly, Colonel. You can count on me to resolve this ... situation ... promptly."

"See that you do, Captain. You are dismissed."

Yes, Colonel, I will find the Madonna. But I swear Herr Himmler will never rest his eyes on it ... as long as I remain alive.

Once he returned to his office, the captain issued a priority directive to all police in the Morbihan district:

> Recovery of the Madonna relic is to be considered a
> top priority.

Foucault called his aide into his office.

"I need to speak to Bishop Jacquette at Rennes immediately."

"I am sorry, Captain. The phone lines are down. It will be some time before they are fully operational."

"Then get me a car - a German car, preferably. With a German driver to accompany me. I have no time to explain myself at every check point in Brittany."

"Immediately, Captain."

Captain Foucault sat back and considered the implications of his meeting with Colonel Reiniger.

> We have to move quickly. War with the Germans is
> one thing. They will look the other way as we squeeze
> Lorient of its fat, as long as they get their fair share.
> But a war between the Breton church and Les
> Boucliers, that is another matter entirely. I cannot let
> either side get their hands on the Madonna. Not if I
> want to squeeze every last drop of blood from this
> miserable port.

"Captain Foucault, I am afraid you are too late. First blood has been spilled, but it does not stain the hands of the Church."

Bishop Jacquette handed Captain Foucault a typewritten memo from the Prefect of Rennes, a summary of a police action taken in the nearby commune of Redon.

Five adult males, Breton peasant clothing, found
murdered in a shed on the outskirts of Redon. A
cross painted in the victims' blood was found on the
inside of the door.

"The mark is obvious, Captain - Les Boucliers. This means Les Boucliers believe the Madonna has been found, and will stop at nothing to recover it. These dead - they are all members of the local parish. I am afraid it means another time of sorrow between the Church and the Separatists after so many years of peace."

"What will you do, Bishop?"

Bishop Jacquette stood and walked over to the tall draped window overlooking the expanse of cemetery to the South.

"What we have always done, Captain. Bury the dead. Then crush the Separatists."

He turned and looked coldly at Captain Foucault.

"What choice do we have?"

A plain-clothed French policeman waited next to Foucault's car and handed him an envelope. He read the report as they rode away from the church courtyard.

Action confirmed. Five dead in Redon. Roundups
beginning.

The French police, under the watchful eye of their new SS masters, would stage five more killings in the days following. Dozens of partisans from competing factions were arrested for deportation to the East. Soon the police would have their own network of camps, and the roundups would increase in frequency and ferocity. For now it was sufficient to inflame this dormant war and let the factions kill each other.

Stoke Military Hospital, England

"Soldier. Can you hear me?"

The soldier simply stared straight ahead. Morphine delusions clouded his thinking and he struggled against the black abyss enveloping him.

"This one is almost completely unresponsive," the orderly told the doctor as he made his daily rounds, a young nurse dutifully following behind him. The doctor stopped and checked his chart.

"Pack him up. Send him to the psychiatric ward. We need the bed."

Nurse Lorrain McPherson knew exactly what that meant. Once in the Stoke psychiatric ward the soldier in the bed would be stashed away, drugged up, and left pretty much on his own. There were simply too many in hospital and beds were scarce.

"Doctor, he is struggling to even breathe. Can't we leave him here a little longer? Someone has to be looking for him. He has to have family somewhere."

The orderly began to remove his chart and unhook the fluids from his arm.

"I got it, doc. He'll be on his way."

The orderly's words floated above him as he struggled for breath. She knelt down beside him, gently whispering in his ear.

"Soldier, do you have a sweetheart? Someone I can call for you?"

Her soothing voice drifted quietly through the perfect void. Scotty opened his eyes. He barely whispered.

"Anisette. Her name was Anisette."

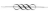

CHAPTER 4

A GROWING SHADOW

Man stands in his own shadow
and wonders why it is dark.
- Zen Proverb

The old man woke at first light, the waves lapping on the nearby shore filling his senses with a subtle illusion of calm. As he blinked back the last vestiges of sleep, the aching in his limbs returned, reminding him this was yet another day. Tiny slivers of light slipped through the cracks in the siding of the rude shack he sneaked into the night before, as he had done several nights past. The dog lay sleeping beside him.

When he first approached the shack days before the dog barked threateningly, but warmed up to him when he offered a scrap of gristle from his worn pack. Each day he brought him a treat - a bone from the garbage of the butcher, a crust of bread from the back of the café. Now instead of barking to alert its master, the dog waited patiently for him and curled up beside the old man at night.

It was a short walk to the beach where he could wash and relieve himself undisturbed. The dirt road dipped to almost the level of the high tide, a path leading to the upper reaches of the beach from where the Vallée de Port aux Goths split - north to the village of Prefailles and south along the bluff where the land rose to form small cliffs. Ever since the British evacuation from nearby Saint-Nazaire and the sinking of that great ship the shore was littered every day along the isolated rocky coastline to the South with something he might be able to sell or trade.

Most of the debris was garbage, but he picked through everything nonetheless. The day before he found a canteen filled with red wine, the day before that a small wooden box with pictures of a pretty young woman. He couldn't read the words written on the pictures, so he threw the photographs back into the surf. But he traded the box for a few rolls at the bakery and was able to eat that morning.

What will I find today?

The dog shadowed him dutifully as he worked through the rocks and small sandy reaches.

A jacket - oil stained, and ripped into shreds. Nothing to salvage. A soldier's helmet caught on a piece of flotsam - he slipped it into his pack. The police had scoured the beach for several days looking for bodies, but they were content the sea had given up all it would. They wouldn't bother with the remaining debris.

The dog began to bark furiously, sneaked forward, and planted both his front feet and crouched low, barking again. He then retreated toward the old man, then back again, repeatedly, waiting for help.

"I am coming. I am coming."

The barking continued.

"What is it? Patience, my friend, I am coming."

He rounded a small outcrop where the bank had fallen away. In the shelter of the tiny cove was something large, dark, rolling in the surf. The way the dog barked he feared it might be a soldier's body, so he stopped at a distance and just watched.

No, it was not a body. He stepped forward as the dog retreated to his feet, running furiously in circles around him.

"Now, now, nothing to get excited about."

He approached the floating debris - it was a pack, one a soldier would carry.

"Ah, maybe something of value here, my friend. Maybe to trade for a piece of meat, eh? One never knows."

He dragged the waterlogged pack further up the beach and looked up - left, then right - to make certain he was not watched. The zipper was difficult to open, but it eventually yielded as his companion whined anxiously at his feet.

"What do we have here? Some clothing?" - a soldier's uniform pants, and a shirt. "Too small for me. But something I can trade. And this ... ah, my friend. A tin of British beef. We will eat breakfast today!"

He carefully laid the clothing out on the rocks to dry, and returned to the pack.

"This will do."

He pulled a small tin box from the side pocket of the satchel. It was bound with heavy cloth tape. The tin box was overlaid with scenes from Paris - a simple novelty store item. But what was inside? Money, perhaps?

"I will open this later," and he reached back inside the pack. "What is this?"

He pulled out something stiff and heavy, wrapped in a woolen cloth. Oil had fouled the cloth - too bad. Clean and dry, he could trade it. Soiled like this ... .

He removed the cloth from the heavy object, and set it down on the sand.

"Ah, our soldier was either a pious man or a thief. Look, my friend, at what he tried to take home."

He picked the object up and held it aloft.

"Very heavy. But just made of wood. It is a nice piece, but I regret to say it will not be worth much. Just another figurine in a land filled with too many Catholics. Still, it may go for a loaf of bread, perhaps."

He stuffed the wooden figure and the tin box into his pack and walked up to the edge of the bluff. The sun rose higher and the wind freshened.

"It will not take long for the clothing to dry. Then we go to the village and see what we can trade. In the meantime," he picked up the can of bully beef and struck it hard against the sharp edge of a rock, "our thief's loss is at least breakfast today."

The dog curled up at his feet, waiting to share in the spoils.

"Go away! None of your trash today!"

The butcher was not interested in trading for the clothing. Perhaps the baker.

Monsieur Carréau and his wife passed the defeat of the French Republic with little fanfare. They continued to buy grain, grind their flour, and bake bread for the small village on the shores of the bay. The local police came by once and announced a set of curfews, to which M. Carréau replied, "So what? I am at my ovens by five in the morning. I go to bed at nine. What do I care of curfews?"

The Germans imposed rationing across occupied France; the Vichy regime quickly followed with a similar edict. Anyone found breaking the strict laws could be ruthlessly punished. For the baker and his wife, however, the problems of the city seemed remote. Life went along as usual in the small coastal village, for a while.

"Old man, what do you have today?"

The people in the village just called him "Old Man." Madame Carréau felt sorry for him, and saved some of yesterday's unsold bread. Trading it was just a pretext. The old man would not take charity.

"Some soldier's clothing, and in decent condition. And a beautiful tin box. Very expensive."

Mme Carréau crossed herself when he pulled the clothing from his pack.

"Not from the dead, I can assure you. From a backpack, that is all."

"Very well. I can give these to the church. This tin box - leave it. I will give it to one of the children when they come for bread. What else do you have?"

"Just this," and he took the statuette out of his rude pack and dropped it onto the table. "A madonna. A very valuable one," he postured. "The soldier was a thief, I think. Stole it from a church as he ran away to Saint-Nazaire."

Mme Carréau lifted it.

"It is very heavy. And so beautifully carved. I wonder where it came from?"

"Beautiful yes, and worth much, I am sure."

Mme Carréau smiled.

"I will give you bread and cheese, for a week, Old Man ... if you promise to take a bath in the outside tub today."

"A bath? You ask too high a price, madame ... but bread and cheese for a week? Perhaps a treat for my friend, too?"

She pulled a large bone from beneath the counter, anticipating his arrival.

"For that, I will bathe - but just this once! Do not make a habit of asking me this, madame."

Mme Carréau took the wooden figurine into the kitchen and laid it on the counter.

"With a little oil, cleaned up, it will look nice in the bakery. Now, I wonder what is in here?"

She cut away the cloth tape from the tin box. The contents had been protected by a soft wax seal, and despite being immersed in the bay for several days were still dry.

"Letters? Nothing more?"

She laid the letters out across the counter. They were addressed to Pvt. Scott Fitch, First Battalion Sherwood Foresters Rifles. They were in English and she could not read them.

She said a prayer over the thought of a dead British soldier somewhere, lost, unknown to family and friends. She thought to give the letters to the priest, and placed them back in the tin box. A customer entered the bakery, so she slipped the box under the counter.

It did not take long for the regulations to strangle even those in rural France. A man who lived just outside of Prefailles was arrested for snaring a hare in the field behind his house - he had already used his allotted meat ration for the week. Claer Mathis who delivered the raw grain the baker ground into flour was arrested for hiding a stash of grain in his root cellar. M. Carréau suspected the police would be questioning them soon.

"You are the baker?"

The uniformed policeman reminded M. Carréau of a toy soldier in his impeccably starched uniform and silly hat.

"Yes. What do you want?"

"I am here to ask you some questions."

"Then you will have to come into the back. I am baking right now."

"Monsieur, you will answer my questions first."

"Not unless you want all my bread to burn. In the back, or come back another time."

M. Carréau walked back into the kitchen and tended to one of the large ovens. The policeman straightened his tunic and followed, obviously displeased.

"Do you know Claer Mathis, monsieur?"

"Of course. He delivers my grain."

"Used to deliver your grain. He was arrested yesterday for hoarding."

"Too bad. I did not know."

"You will receive your ration of flour on Tuesday from now on."

"I grind my own flour."

"Not any longer. All baking will be done on official flour, delivered from Saint-Nazaire. There will be no exceptions."

"And what of the flour I still have?"

The policeman was not certain how to answer.

"I will have to check with my superior, monsieur."

"And you will tell me when?"

"When I return next week."

"I will have baked it all into bread by then."

"See that you do not exceed your quota, monsieur."

"I have read the new regulations. Are you finished?"

"I do not like your attitude, monsieur."

"I am a baker. I do not care about your politics or your regulations. I bake bread so my neighbors can eat. Nothing more."

The policeman, flustered by M. Carréau's obstinacy, looked around for some minor violation to use to his advantage. The baker pushed past him with a tray full of buns and placed them on the front counter. The policeman followed and stood looking around.

He noticed a wooden figurine on a shelf behind the counter.

"The madonna statue. You are Catholic?"

"Not every statue belongs to the Catholics. I am Reformist. What is that to you?"

"The authorities graciously have agreed to let you continue to practice your faith, at least for now."

"Very kind of them." The sarcasm in his voice was not lost on the policeman.

"Tell me, monsieur, where did you get that statuette?"

The sudden interest of the policeman caught M. Carréau by surprise, and he raised his guard.

"It has been in my wife's family for generations. It makes an adornment that pleases my customers - not that it is any of your business."

I will make it my business, baker. Everything in Prefailles is my business.

"I will take a loaf of bread, monsieur, and will call upon you next week."

"As you wish."

M. Carréau reached into the glass case and pulled out a loaf of bread. The policeman slipped it under his arm and walked out of the bakery without paying. The baker thought he asked a few too many questions.

The car skidded to a stop. Two armed men immediately exited the side doors and stormed into the bakery.

"What do you want?" M. Carréau demanded from behind the counter.

"You will remain where you are, monsieur."

The door opened again and a uniformed police officer stepped through.

"I am Captain Foucault, Prefect of Police, the Morbihan district. What is your name?"

"Mikel Carréau, baker of bread. You are not the Prefect of Loire Atlantique. This is not Lorient, or the Morbihan district. What authority do you have here?"

"I will ask the questions, monsieur. You work here with your wife? She is where?"

"At the church this morning."

"I have been told you have a religious artifact here in your bakery. Where is it?"

First the nuisance policeman and now the pompous captain. What is his interest in this?

"You are mistaken."

"Monsieur, you are lying to me. You will tell me immediately where the madonna relic is being hidden."

"There is no relic. Look around for yourself."

"I will do just that."

Foucault barked an order and the two uniformed police began to ransack the small bakery.

"Stop! What are you doing? You are destroying my bakery!"

The police continued their search. After ten minutes they reported there was nothing to be found.

"I told you, there is no madonna. You are mistaken."

"And yet it was seen here in your shop. You are a liar, monsieur, and are under arrest!"

"Arrest? What for?"

"You are a thief, and we deal with thieves, monsieur. Perhaps with some persuasion you will tell us what I want to know."

The two armed policemen grabbed Mikel Carréau and dragged him from the bakery. As he struggled, one of the men slugged him with a small lead baton. Blood gushed from his head. Dazed, he was stuffed into the back seat of the car.

Mme Carréau returned home from church where she had taken the madonna to find the bakery empty, the shelves ransacked, the bread burning in the ovens. The baker disappeared into the night and fog of German-occupied France.

Chapter 5

Headquarters

All things are in a state of flux.
- Heraclites

Present Day

I spread the remaining contents of the "Madonna" file out across the table. Stapled together was a set of orders - two pages. The first was typed on plain paper from Third Army Headquarters, short and to the point. I examined the paper. It had been neatly folded, showed signs of wear along the edges, and some smudging of the ink.

HEADQUARTERS
THIRD UNITED STATES ARMY
AFC 403

4 AUGUST 1944
SUBJECT: Temporary Orders, Pvt. S.H. Woodard

TO: Commander, OSS; GEN W.H. Donovan

1. Private Sidney H. Woodard, #39859283, is assigned
to Third Army HQ command as a forward
intelligence observer.

2. Command authority, Maj. C.R. Codman, Third Army HQ company.

3. Reporting command, Cpt. A.F. Kennedy, Third Army Liaison, OSS.

The order was signed:

G.S. Patton

In researching another project many years ago I uncovered a copy of a document from the director of the OSS, Brigadier General William Donovan, to the president. Donovan lobbied Roosevelt to grant him freer authority to assign OSS agents to the forward division and corps units instead of holding them at the "Army" level - meaning back behind the controlled support areas. Donovan had convinced General Bradley shortly after D-Day to allow some agents access to forward units, but SHAEF favored the British system of keeping agents in reserve.

This order convinced me Patton had been privy to the Bradley communique from Donovan, and leveraged this to bring Sid from his reserve assignment in Dover to France. I hoped the rest of the file would tell me why.

The second document was more mundane. Sid Woodard, Service #39859283, was ordered to report to Third Army headquarters company, Rennes, France on or before 8 August 1944. He was ordered to report to Captain A. Kennedy, OSS Liaison, for further orders.

I thought about the juxtaposition of these two papers. I could certainly understand the importance historically and nostalgically of the orders signed personally by General Patton. But why did he save the second document? Or more importantly, why did he include that document specifically for me to see?

August 1944; Rennes, France

"General, I need a moment, on a delicate matter."

"What is it, Major?"

Major Codman, the aide-de-camp to General Patton, knew better than to interrupt the general in the middle of a planning session. Third Army was fanning out through the Breton peninsula under orders from General Bradley, despite Patton's strong objections.

"Brad, we should be moving east, pushing the damn Germans, not mopping up in the West. The Germans are going to destroy the ports anyway - why waste the men and ordinance?"

Bradley was not about to deviate from the original plan for Operation Cobra, even at Patton's insistence. So the general ordered supplies - guns, ammunition, and explosives - air dropped to the resistance now organizing as the French Forces of the Interior - the FFI. The FFI would help clear the pockets of Germans from their homeland and allow Third Army to continue its armored thrusts toward the Brittany ports. Patton set up temporary headquarters in the administrative building in Rennes, captured earlier in the day.

"I have Monsignor Jacquette of the Rennes Diocese in my office. He wishes to make a special request of Third Army."

"Dammit, Chuck. Can't it wait? We've got to keep moving. I don't have time for this!"

"General, I think you need to hear the monsignor out."

Major Charles Codman belonged to a privileged New England family, a graduate of Harvard, and served with distinction in the air corps in the first war. He wore both the Silver Star and the French Croix de Guerre. When Germany invaded he was working as a wine buyer on a trip to France and barely managed to escape, catching the last plane out of Bordeaux for Lisbon. He reenlisted in 1942 with the rank of major, and joined Patton's command in North Africa. Codman spoke fluent French, and Patton trusted the fifty-two year old major to watch his back.

"All right, give me five minutes, then bring him in the office."

The general finished reading his briefings, cleared the maps and situation reports from his desk, and rang the clerk in the front office. Major Codman opened the door and led the French clergyman into his office. Patton stood and adjusted his uniform.

"General Patton, *permettez-moi de vous présenter le Révérend Monsignor Ansell Jacquette.* Monsignor Jacquette, General Patton."

"*Mon general,* how gracious of you to see me on such short notice."

"My pleasure, Monsignor. I commend you on your excellent English."

"Thank you, General. I understand you speak fluent French."

"Oui, Monsignor. If you would prefer."

"This is an excellent opportunity for me to exercise my English, if you do not mind, General."

"Not at all."

"Please, General, let us be seated."

Protocol demanded even a general wait for the monsignor to sit, and Patton - despite his infamous caustic behavior - understood the importance of proper protocol. He motioned for Major Codman to remain.

"How may Third Army be of assistance, Monsignor?"

"General Patton, I have come on an urgent mission on behalf of the Church."

Patton glanced momentarily at Major Codman. There was something about the tenor of the monsignor's voice.

"Your army is moving very rapidly through Brittany, General. This creates disruption and chaos that those who may not share your command's sense of justice and honesty may choose to take advantage of."

Cut the crap. What are you after?

"The Germans are abandoning their posts and retreating toward the coast. They are being pursued not only by your armies but by French citizens armed by the Allies. This creates a very dangerous situation, General."

"With all due respect, Monsignor, we rely on the FFI to clear pockets of resistance. Our tanks need to rapidly push forward to exploit the advantage we have gained," Major Codman interjected.

"This FFI as you call it, they are an undisciplined force, many without ties to the Church. They often seek revenge for past injustices inflicted by the Germans and use your weapons to engage in horrendous acts of violence."

"Just what is your point, Monsignor?" Patton knew the monsignor was skirting the real reason he was here.

"During the occupation the Church sought to ensure the safety of our parishes and their people through cooperation. There was really no alternative, you see, but this truth is often ignored. Acts of retribution against these policies have become commonplace. Once the agitators among the population began to harass the Germans, they also turned against the Church of France. Many small parishes have broken away from control by the Church and act openly in defiance of its edicts.

"These separatists often protect those in the growing black market. We have taken certain steps to protect our most vulnerable churches and our priests, but I am afraid violent incidents have already occurred."

"I can assure you, Monsignor, that no units under my command will participate in or countenance violence against the Church. As for the FFI, we are already moving quickly to establish better communication with the isolated factions to coordinate their operations. If there are any rogue elements out there, we will deal with them, Monsignor."

"Your assurances are comforting, General."

That's not why you are here.

"There is another issue."

I thought so.

"The Church is afraid certain property may have already disappeared from some of the more isolated parishes, particularly the separatist churches. Relics have special importance to the people of the peninsula.

"There are rumors a valuable figurine may have fallen into the hands of the black marketeers. The Madonna Rosa is invaluable to the people of Brittany as a symbol of our faith."

A madonna? Major Codman glanced back at Patton. The change of inflection in the monsignor's voice hinted there was more lurking beneath this carefully contrived dialog than the monsignor was telling.

"There is an island off the coast of Lorient called Belle Isle. Citadel Vauban overlooks the harbor at Le Palais and is occupied by a sizable German garrison. The Church has reason to believe the German commander may be a member of a well-organized black market, and possibly holding this relic at the Citadel. He certainly could use the icon to bribe his way to Spain or Portugal - or worse, to send it to Berlin in exchange for a change of duty.

"There are separatists in Brittany who have tried to ally themselves with the Germans. They are rumored to be in league with black marketeers, and may indeed be the thieves holding the relic - or at least responsible for stealing it."

The black market - that would explain why a regular army commander might risk such an extreme move to avoid surrender.

"What do you want from Third Army?"

The general's fierce stare told Major Codman that Patton also did not trust the monsignor.

"An invading army unmasks the intrigues of men, General. At the same time it empowers others to travel in darkness. The thieves must be found, and the Madonna Rosa restored to its historic refuge."

The monsignor stood, and General Patton stood after him.

"Brute strength directed against the fortress will most certainly put the relic at grave risk. We hope there may be alternative means to ensure the return of this precious artifact.

"The Nazis failed in their attempt to steal the land of the Breton people, thanks to the Allied liberation. If they have taken the

Madonna, however, they will have succeeded in stealing our soul. I have promised God I will not surrender to the days of darkness."

"Before Third Army broke through into the peninsula, the Germans succeeded in shoring up the artillery defenses at Lorient and Saint-Nazaire. Both of these ports are now effectively cut off from land transportation, leaving U-boats as the only source of supply."

The intelligence officer stood before a large map of the Brittany coast with a pointer and grease pen and drew arrows showing the thrust of Patton's tanks.

"We have sortied against the submarine pens in Lorient and have reduced their efficiency. The town itself has been bombed mainly to rubble making the efficient movement of supply difficult."

Patton began to squirm in his seat. This intelligence briefing was more fantasy than reality - he knew it, and so did General Bradley.

"The next objective is to drive through to the Quiberon Peninsula, seal off the German retreat from Brest before pushing back west to Lorient, eventually securing a port for supply."

The Combat Command officers of units A, B, and C anxiously awaited orders to move through the open countryside to the East and South of Paris - heading West was not one of their favorite subjects. The generals meeting in Bradley's command headquarters sensed a fight was about to break open.

"The attack on Lorient is scheduled for August 9. RAF bombers will sortie the night of the 8th. American bombers will follow during the day to soften up the defenses and neutralize their resupply capability. We expect to break the German defensive perimeter by mid-day and take Lorient by nightfall."

"That's a load of horse crap."

Patton had heard enough. General Bradley weighed in to smooth the conversation over.

"Now, George. Lorient and Brest have been identified all through the Overlord planning phase. Ike fully expects these strongpoints to be neutralized and the ports taken before we can swing east. This is not negotiable."

General Bradley had anticipated a harsh criticism of the plan by General Patton and had cemented his position with a call to SHAEF headquarters before the meeting. Typically, he pushed his decision to follow the initial COBRA plan onto Eisenhower to thwart the objections of General Patton.

"Brad, what the hell are we pushing armored columns forward just to stop and piss on Lorient? The Germans have unfettered access to the Bay of Biscay for resupply with their submarines, and enough artillery to stall us off for weeks. The submarine pens have taken direct hits and still are fully operational. We should bypass these strongpoints and let them sit out the damn war."

"George, we have been over this before. Ike wants these ports taken for supply purposes. Operation Chastity has been a part of Overlord since mid-July."

"Brad, the tactical situation is different from what it was in mid-July. And what about Belle Isle?"

General Bradley looked up in surprise.

"Belle Isle has figured in the Operation Chastity planning."

"We have intelligence the Germans have a substantial garrison there, and artillery. Lots of it. They command the sea approaches. Is the British navy going to support our attack by sealing off the bay? If so, they will have to isolate and neutralize the garrison at Le Palais."

Bradley looked at his aide who frantically made notes on a white pad. He wrote across the top of the page in letters large enough for General Bradley to see from his seat, "NO CURRENT INTEL BELLE ISLE".

"I'll have to get back to you on that, George," was all he could reply.

"I don't want my tanks sitting there being pounded by German artillery from that damn island."

"We'll take a look at this, George. In the meantime, it would help if you shared your intelligence report with us on this."

"What we know now is second-hand. But I want to get a closer look at what's going on out there. Once you start dropping bombs again I lose my chance to get valuable intelligence."

Bradley began tapping his pencil on the table - and Patton knew he scored with his intelligence plea.

"I asked 8th Air Force to move up their attack, and took some pushback from them over it. They prefer to attack sometime after the 15th. The RAF will concur with that delay - it gives them both a chance to put more planes in the air. If I give you a week can you get me that intelligence?"

"Already working on it, Brad. Consider it done."

"I will expect a report, George," General Bradley countered, cautiously.

General Patton read the report on the progress of Operation Chastity late that night over a glass of wine with Major Codman.

"Christ, Major. This Chastity thing is already a mess. Without complete control over the sea approaches shipping will be a sitting duck. This idea of building a deep-water port on Quiberon is a load of goose-shit. We can't even supply the FFI effectively - and we need them to clean up these pockets of Germans scattered all through the peninsula. We're missing the drop zones. Some of these weapons are falling into the hands of the very German troops we want to flush out. And this lack of coordination - we need to get this under control and get the hell out."

He stood and began to strut around the room.

"It's all about mobility. Dammit, Chuck, we showed them how tanks needed to be used, and we aren't a month into this thing and already Bradley is talking static warfare. We have to keep the drive moving east. The Germans cannot sustain a counter-attack with Third Army crawling up their ass."

"What can we do, General?"

Patton breathed in the heady aroma of a fine Bordeaux and savored its calming bouquet.

"We need to get this tick off the hound. Who do we have as liaison with the OSS?"

"A Captain Kennedy, general."

"Kennedy. Why do I know that name?"

"He organized the Seasalter speech."

"Oh, yes. My kidnapping. Whatever happened to that soldier ... what was his name?"

"Woodard, sir."

"Woodard, yes. A real cracker, that one. He's got balls. Did he work for Kennedy?"

"I don't think so, General."

Patton sat back and closed his eyes.

"A good wine helps me think, Chuck. This Citadel problem, it's been spinning around in my mind ever since the monsignor left. It's a good bet there's a lot more to this story than the monsignor was telling us - or our own intelligence."

"I believe that as well."

"It makes no sense to try and storm Lorient or build a separate harbor at Quiberon if they have a large artillery presence offshore. Look at this map," and he pushed the papers aside to uncover his most current situation map.

"This is Belle Isle. From here a well-trained artillery battery commands the approaches to Lorient to the Northwest, Vannes to the Northeast, and Saint-Nazaire - almost due West. The Brits cannot sustain surface action without first reducing the battery from the air."

"That target is awfully small, General."

"Those B-17s will blow up a lot of fish attacking this small port, Major. That's about all. And the Brits at night? No, I can't see either air force accomplishing much."

"What about the bombing of Lorient?"

Patton stood and walked around the room.

"We've been hitting Lorient since May '43 and still the submarine base is basically undamaged. The city itself - nothing but rubble. It makes a perfect defensive nest for German soldiers. What the hell good does it do to take the port only to have it destroyed and out of operation in the process? No, Chuck, this is a fool's errand. These ports are the wrong targets - at least for the armored units. I need a good excuse to bypass Lorient and just seal it off."

"Something bothers me, General. Why did the monsignor link the FFI and the madonna story? If the Germans have it, what does the FFI have to do with it? And all this propaganda about the 'soul of Brittany?'"

"He came off like some god-damned over-baked ham. He's not telling us the truth, Chuck. That's for god-damned sure."

Patton sat back in his fine smoking jacket, set his wine glass on the side table and lit a cigar. He took a long pull on the cigar and closed his eyes.

"Major, I keep thinking about that Jaguar driver."

"Woodard, sir?"

"Yes. Cocky bastard. Never did like those damn spooks, sneaking around like that. But maybe that's what we need. Someone to stick out there and see what's really going on."

"He does speak fluent German, General."

"Yes, so I read. I'm surprised he was not shot in all that nonsense."

Patton reached for the wine glass and after a long stare at the deep color in the glass, took a carefully measured sip.

"I've got a week to get someone out there and see what is going on. Get that Woodard character here. Go straight to Donovan at OSS if you have to."

"I can prepare orders, General."

"Good. Do it right away. Assign him to Kennedy, but give him a free rein. There is a connection between this artifact, the Citadel on Belle Isle, and the FFI. I can feel it. And I don't want Third Army bogged down by some god-damned religious civil war."

"I will prepare orders for Kennedy tonight."

"Good. Have Woodard in my office at 1400 tomorrow afternoon."

"Yes, General. And I suggest we bring in a liaison with British intelligence as well - in case there are plans for raids in the area, if nothing else."

"Good idea. Ask for that woman - what was her name? The one pulling double duty in Dover?"

"Carlisle, sir."

"Yes, yes ... Carlisle. Seems she earned a promotion over all that nonsense. A first-class popsie, that one - but worth her stuff, and I want her."

"Consider it done, General."

Major Codman packed up his briefcase and headed back to his office. General Patton savored the Bordeaux and closed his eyes, surrendering to the sublime darkness of sleep.

Captain Carlisle stepped into her temporary office, closed the door, and pulled her orders out of her valise.

> TEMPORARY ASSIGNMENT
> Liaison, SOE - OSS, special request
> Report: Maj. C. Codman, US Third Army HQ
> Rennes

Major Codman had given her a small briefing file and left the young captain on her own. She knew as an "unattached" officer, especially a woman, her rank would afford her little help on this assignment. But she was used to getting her way in this man's world.

"I wonder who this operative is."

Her primary assignment was to monitor the communications from an OSS operative to see if they presented any targets of opportunity for Bomber Command. According to Major Codman's file she was supposed to ensure no bombing missions jeopardized the deep-cover operative. She could only laugh at the contradictions in these orders.

"Well, at least this is just temporary," she added, and opened the door.

"When the American gets here, please have him come in immediately."

"Yes, ma'm," the clerk replied, somewhat caustically. She didn't like taking orders from a woman, especially a Brit.

"They only give a dolly like that a promotion for a little slap and tickle, if you ask me," she would later say to her roommates.

Present Day

The last two documents were stapled together. The topmost one was a letter written on the stationary of a church in Vannes, on the Breton peninsula near Lorient.

15 Sept 1952
Monsieur Woodard,

In reply to your recent letter I must take exception to your suggestion the church played a role in supporting the underground activities of French collaborators at Lorient.

The matter has been reviewed by the courts and those responsible for wartime acts brought to justice. No inquiry has verified complicity on the part of the church in these matters.

I suggest those who profess knowledge of these allegations do so for personal gain. I would sincerely hope you respect our position in this matter and recognize these accusations for what they truly are.

Sincerely, in God's Trust,
Monsignor F. Renault

Beneath it was a single-page handwritten memo from the desk of then CIA Director General Walter Bedell Smith stating simply,

The Agency will not support further inquiry into recovery of the religious relic.

B. Smith

I knew Sid had decided not to join the CIA following the war. The Office of Strategic Services morphed into the CIA, and according to

Sid became far too conventional and bureaucratic for his liking. He opted instead to serve as a contractor for the Company - he liked his independence.

Yet here was a direct intervention by the director - a general who served as Eisenhower's chief-of-staff at SHAEF. I knew from past conversations Sid and Walter "Beetle" Smith had crossed paths before.

What was General Smith referring to - the "religious relic?" What exactly was this relic? The fact the army was "no longer" supporting its recovery indicated this was once someone's assignment - perhaps Sid's. Since Sid did not join the CIA, it made sense to believe it was something he did while still under the command of the OSS during the war.

I looked further through his notes and found one cryptic entry:

> Arrived military airfield - Arromanches.
> 8 Aug 44

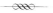

CHAPTER 6

DRAWING THE SWORD

All things are ready, if our minds be so.
- William Shakespeare

The duty sergeant did not bother to look up from his desk.

"What do you want?"

"I need transport to Rennes, Third Army HQ."

He looked up from his crossword puzzle and dropped his eyes menacingly at the uniformed private.

"You think this is some god-damned taxi service?"

Sid shrugged, turned abruptly, and left the transport office, walking the short distance to the Arromanches Military Airfield command tent. A young private manned the duty desk.

"Say, Bud. Who is your CO?"

"Major Dougherty."

"And the field exchange number for his office?"

"What do you want that for?"

"Signal Corps. Following up on a complaint of telephone problems. His exchange number?"

"Twelve." The private looked at Sid suspiciously.

"OK, thanks. I'll be poking around a little, checking line cross-connects - technical stuff. Don't pay me any mind."

Sid left the command tent and crossed the compound to a small building that showed obvious signs of a comm shack - wires stretching out in long lines on hastily erected poles. He stepped through the front door.

"This is a secure area, Private."

"Don't mind me. Woodard. Signal Corps. I have orders to check some faulty telephone connections," and he reached into his breast pocket and pulled out a set of orders and waved them around in the air, then stuffed them back haphazardly into this shirt pocket. "I need a mobile set. That one will do."

Before the operator could object, Sid grabbed the handheld telephone receiver and left the shack. The duty operator didn't bother to call the field MPs for verification. After all, he was just fixing some telephone lines.

Sid walked up the line of buildings and stopped by a supply shed adjacent to the transport office that had a telephone line entering the top of the outside back wall. He moved a nearby wooden crate over to the wall, climbed up to where he could reach, and clamped the mobile handset on the wire. He turned the hand crank.

"FMA Communications."

"Exchange 12."

The line went quiet for a moment, then erupted with a short burst of static as the call connected.

"Major Dougherty."

"Major! What the god-damned hell is going on up there! You stupid pricks in the rear couldn't shit your way past a goose if they fed you a prune pie!"

"Who is this?" The major's indignant tone made Sid laugh, almost spoiling the charade.

"Who is this? I'll tell you who, you polished-brass pin head. It's General George God-Damned Patton! What's the meaning of denying my man Woodard a god-damned car to drive to headquarters? I want to talk to your superior officer - now!"

"Excuse me, General. Sorry, General. I didn't know one of your men was looking for transportation - Woodard, you say?"

"Didn't know? What kind of horses-ass outfit are you running up there, Dougherty? You get Private Woodard a god-damned staff car within the half-hour and push his puny ass down the road to HQ, or I'll personally come up there and crawl up your butt with a corn cob. You got it?"

"Yes, sir, General, sir. I will see to it myself, sir."

The line went dead.

Major Dougherty ran out of his office and hurried away to the airfield's transport shack. Sid was waiting quietly, sitting on the steps, his rucksack lying on the ground.

"Are you Private Woodard?"

"Yes, sir," and he didn't bother to stand. Major Dougherty tried to catch his breath.

"You will have your car in just a few minutes," and he raced up the steps. He closed the door behind him, but Sid could hear the screaming clearly from where he sat. In a moment, Major Dougherty emerged, face flushed, followed by the frantic duty sergeant who raced out the door, across to the motor pool, and emerged moments later driving an olive green officer's staff car.

"Sergeant Miller will drive you, Private. And please give my compliments to General Patton."

"Thank you, Major. I'll be happy to mention you when I join him for a cigar this afternoon."

Barely suppressing a smile, Private Woodard opened the passenger door, tossed in his rucksack, and settled back for a nap as the staff car drove off to the South toward Third Army headquarters.

Third Army HQ, OSS Liaison Office

"These are unusual orders, Private Woodard."

Captain Alexander Kennedy. Your name is familiar. We meet at last.

"Yes, sir. I'm not really certain just what I am supposed to do here, Captain."

"Well, why would you? They don't exactly consult with privates when they issue orders, now do they?"

They don't consult with pencil-pushing captains either, you over-stuffed prick.

"No, sir."

"Your orders came from Major Codman of HQ Company. You realize, don't you, that Major Codman is General Patton's aide-de-camp?"

"No, sir."

"Well, he is. So you won't be bothering him with routine reports, Private. I am your CO. You will file your operational reports with me directly. Do you understand?"

"Yes, sir."

Fat chance. I wouldn't be ordered directly by the general's aide if this weren't something he wanted kept secret from the command structure.

"You will be briefed at 1400 hours. I will attend the briefing of course, as your commanding officer. Building 4. 1400. Dismissed."

"Yes, sir."

Sid turned and left Captain Kennedy's office, barely managing to keep from laughing out loud.

How did a prig like that ever get into the OSS?

1400 Hours

Officers milled about waiting for the briefing officer to arrive. The briefing room remained closed to safeguard against the tendency, especially of junior officers, to discuss their reports with other officers before formally presenting their briefings. Captain Kennedy arrived promptly on time and barely acknowledged Private Woodard. Only officers would be allowed in the room when it opened; any enlisted men summoned to appear would have to wait until called upon individually.

Colonel Barrister, the staff officer on duty, strode briskly down the hall, opened the briefing room door, and stepped inside. That was the cue for the other officers to follow - by rank, of course. Sid had to laugh at the spectacle - chickens following a pecking order.

"Wait until you are called," Captain Kennedy snapped as he entered the room in turn.

The door shut behind the last lieutenant in the line and the hallway was quiet. A petite WAC lieutenant stepped quietly down the hallway and approached Sid.

"Private Woodard?"

"Yes, ma'm."

"Follow me, please."

She turned and walked back the way she had come. Sid was all too happy to follow her, admiring her slim figure as they walked to the far side of the building, passed through a senior officer's outer office, and entered the rather spartan office behind.

"Major Codman will be with you shortly. Please have a seat."

Codman? This is getting interesting.

As he waited, Sid heard a disruption in the outer office.

"No, I am afraid you cannot see the major … I don't care what your orders are, Lieutenant … no, Private Woodard is waiting for Major Codman. You will have to wait … no, you may not enter! Lieutenant!"

The door opened brusquely and two uniformed MPs stood in the doorway. One brandished a threatening baton.

"You Woodard?" The one with the baton tapped it menacingly against his palm.

"Well, that depends … ."

"You are under arrest, Woodard. Get up."

"Sorry, I don't think so … ."

Before the two MPs could grab him, the door behind them burst open and General Patton entered the office followed by his aide, Major Codman.

"What the god-damned hell are you two doing here?"

The MPs snapped to attention.

"I have orders to arrest the private, General, for misappropriating a motor pool car."

Patton turned to glare at Private Woodard.

"Seems you have a knack for that, Private!" He turned to the MPs. "Get the hell out of this office. And tell whoever issued those orders to stuff them up his ass!"

"Yes, sir!" The two MPs fled as quickly as they could from the building.

"Get in here, Woodard!"

Patton stepped into the office and sat behind Codman's desk, and the major took a seat next to the private.

"Stole a god-damned staff car, eh, Woodard?"

"Borrowed it, General. It's still parked outside."

"Thought you preferred a sports car."

"Yes, sir, but the Baron wouldn't part with it."

Patton glared at him.

I like this petulant bastard.

"I have things to do, Woodard. Let's get to it. Major."

"Private Woodard, I am Major Codman, the general's aide. Despite your official orders assigning you to Captain Kennedy, you answer only to me. No reports or briefings are to be made on this assignment to anyone else unless specifically directed. Do you understand?"

"Yes, sir."

"The file you will receive from Captain Kennedy is all we know about a possible ancient church relic that has disappeared. The general has given the Church his assurances Third Army will try to recover the artifact - some sort of madonna statue."

"What's so important about a church relic?"

"Not a god-damned thing," Patton boomed. "But there is something going on in all this I don't like. Look, Woodard, Third Army is going to drive like hell to the Quiberon Peninsula to cut off the German retreat and seal off Brittany. But then that becomes a mopping up operation. Part of that will be assigned to French forces fighting as the FFI, and the rest to 6th Armored Division - at least for the time being. I don't want Third Army stuck in the mud of Brittany."

Major Codman continued.

"We believe there is animosity between the Church and the FFI, perhaps even collusion with the German military that we believe will hole up in Lorient and the other ports. The last thing we want is open warfare between the FFI and the Church in our rear."

"Look, Woodard," Patton interjected. "Something is going on out at a place called Citadel Vauban, on Belle Isle outside of Lorient. It's all in the file. We believe they have a large artillery garrison on the island, one that could threaten any attempt to take Lorient by sea as well as rain hell down on my tanks if we cannot keep them moving east.

"The Germans have stolen much of the valuable art and treasures of France - and this madonna may just be a part of that. The Citadel could be one of the places they are stashing it away - then moving it out by submarine. Plans to attack Lorient by air, which may also include the harbor at Le Palais, have been temporarily postponed so we can find out exactly what the situation on the ground at the Citadel really is.

"I need someone with your unique talents to do this, Woodard. You will be on your own. The major will cover your back as best he can, but chances are you will be outside of army control. Make this happen, Woodard. I don't want some god-damned political hornet's nest slowing up Third Army when we move east."

Major Codman handed Sid a large envelope.

"Third Army captured one of Organization Todt's engineering companies as it tried to evacuate south from Cherbourg. We have several of their officers here in Rennes under interrogation. We have doctored a set of identity papers to use as your cover. I understand you have used this cover before."

"Yes, sir."

"I have a set of orders for you that will help you put together whatever else you need to get started. Once you leave the controlled zone you need to destroy them. Beyond that, you are on your own."

"And what of this artifact? Do you want me to try and recover it?"

Patton leaned forward in his chair.

"We don't have a lot of time, Woodard. Something is brewing up north. We are preparing for a possible German counter-attack against our supply lines, and that may free up Third Army from Brittany. So you have to get in, get the intelligence on what is happening at that damn fortress, and get the hell out."

"Can I keep the car?"

"No, god-dammit!" Patton stood and stomped briskly toward the door. "But if you stole a Jeep, it might take a while for anyone to find out." And he left the office.

Sid looked at Major Codman.

"What about Captain Kennedy?"

"Report to him when you leave, but keep the content of this briefing private. Do you have any questions?"

"No, sir."

Sid stood to leave.

"You will be working with a British officer - strictly as a liaison. We don't want any surprises interrupting our efforts. And Private, it's more important we have clear intelligence than it is to find the artifact. And there is not much time … ."

"I understand, Major."

"Sit down, Woodard. And pay close attention."

Kennedy stood and began to parade around his office.

"Inside this packet are your briefing papers. They are quite specific."

Sid saw the packet remained sealed and knew Captain Kennedy had no idea what was inside. For his part, Kennedy assumed Private Woodard was there to help him coordinate with the French resistance.

"This is a relatively simple matter. We are trying to coordinate with the French fighters and need additional intelligence. These FFI. Rabble, mostly. I'm going to go and meet with the various leaders and try to bring some degree of discipline among them. Most of them are simple opportunists - looking for a way to steal arms and supplies for the black market - I know this for a fact.

"The worst of them is a man who presumes to call himself a colonel - Verbon is his name. He leads the biggest faction, and has become a thorn in the side of Third Army. This Colonel Verbon will be brought under my control, or I will cut his head off like a damn snake.

"With your help we will identify other rogue factions within the FFI, surround the area where they are operating, and seal off the escape routes. Loyal FFI will be sent in to attack - that keeps the US Army out of the whole mess."

"A police action, Captain?"

"Hell, yes! The Army is empowered to do this - whatever the hell it wants! Anyone inside the circle will be arrested. Or shot! This will send a clear signal to the renegade resistance groups about who is in charge."

"And just who is that, Captain?"

Kennedy looked him, annoyed.

"Me, that's who! Do you understand your orders?"

"Yes, Captain. I understand my orders."

I understand you don't have a clue what my orders really are.

"Good. This is very important to me. I expect results, Woodard. Dismissed."

"Yes, sir."

Private Sid Woodard walked down the long hallway accompanied by a spit-polished corporal who led him to the temporary office marked "SOE LIAISON." He knocked on the door, irritated at being held up at the last minute by this little bit of cross-service protocol.

"Enter."

He stepped into the room, and let out a small groan.

"You are at attention, Private!" Captain Carlisle snapped.

"Yes, ma'm."

She could feel the sarcasm in his voice.

I'm not taking any crap from him.

"So, we meet again, Private. Let's get this over with. I am sure you are anxious to take the field."

"Yes, ma'm."

"My job, Private, is to coordinate any intelligence you may gather between the forces. Specifically, to ensure no secondary targets jeopardize your mission while no targets-of-opportunity are left on the table."

"Sorry, ma'm, but I will not be carrying a radio."

"So I am told." She handed him a small envelope. "Let's hope you get back to the American lines in a timely manner."

"I officially report to Captain Kennedy," Sid smiled, hoping a little dig would set her off. She did not take the bait.

"That is not my concern, Private."

She stood and straightened her perfectly pressed uniform.

"Everything you need is in the envelope. Good luck."

Sid saluted, almost half-heartedly, and left the office. The corporal met him in the outer room and escorted him out of the command building.

"Tough luck to have to report to a woman. A bit prim and prissy, if you ask me."

"An officer? I would't waste my time."

The two men chuckled at the underhanded, slap at the pretty captain as Sid left the building and walked back to his temporary quarters at the Mercure Hotel.

In his hotel room Sid broke out a map of the Brittany peninsula. He had little time. If he could get to the German lines while the situation on the ground was still chaotic, he may have a chance to slip through and get onto Belle Isle. If he waited too long, he likely would end up dead.

He finished off his third glass of scotch and thought of Captain Kennedy.

What's his angle? I don't trust that prissy pinhead. I have a suspicion I will see him again.

He studied the map, then drew a large circle around Lorient.

Captain Janine Carlisle completed her daily work, cleaned up her desk, and walked through the maze of clerks who looked after her with some slight disdain. She could feel their eyes following her as she left, but was resigned to not let these "little clerks" get the better of her.

The summer evening hung warm and humid as she walked down the street. She decided to pass on stopping for a glass of wine at the little café on the corner by her hotel. Instead, she crossed the street and walked another three blocks.

At the entrance to the Mercure Hotel she stopped for a moment, looked up and down the street, and stepped through into the lobby.

—⦿—

Chapter 7

Festung Lorient

And after all, what is a lie?
- Lord Byron

The guard stepped out into the road and brought his carbine to the ready.

"Halt!"

Sid intercepted the thrust of the 4th Armored Division driving south and west from Rennes pushing the stunned German forces retreating toward the port of Lorient. He had passed a steady stream of tank-escorted truck convoys carrying gasoline and material in a Jeep he had borrowed from the corps motor pool when the sergeant was shooting craps. He met the sentries of the supply company feeding the forward attack companies where the 4th captured the bridges over the Blavet River near Baud.

"Stand down!" Sid turned the Jeep off. "Destination?"

"I have orders to report to Colonel Clark, Combat Command A. Where can I find him?"

The sentry turned and spoke to his cohort who raised his carbine and pointed it directly at Sid.

"You? A private? You want to see the colonel? CCA is a little busy right now, GI."

"Yeah, well, you might want to take a look at these orders - especially who signed them, Bud."

He took a sheet of paper from his tunic and presented it to the sergeant. After a brief examination, he handed them back and glared at him.

"So what? Phony papers with Patton's name on them? I've never heard of a general signing orders for a dumb dogface before."

"OK, I see. Perhaps you want to call his command center - talk to Major Codman." Sid fired up the Jeep. "Tell him hello for me," and he drove on through the sentry post while the sergeant contemplated shooting him in the back.

"You gonna call command?" his partner asked.

"Are you nuts?"

Colonel Clarke was just finishing a briefing when Private Woodard was escorted into his tent.

"What's this about?" he barked.

"Private Woodard, sir. I have been ordered to report to you."

"By who?"

"My orders," and he handed Clarke the paper. The name on the bottom caught his immediate attention.

"What is your assignment, Private?"

"Classified, sir - sorry. What I need to do is get close to the enemy lines as quickly as possible."

"Well, Woodard, the lines are pretty unstable right now. The Germans are falling back to Lorient and have been setting up temporary defensive nests along the way. Generally don't know where they are until they open fire on you. You have transport?"

"Just a Jeep."

"Well, that's a good way to get killed quick … Corporal!" He barked loudly and an aide quickly entered the tent.

"Yes, sir."

"Take Woodard here over to 25th Recon. He can follow them forward as far as he wants. After that, you're on your own."

"That'll do fine, Colonel."

Colonel Clarke looked down at a situation map.

"You got a death wish, Woodard?"

"*Ich will nicht sterben, Herr Oberst* - I don't intend to die."

Clarke looked up over the top of his reading glasses.

"Dismissed."

The light tanks of the reconnaissance division rolled down the road marked A213 on the map. German units set up hastily built machine gun and mortar nests to delay the American attacks, and give the illusion of greater strength than there really was. It was up to recon to flush these units out and determine if they represented a greater strength. Standard procedure for recon was to immediately attack any enemy resistance with armor then push the defenders back away from lightly manned positions, relying on shock tactics. If the enemy was dug in with heavy weapons, especially anti-tank guns, they would withdraw and radio their position to headquarters.

Sid followed the 25th sandwiched between a light tank and an armored troop carrier to shield him from an initial machine gun attack. If you survived the first thirty-seconds of an ambush you stood a pretty good chance of living until payday.

The column stopped where A213 met a small stream crossing. On the far side the road branched.

"Captain, that 'Y' looks like a good spot for an ambush."

Captain Ansel Merrick took a long look through his field glasses.

"If we charge that position, Sergeant, we will have to expose our flank either right or left."

"Let me take a squad and circle around before they take a bead on us. If we come in from the right flank first, we can get a good look and see if they have something set up."

"Take a squad. If you can, attack the rear of their nest. We will charge the front with armor if we hear the small arms fire. If they have 88s, withdraw and radio back."

The sergeant assembled his squad, pulled a bazooka team from the troop carrier, and slipped through the low marshy ground to the right, heading for the flank. Sid watched in amusement.

Glad I'm not going out there. I hate this marshy crap.

Fifteen minutes later the silence was shattered by the report of a bazooka, an explosion, and a hail of small arms fire.

"Ahead. Attack right, tanks one and three. Tank 2 attack left and cover."

The orders went out over the radio and the light tanks roared into action. At the "Y" the lead tank broke right, spreading a hail of machine gun fire into the cover as it charged forward. The second tank, now taking some machine gun fire itself, broke left, exposing the machine gun crew as it had to turn to continue fire. The third tank charged right then broke into the brush, running straight over the top of the German machine gun nest. In a matter of seconds, the attack moved quickly down the road.

The orders came by radio.

"Follow right - 1 click."

The troop carrier drove into the "Y" to the right and met the tanks on the road one kilometer - one "click" - further ahead. Sid followed in his Jeep.

Captain Merrick stood examining his map, talking to the sergeant that led the ground patrol.

"Right about here, Captain. The forward nest looks like an attempt to draw us further up the road. They have a wheel mounted gun here, where the road takes a bend. Not an 88, but it could do damage to these light tanks. Machine guns on the other side provide crossing fire."

"I haven't heard back from tank two."

As he spoke, tank number two rolled back toward them from the starting point and rolled to a stop.

"Like you thought, Captain. They've set up down the left side with some heavy field guns. My guess they were hoping to drive us left after stopping us on the right road."

Captain Merrick marked the locations of the two German strongpoints, and ordered the recon patrol back the way they came.

"You following us, Private?"

"No, I think this is where I get off, Captain."

"You got a death wish, Woodard?"

"Funny - you're the second one to ask me that this afternoon. No, I got a handle on what I need to do."

"OK. You're on your own. Don't be calling us for help."

"Wouldn't think of it, Captain."

The squad retreated back up the road. Sid knew he had bought some time to prepare his next move, anticipating the Germans would move forward to reclaim their dead at the "Y" before deciding their next holding move.

He tracked back to the "Y," parked, and waded through the brush to the German machine-gun nest. Three soldiers lay scattered about the ground. Two were mutilated badly where the tank rolled over the top of them. One avoided the crushing, but took a round through the chest, killing him instantly.

Sid grabbed him by the arm and dragged him back to the road. Gathering his pack, he stripped off his own uniform and donned civilian clothing. He dressed the dead German in his own field jacket and shoved him into the driver's seat of the Jeep, using some rope in the back to tie him in an upright position behind the wheel. He removed his own helmet and placed it on the dead German's head.

He was running short of time. He took his belt and fastened it to a cleat in the floor, then to the steering wheel so he could lock it in place quickly. Removing a shoelace from the boot of the dead soldier, he passed it through the bracket holding the accelerator lever and fastened a loop - this allowed him to tighten the pedal down to the floor with a quick tug. He slipped into the seat, reached over and pushed in the clutch with his hand, laying over the seat. He managed to reach up and start the Jeep, jammed it into gear, and began to careen somewhat out of control back down the right side of the "Y" - straight toward the ambush that lay ahead.

The bend the squad sergeant described lay ahead. As he steered around, he pulled on the belt, tightened the steering wheel lock, pulled the shoe-string loop forcing the accelerator to the floor, and bailed out the open passenger side. Still in first gear, the Jeep whined at full throttle, but still ran slow enough to make an easy target. Just as Sid took cover behind in the brush, the machine guns opened up, ripping into the Jeep as it careened past. A single blast from the field gun and the Jeep - with its dead German passenger - burst into flames, blocking the way.

Rifle soldiers moved quickly forward and took positions alongside the road, expecting an assault force to follow immediately. Frozen in position anticipating an attack, and focused on the road, no one saw Sid as he slipped behind the German positions and through to the open ground behind, moving quickly along the side of the road and avoiding the marshy ground to his right. He covered three kilometers as quickly as he could, and - winded - took cover in the brush and waited.

As he expected, the German ambush squad - seeing no attack to follow the Jeep - was recalled to join the major force down the left side of the "Y" and away from Sid's position. No one bothered to check the remains of the Jeep driver as the fire still burned. Sid left the safety of the brush and started back down the road.

His objective - Lorient.

Sid carried false identity papers as an officer of Todt, the paramilitary construction organization building the defensive facilities. Todt managed some 15,000 workers in Lorient at the height of its building program that despite the completeness of the submarine pen facilities was still underway.

He decided to take a direct approach to get to Lorient.

"Halt!" Sid stepped out into the road and stopped a small convoy of Wehrmacht soldiers heading down the road just past the railroad junction south of Hennepont. By the looks of the column they had been mauled pretty badly.

The driver of the Kübelwagen stopped as the young officer in command of the column stood and unholstered his pistol.

"What do you want? Get out of our way!"

"What do I want?" he indignantly spat, and with a fierce scowl trudged to the passenger side of the vehicle and motioned to the soldier sitting in the back seat. "You, move over!" He didn't bother to address the officer. "Take me to command headquarters, immediately."

"You do not give me orders. Who are you?"

"Who am I? Who am I? Are you serious? Do you know what General Farhmbacher will do to you if he finds out you have detained me even a minute longer? Driver - do you have a radio? Contact the general's aide for me, immediately!"

Sid was hoping the column was outside of radio control.

"Enough! You will tell me immediately who you are, and show me your identity papers, or I will shoot you where you sit!"

Sid stood and faced the young officer without flinching.

"I am OT-Einsatzleiter Steiner, on a special assignment for General Farhmbacher to report on the progress of the destruction of the bridge at Hennepont!"

"The bridge has not been destroyed."

"I know that, you idiot! Why do you think I am in such a hurry to get back to the general? Von Rundstedt ordered the bridge destroyed, on a direct order from the Führer! Maybe I should tell him just who is preventing me from reporting. What is your name?"

"I am Hauptmann Klugge. I am in command of this unit ... ."

"Not any more, Klugge. Get out!"

"What?"

"I said get out!" Sid shouted, his face red with fury. "Get out or I will order the driver to shoot you!"

The young captain, flustered by the upbraiding in front of his men, hesitated for just a moment.

"Get out!" and Sid reached for the rifle the soldier in the back seat was holding.

"All right! All right! We will get this resolved once we get to Lorient."

"That's right, Captain - just before the general orders you shot! Driver - drive on. Now! The general's headquarters!"

The driver of the car looked helplessly at the captain then gunned the engine, leading the small column away, and leaving the dumbstruck Captain Klugge standing alone in the road.

Sid "OT-Einsatzleiter Steiner" Woodard waived the sentries aside as the column sped at top speed toward the city. When the driver stopped in front of what Sid guessed was Lorient command headquarters by the flags and military vehicles staged in the plaza, he stepped alone out of the car.

"Your name, driver."

"Gefreiter Harmut, Herr Einsatzleiter."

"Well, you are Oberefreiter now, Harmut. On the personal order of General Farhmbacher. Now be off with you."

The bewildered driver drove off, leaving Sid standing alone in front of the German command headquarters of Festung Lorient.

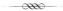

CHAPTER 8

LA GUARDIENNE

A living faith will last in the midst of the blackest storm.
- Mahatma Gandhi

Five men armed with light machine guns waited for Captain Kennedy and his driver where the main road crossed the river La Vilaine near the commune of Le Pont Réan, south of Rennes. A ramshackle company of FFI supplied by Allied airdrops had secured both the highway bridge and the railroad trestle downstream after a pitched battle with German troops. This allowed the Fourth Armored Division to bypass a key German strongpoint and cut off its line of retreat to Brest. Isolated pockets of Germans remained scattered west of the river. Clearing out these stragglers would be left to the FFI.

Kennedy detested these insolent French peasants.

"Undisciplined, and totally unable to follow orders," he protested to his commanding officer when he received his orders. "They hate the Germans, but hate each other even more. The FFI are just a hodgepodge of warring factions, incapable of working together."

Nonetheless, the OSS was tasked with coordinating intelligence gathering from the scattered FFI forces. For the Germans caught in the traps laid by the FFI, the "insolent" French irregulars proved to be vicious fighters who did not take prisoners.

"I am Lucas Prebont. I will interpret. Follow me."

The man hasn't bathed in weeks. My God, the smell! No wonder the Germans are retreating.

Kennedy's Jeep followed the battered car up a one-lane frontage road that branched off the highway and followed the river north a short distance. The fighters had commandeered a large barn for an assembly area; inside they stashed the carbines, machine guns, and explosives. Even more important were the massive stockpiles of foodstuffs the resistance distributed to the local inhabitants to ensure their cooperation.

The vehicles pulled up to the barn and Kennedy got out to stretch.

"I would not waste too much time enjoying the sunshine, Captain. A German sniper would like nothing better than to zap an officer."

The other men laughed as Kennedy hurried inside and out of any potential line-of-sight. The men fanned out and formed a protective perimeter in the woodline that defined the small farm just in case.

The blackness inside the unlit barn swallowed the bright sunshine and Kennedy stopped to adjust his eyes. When he could see again he could make out a small table where a single man sat, a bottle of wine, a loaf of bread, and a map on the table in front of him.

"You are Captain Kennedy?"

"Yes."

"I am Luis Verbon. Have a seat, Captain."

Luis Verbon commanded the FFI faction known as Les Boucliers. For years he hid from the Germans with a death sentence hanging over his head. He had fought in the woods when the only weapons the resistance had were those they stole from dead German soldiers.

Kennedy had read his file carefully. The Germans were correct to fear this man.

"I was told you would have a report for me, Monsieur Verbon."

"Colonel Verbon."

The man's weather-wrinkled face, deeply tanned and covered with a week-old scruff of beard, told of the years of running, and killing.

"Colonel, I am corrected."

Colonel, indeed. This rabble dares to pretend it is a military unit?

"My men took the highway bridge at Hennepont three days ago and held it long enough for your tanks to cross, forcing the Germans back. They tried to destroy the rail bridge but failed to detonate the charges before my men attacked. We cleared the last of the explosives this morning."

The conversation lagged as Verbon stopped to let the interpreter translate for Captain Kennedy.

"How many prisoners did you take?"

Verbon looked with disgust at the impeccably dressed and clean-shaven captain.

"We take no prisoners."

Kennedy waited for the translation, then frowned.

"Colonel Verbon, prisoners are the most important source of intelligence on the disposition of German units, especially artillery and machine gun positions. I must insist your men refrain from killing German soldiers that may want to surrender."

"Refrain from killing?" Verbon stood, defiantly. "These men, Captain, have survived four years of German occupation. They have seen their brothers, their parents, their sweethearts hauled out in the middle of the night and shot outside their front doors. Many have simply disappeared without a trace. They have withstood the rationing, the beatings, the rape of their women. You go and tell them to let the German dogs whimper with their tails between their legs. As for me, I will kill any German I find, even if the mutt is begging for his life."

As the interpreter tried to keep up with the rant, Kennedy knew he would not have the cooperation he wanted from this man. But still he had his orders. The arms shipments would continue, the FFI would continue to kill isolated German units, capture and hold bridges, and clean up behind the quick thrusts of the tanks and mobile infantry.

The two men stared at each other. The standoff was broken when a small boy ran toward Colonel Verbon, nearly out of breath.

"*Papa! Papa! La Guardienne. La Guardienne, elle est ici!*"

Kennedy looked over at his interpreter.

"What did he say?"

"The Guardian is here. Watch what you say, and be careful with your movements."

Careful? Careful of what?

Colonel Verbon turned and quickly followed his son to the back door of the barn. Kennedy watched as two armed men entered through the back door. Unexpectedly, the silhouette of a slight woman appeared backlit by the harsh sunlight outside. He could not yet make out her face, but he saw Verbon suddenly fall to his knees and make the sign of the cross. The woman reached for him and gently touched his shoulder. Kennedy could hear them speaking in low tones, but even the interpreter could not make out what was being said.

The woman turned and looked in his direction. Verbon stood, appeared to argue with her a moment, then bowed his head slightly as the woman walked through the doorway and into the barn. Verbon followed dutifully behind her.

Who is this woman?

"Good afternoon, Captain," she spoke in perfect English.

In the middle of the dirty, foul-smelling rabble that called itself an army stood an old woman. She walked with a slow but graceful gait, her simple peasant dress flowing over the ground, adorned by a soft, silken shawl. The men in the barn deferred to her as if she were royalty. Even Colonel Verbon.

"Good afternoon, madame. And to whom do I have the pleasure?"

The men murmured among themselves. The woman ignored them and stretched out her hand.

"I am Madame Crochet."

"My pleasure, madam."

Kennedy took her hand and kissed it formally, his eyes never leaving hers, studying her face, wondering who she was. She absorbed the intensity of his stare like a drop of rain falling upon a spring field.

Whoever this woman was, Kennedy could feel the anger building among the men in the room. The intensity of their stares fed him, infused him with power over this motley collection of thieves and murderers.

One of the men moved forward and wiped off the chair meant for Kennedy. The woman thanked him and took a seat. Kennedy walked around to the other side of the table where the colonel had been sitting. He left Verbon standing, fuming, in the background.

She turned and spoke quietly to her countrymen. A low murmur swept through the room, but the men dutifully did as she asked and left by the back door, waiting outside. All except Verbon.

"Luis, I wish to have a private word with the captain."

"Leave you alone here? I will not!"

"Yes, Luis, you will." She smiled a serene, gentle smile, absorbing his anger. "What I wish to discuss must be in private."

Kennedy knew she was not asking, but commanding, and however reluctantly Verbon backed away. He shot Captain Kennedy a threatening glance, then turned brusquely and stomped out of the barn.

"Forgive Luis, Captain. Our people have suffered greatly under the occupation. Now that the Germans are in retreat and your army is supplying his men with guns and ammunition, he feels it is his duty to avenge our suffering."

"And you agree with this?"

"I am not a soldier, Captain."

"But these men, they treat you like royalty."

"Somewhat misplaced, I am afraid. I am but a servant of God."

"You are a nun?"

She smiled, and quietly lowered her eyes.

"I serve in other ways."

The ambiguity of her reply intrigued him.

"You speak excellent English."

"I am also versed in Latin and German."

This woman beguiled him. Who was she? She was evasive, yet so casual and calm. She commanded what appeared to be blind obedience from the men.

"I wish to not interfere with your talks with Luis, but when I heard he was to meet with a member of the American intelligence, I decided to come."

"How may I be of service?"

This man has manners, from high society. But he has the eyes of a snake.

"I am from the commune of Redon. Our church has been the sanctuary of a sacred relic for hundreds of years."

"And just what is this relic, madame?"

She dropped her eyes for a moment before turning her face upward, ever so slightly.

"It is called the Madonna Rosa, Captain. Legend says it was carved from the cross upon which the martyrs of Lyon were executed."

"Martyrs?"

"Victims of the Roman persecutions in Gaul, Captain. The Romans tried to extinguish the light of Jesus in the northern province of Gaul. Many were killed in the amphitheater of Lyon, but none so brutally as the virgin slave who is now known as Saint Blandina. She stood facing torture and unimaginable horrors but refused to renounce God to save herself."

Saints? Nonsense.

"A Christian in hiding carved the Madonna from the wooden cross upon which she died. It followed the survivors of the persecutions as they fled west into Brittany and established their own villages, including Redon. They carried the sacred Madonna of the agony of Saint Blandina before them for protection."

These people believe this superstitious dribble?

"When the Roman empire turned to Christianity the Church coveted the Madonna. Under the guise of clearing marauders from the land they attacked the separatists holding the Madonna and slaughtered them at the river, not far from this very spot. The Madonna was held captive to guarantee the fidelity of the independent Bretons until a noble of one of the rebellious houses stole the relic. In turn, a group of bandits stole the relic from the nobles as they fled the Revolution.

"The lone survivor of their attack was a young servant girl. She was spared by the local priest and consecrated to be the first of the Les Guardiennes - an order of women ordained with the blessing of Saint Blandina to protect the Madonna."

La Guardienne. That was the name the boy used to describe her.

"When the army of the Republic fell in 1940, German forces descended upon the villages, looting anything of value they could find. The church at Redon was ransacked by soldiers of the SS looking for the relic. It had been taken into the hills to find safe haven. But we were betrayed by those seeking gain from the German invaders. My daughter was killed. My granddaughter Anisette was captured and taken away by the SS. She is the last to have seen the Madonna."

"She was taken by the SS? How do you know she is even alive?"

"The Germans came to Redon with just one purpose - to find the Madonna Rosa. They would not kill the only Guardienne who knows its secret. But as your army advances, the Germans will become more desperate."

"What do you want, madame?"

"Help us, Captain. Help us find my granddaughter before the Germans seek their revenge against her. Only Anisette knows what has happened to the Madonna."

"Really, madame, this is the responsibility of the police, not the army."

"You seek assistance in fighting the Germans, Captain. Help us find Anisette, and in return, the forces of the French resistance in Brittany will do your bidding, as violent as it is, and follow your orders. If not, they will act on their own, and I fear the consequences of such action for all of us."

Kennedy looked at her suspiciously.

"You can guarantee their cooperation? Under what authority, madame?"

She rose, dismissing his question.

"Soon France will be rid of its German oppressors. But before the soft green grasses return to the fields, the thistle is the first to grow - an illusion of peace held in its thorns. Without the Madonna, peace will not return to Brittany, Captain."

She raised her silken shawl and placed it gently over her head. Kennedy rose. She extended her hand to him, turned, and left as discretely as she had arrived.

Colonel Verbon approached Kennedy and grabbed him forcibly by the arm. Kennedy noticed a small red rose tattooed between his thumb and index finger.

"Do what she asks of you, Captain, or I will slit your throat as you sleep."

Kennedy put down his scotch, lit a cigarette, and watched as the woman finished dressing.

"You wish for me again, *Capitaine*, or perhaps another girl? Perhaps two next time?"

She didn't smile. She made no pretense. Alexander Kennedy was not really listening.

"What do you hear about this thing ... this Madonna Rosa?"

"La Madonna? I hear many things, *Capitaine*, from many men. They say it is very valuable. Many jewels, and the gold ... it is so heavy. Perhaps it is just the talk of men with too much drink. Men who want to impress the ladies."

Jewels, and gold. Yes. I have thought of that. The Catholics like their treasures.

He looked over at the small cabinet in the corner of his billet in the center of town, knowing the small safe was discretely hidden from sight.

Just like the church in Arromanches. That was too easy. But this ... this is a big deal. I've got to plan this out carefully.

The next day Kennedy met with other bands of FFI in various locations, but none of the meetings were anything but routine - situation reports, hand-drawn maps showing the locations of pockets of German soldiers, and the escape routes slowly being closed by the resistance. He promised more arms, more food, and closer communication before returning to headquarters.

"I want a complete report, Kennedy. Deliver it to me personally by 2100 hours."

His commanding officer was in no mood for excuses. Something was happening, and while Kennedy completed dictating his meeting with Colonel Verbon and the mysterious woman who wore the silken shawl, headquarters company prepared for another move. When the report was finally transcribed, Kennedy slipped it into a large envelope, sealed it, and headed for his meeting.

"I'm sorry, Captain. But the colonel has been called away."

"I am supposed to deliver this to the colonel personally. When will he return?"

"Not until tomorrow, Captain."

Exhausted by the long drive through Brittany, Kennedy left the headquarters compound for dinner in a local restaurant, and sought out his favorite prostitute and a bottle of cognac.

His commanding officer burst into his office early the following morning as Kennedy nursed a violent headache.

"Be in my office at 0800. We are moving east."

The Germans had dug in and mounted a counter-attack against Patton's extended flank, threatening Allied supply lines. Alerted by Ultra intercepts, elements of the First Army blunted the attack, and although the fighting continued for a few days, after the first twenty-four hours the offensive was effectively destroyed.

The Canadians began to move south toward a town called Falais. Patton struck back, swinging beneath the German counterattack and began to quickly close the pincer. Headquarters needed an intelligence officer at the front and Kennedy was the only one available on such short notice. He left the colonel's office and was driven to his billet with only five minutes to pack. He managed to retrieve the small safe before he was driven to the front.

He forgot about the envelope.

The battle at Falais Gap would destroy the fighting ability of the German army in Normandy. The carnage on the ground at Falais was likened to a recreation of Dante's Inferno. General Eisenhower would later write,

> It was literally possible to walk for hundreds of yards
> at a time, stepping on nothing but dead and decaying
> flesh. (2)

Third Army raced across central France attacking the fleeing Germans as they retreated to the Rhine. The corps headquarters was ordered east, and Colonel Verbon's threat dissolved into the night and fog of war.

"What about Woodard, Major?"

Major Codman looked up at his aide as they prepared to follow General Patton with the headquarters company.

"Woodard? We have not heard from him. He's on his own, Lieutenant - if he's not already dead."

CHAPTER 9

TICKS ON THE HOUND

Never yield to the apparently
overwhelming might of the enemy.
-Winston Churchill

Sid did not linger in front of Lorient Wehrmacht headquarters - he
headed for the waterfront, the one place he knew he could find a
doorway into the underworld of the city. He found a safe place to
hide for the night and catch some much-needed sleep.

At first light he cautiously slipped out onto the streets of Lorient,
watching, waiting. When he saw two German soldiers turn the corner
in front of him he pressed back into a doorway along a rough stretch
of side street two blocks from the quay. He watched them as they
called to a young French boy who exited a rude doorway.

"You, boy. Come here."

The boy stopped. One of the soldiers took a quick look around.

"Apple? You have apple?" he called out in broken French.

"Fifty," the boy replied.

"Fifty? Ten."

The boy turned and walked away. One of the soldiers ran after
him and grabbed him by the collar of his coat.

"Twenty. No more."

"Thirty."

The soldier withdrew a stack of German script from his pocket and counted out ... twenty-five. The boy looked up and down the street, removed a fresh apple from his coat pocket, took the script, and disappeared down and around the corner away from the soldiers.

The soldier took out a small knife and cut the apple in two, giving half to his companion. They continued their walk up the street. After they passed, Sid slipped out of the doorway and followed in the direction the boy had disappeared.

"Twenty-five? Mon dieu, how does he do it, Henri?"

"He is a devil, that one. He learned it from his mother!"

The two men laughed.

"Pay me." The boy stood defiantly in the kitchen of the café waiting for his cut. His father, Henri Gireau peeled off his share of the payment and the boy headed for the back door. Sid waited, listening. He grabbed the boy by the arm as he hit the street.

"Come with me. If you cry out, I will kill you."

The boy fell into step beside him as Sid hurried up the street, then ducked into the alley.

"So," the boy started. "What do you want? A woman? Wine? I can get you anything. For the right price."

"I have marks."

The boy raised his eyebrows. What was this man who spoke very poor French, probably a German spy, doing with German Reichsmarks instead of francs or military script? That was rare, especially on the docks.

"Marks can buy anything, monsieur."

"I need papers. I think you know where I can get them."

The boy backed away.

"No, monsieur. I do not know of such things. An apple, maybe a cut of pork."

Sid pressed him back against the wall of the warehouse.

"I think you do."

"Please, monsieur. I am just a boy."

"Cut the crap, boy," Sid spoke in English. The boy looked at him in surprise.

"*Américain? Tu es Américain?*"

"Yes. And I saw you, in the café. And with the German soldiers. You know how to contact the right people."

The boy sized him up for a moment.

"And what is it worth to you, *Américain?*"

"It's maybe worth not turning you in to the Gestapo."

"Ten marks." The boy did not even flinch at the threat.

At the inflated exchange rate, this was two hundred francs - a relative fortune on the local economy if his money weren't counterfeit. With the inflation on the black market, one could only guess. (3)

"For the papers?"

"No. To bring the man to you. That is all."

"Three."

"Seven, or I go to the Gestapo." The boy held out his hand.

"Two now. Two when you show."

"Pay now."

Sid turned and began to head back to the street. The boy grabbed him by the arm.

"OK, OK, *Américain*. Two now. Three later."

"Five? Done."

Sid guessed the boy would pocket the down payment, and only share the payoff.

"Come with me."

The boy led Sid down the alley and through a broken doorway into one of the abandoned warehouses damaged by Allied bombs in the frequent aerial and artillery attacks on the city. It was a convenient spot for a clandestine meeting - or an ambush.

"Wait here. I will be back in one hour." The boy disappeared out the door.

The room had once been an office, Sid figured. He took the hour to carefully inspect the nooks and crannies - and especially the exits - before he decided just where he would wait. He knew the boy would not just walk through the front doorway with the men from the maquis. Chances are they would try to surprise him and keep the upper hand. Perhaps they would just kill him for whatever currency he had. In any event, he would be prepared.

Sid picked a vantage point on the loading ramp above the office. From there he could see the approach along the alley, the open space in the shell of a warehouse to his back, and an emergency exit he fashioned by prying off a few planks on a side wall. He knew there could be other ways to approach without being seen, but he had to trust this makeshift setup. From here he could disappear along the sidewall and out the back to the port with ease if it was a trap.

The hour passed, and no one showed.

I wouldn't show on the hour either. Too obvious.

Another hour passed, but Sid remained in his place. He figured the area was under a close watch, and his contacts would arrive only when they felt it was safe. If he tired of the wait, it only proved to them he was lying to the boy.

The first movement came from the side. Sid saw a man steal carefully toward the office using several old packing crates to conceal his path. He carried a small machine pistol - the lookout. If there were any hint of trouble, this man could slip away quietly and warn the others. If there was a firefight, his pistol could lay down a blast of suppressing fire sufficient to allow everyone to escape into the maze formed by the bombed out buildings.

Two more approached through the open back warehouse fifteen minutes later, coming off the quay. Sid could see they were also lightly armed for mobility. Neither of these would be the contact. This was the protective firepower no one was supposed to see.

A lone man wearing a beret sauntered slowly along the alley, in plain sight. He stopped, lit a cigarette, and openly smoked in the street. This was a test - an open invitation to any German soldiers who may be within view. A single civilian with a cigarette would draw them like flies and they would try to barter for smokes, or just steal them. No one showed.

As Sid waited for the man to enter the door, a slight noise behind him caught his attention. He turned and saw the boy moving along the upper storage ledge - the same route Sid had taken to reach this lookout spot.

Smart kid.

As the boy passed in front of him, Sid grabbed him quickly and smothered his face with his hand. He reached his arm around the boy's throat and pulled him back into his small recess.

"Ssh," he hissed, quietly. The boy simply looked at him with widened eyes.

The man in the street tossed his cigarette into the gutter. At that prearranged signal, the two from the back warehouse burst through the door into the office, weapons drawn. At the same time the man pushed through the front door. The office was empty.

"Pascal?" The man who entered the front door cried out.

The boy tried to speak.

"You are Pascal?" Sid whispered. He nodded his head. "Who is the man?" Sid loosed his grip just enough.

"Papa!" he cried out before Sid clamped back down on his mouth again.

Sid thought for a moment.

"Place your weapons on the floor so I can see them. And tell the man behind the side wall to do the same. Do it now, or I slit the boy's throat."

"Pascal?" the man cried.

Sid loosened his grip again, enough for the boy to cry out, "Papa!"

The man took a breath, a scowl on his face, then barked an order to the others. The first man entered through the office side door and they all placed their weapons on the floor.

"Now step back, against the wall. We are coming down."

Sid pulled his pistol and pointed at the boy's head, just to remind him who was in control. He nodded his head, and the two climbed back down to the main floor and entered the office. Sid kept his hand on the boy's collar for good measure.

"Let the boy go, then we talk." The man wearing the beret watched Sid carefully.

"I have no reason to harm the boy. Just making sure we all talk nice."

Sid released the boy who turned and kicked him square in the shins. The men in the room laughed.

"Who are you?"

"I am OSS, American army."

"And what are you doing here, behind the lines?" asked the man wearing the beret.

"I am counting German artillery installations."

Henri Gireau did not believe him, but it made no difference.

"How did you get past the German sentries?"

"I faked my way in - by browbeating a stupid German boy masquerading as a captain."

One of the men sidled up to the leader and whispered into his ear.

"You made quite an entrance, I am told. The Germans are on a high state of alert looking for you. That will cost you more."

"So we can do business?"

"If you have the money."

"I have the money."

"You need papers. That will cost you plenty. And your money - it is counterfeit, I suppose?"

Sid knew it was pointless to lie to this man.

"Of course."

"Let me see one of the larger bills."

Sid expected this, and handed him a hundred mark note from his shirt pocket.

"Very nice. British. They make the best forgeries. OK, we can do business. What kind of papers do you need?"

"I want to be able to move freely. I speak fluent German. I have masqueraded as a member of Todt before."

"No, that will not work. They are looking for such a man after your stunt yesterday. We will talk this over and come up with something suitable."

"When?"

"Tomorrow. You will need a place to hide until then. You will come with us."

He pointed to the pile of weapons on the floor, and Sid put his pistol away. The men retrieved their weapons and one of the men checked the street.

"It is clear."

"OK, we can go. Do not hurry. You and Pascal will follow me. Understood?"

"Yes."

Just then another man Sid had not seen stepped into the office from the side warehouse, a machine pistol at the ready. Sid looked at Pascal's father and he smiled.

"This is Marcel. One cannot be too careful."

As Sid turned to follow, the boy stuck out his hand and stopped him.

"Three marks," he demanded.

"The papers - they will not be ready until morning. Until then, you stay with me ... where I can see you. Or I will shoot you myself."

Henri Gireau led him through a labyrinth of streets, alleys, and bombed out buildings as they travelled along their own unique path through Fortress Lorient. The impressive show of force the resistance cell brandished during their meeting turned out to be mostly bluff. The four machine pistols lacked ammunition. Most of their weapons were outdated and crude, suitable for killings wharf rats but not much else. Sid found out quickly only the unseen Marcel had any ammunition at all, and few rounds at that.

The constant threat of German patrols honed their habits and sharpened their response, however. Despite their lack of firepower they remained a considerable threat - innovative and resourceful, using the chaos of the rubble-filled city to their advantage. Poorly escorted supply trucks were their prime targets.

Henri Gireau captained the coastal boat *Sorcière* and moved cargo regularly between the mainland and the string of islands off the mouth of the harbor at Lorient - including Belle Isle. When the Germans invaded Gireau and his family were forced from their apartment at gunpoint to make way for occupation soldiers. They moved aboard the *Sorcière*. He operated only under direct orders of the Lorient harbor master.

German soldiers hauled his daughter away one night to serve in one of their brothels. His wife disappeared when she left the *Sorcière* to meet a black marketeer to buy some bread. Young Pascal never knew what happened to his mother. Gireau joined the resistance in retaliation.

"So, what are you really doing here, *Américain?*"

Sid had given a lot of thought to how he would answer these questions. He knew this man would not trust him unless his story was plausible, and his actions believable.

"The Germans have extensive artillery spread throughout the occupied zone and the surrounding islands." At the mention of the islands, Gireau raised his eyebrows. "The British surface fleet will not try to penetrate the bay - it is busy protecting the supply convoys between Britain and Normandy. That leaves the U-boats a free hand to resupply Lorient by sea."

Gireau sat back and contemplated Sid's explanation.

He is hiding something. Patience, Henri.

"We do not have good intelligence on the strength and disposition of the artillery or the structures of the submarine pens. I was sent in to find that information out."

What about the islands?

"Well, *Américain*, you ask a lot for a man we still do not trust. Tonight we attack a supply convoy. I can either leave you here with a guard or take you along. Perhaps you are willing to earn your keep."

Sid followed Henri through the rubble of bombed out Lorient to the *Sorcière* moored along the quay next to one of the old warehouses.

Five men waited inside; it took a bit of explaining to get them to relax around Sid, but the men eventually got down to business.

"The U-227 docks tonight. The supply boat will be unloaded at Scorff and the supplies ready for distribution by morning. Le Cercle will be driving the last truck of the convoy ... ," and the man drew his finger along a route on a makeshift map of Lorient. "The driver will fail to make this turn and will instead turn down the alley where the truck will be emptied."

"The Black Circle - what is this?" Sid had not heard this name before.

"The Black Circle - Le Cercle Noir. They control the black market in Lorient and Saint-Nazaire. They offload the submarines and distribute the supplies according to the manifests."

"Yes, two for you, one for me!" The men laughed.

"So they steal from the cargo?"

"It is an effective organization. The Germans pay them to unload the cargoes and they siphon even more off the top."

"What of the police?"

Again, the men laughed.

"Who do you think runs the Black Circle? That Nazi lapdog, Foucault, Prefect of Police for Lorient. Except this is a dog who feeds himself by biting his master's ass."

"And what of the bombing?"

"It is too dangerous to keep the goods here. The Circle moves them offshore, then by boat to Saint-Nazaire and other ports once payment is made."

"They operate through the Citadel?"

At the mention of the fortress, the men stopped, and looked at Sid suspiciously.

"What do you know of this place?"

"Not much, except this is a likely spot - remote enough, too small to be a good bombing target."

The men looked at each other.

"The Citadel is on Belle Isle, at the harbor of Le Palais. It is an old fortress the Germans control. The garrison is small, but it guards the entrance to Lorient with artillery. It is isolated and secure from prying eyes. The Germans move supplies through the Citadel. Their munitions come by boat from the fortified complex at Keroman on the mainland. These boats return with goods unloaded from submarines - mostly foodstuffs and coal oil. Truck convoys move these goods to Lorient where a portion disappears into Le Circle's private warehouse."

"And the garrison commander?"

"Part of the Circle, or course."

One of the men spit on the floor.

"And you take what you can from the Circle?"

"We do what we can."

"You attack the convoys?"

"We are the ticks the Germans cannot scratch off, nothing more. But it is enough to keep food in the mouths of our children and coal oil in the stove in winter."

Ticks, indeed. Sid would learn all too quickly the ferocious bite of these maquis parasites.

"So, what do you think of our little operation, *Américain?*"

Sid poured himself a cup of the black swill that masqueraded as coffee from the pot on the coil oil stove in the galley.

"You are short of ammunition, short of firepower, and your attack plan is flawed."

The man called Marcel grabbed Sid by the front of his shirt and pulled him close.

"You can do better, I suppose? With what little resources we have?"

"Yes I can, and you'd better let go or you will miss the attack."

"Stop. We do not fight among ourselves. Save it for the Germans." Henri lit a cigarette and offered it to Marcel. "What do you mean, you can do better?"

Sid straightened his collar then snatched the cigarette from Henri's outstretched hand and took a drag before passing it along to Marcel.

"Your plan calls for machine pistol fire to separate the column from its guard and force it along the path you choose. You do not have sufficient ammunition to achieve the rate of fire you need, let alone to suppress a counter-attack."

"And you have a better idea?"

"You need to use explosives."

"And you happen to have grenades and satchels, do you?"

"No, but I can show you how to make effective satchel bombs."

"With what - fertilizer? Do you think we do not know this? The Germans have shipped most of the ammonium nitrate north that was once stockpiled here. What little there is will accomplish nothing."

"If used conventionally, I would agree with you. How much do you think you can get your hands on? And a couple buckets of nails?"

The four-truck supply convoy left the secure compound of the Scorff submarine pen escorted by a lead truck with five soldiers and a mounted machine gun. The convoy turned left and crossed the Scorff River bridge before turning along the river toward the industrial sector of Lorient. Once safely in the distribution warehouse the supplies entered the ration system where it would be apportioned by status, political expediency, and bureaucratic rank. What was left, if any, was slated for general distribution.

One of the trucks would never be unloaded. Carefully screened while still under the watchful eye of the Wehrmacht, the truck would peel off from the convoy at a predetermined point and head - less conspicuously - to the private warehouse of the Circle. A portion of the goods would be offloaded and distributed as bribes to German and local officials. The rest would be loaded on small boats for transport back to Belle Isle where it entered the black market supply chain run by police captain Foucault - and commanded extraordinary inflated prices.

A small lorry waited at the end of Rue de l'Ecole with one of Henri Gireau's men at the wheel. The gas tank of the stolen truck was packed with one of Sid's "little creations" manufactured from the meager explosive materials the maquis had on hand.

"It's not about the force of the blast, but the effect of the chaos it creates. That's what matters. Force alone is an illusion," he lectured as he showed several of the men how to maximize their meager resources. "Knowing the route the convoy will take is our hole card."

The first truck of the convoy passed the turn to Rue de Poulorio, not much more than a small feeder alley between warehouses. Suddenly a battered old truck heading from the opposite direction turned sharply, plowing into the front driver-side fender of the lead truck. The shock sent the driver hurtling forward into the steering wheel, momentarily stunning him as the two trucks crashed. Two soldiers in the back flew out of the bed of the truck and sprawled on the ground. Before the other soldiers could react, the attacking truck exploded with a horrendous noise - smoke, a flash of fire, and bits of nails and glass tearing into the faces and hands of the men and blowing out the truck windshield. Panic immediate beset the remaining drivers, certain the soldier's vehicle had been destroyed in the fire blast along with their covering machine gun firepower.

"*Schnell, schnell!*" the driver of the second truck screamed, and jammed his truck into reverse. He pushed into the following trucks, forcing them all to back down the main road some twenty meters, and turned sharply onto Rue de Poulorio. He gunned the engine, taking the rest of the convoy with him - and away from the soldiers and their machine gun.

"Now!" Sid called out. The men ignited a series of small blasts as the convoy sped down the alley. The trucks were splattered with nails, blowing out the side windows, the steel fragments tearing into flesh. Panic ripped through the drivers. First one truck, then another, then a third sped past the turn to Rue de l'Ecole and into the trap.

At the signal, Marcel Regeant gunned a stolen truck parked on the side street and rammed its way between the third and fourth trucks - the one earmarked for the Circle. The driver of the fourth truck jammed on his brakes but was too late to avoid the crash. He hit Regeant's truck just behind the driver's side - exactly where they had planned - the force spinning the truck sideways and jamming the convoy truck into the side building.

Two men dashed from the building's back door and grabbed the driver, hauling him to the ground, striking him a sharp blow to the head. As he lay bleeding and unconscious, the men jumped behind the wheel as Regeant detonated a small incendiary device and the decoy truck burst into flames. He jumped into the loot truck as the engine roared to life and drove away - up Rue de L'Ecole, disappearing around the corner heading back to the east side of the river.

In a few moments the attack was over. The bulk of the convoy sped away while the truck with the machine gun, now turned, tried to catch up. Sid watched in amusement as the soldiers roared back up to the scene of the crash and sped past the now burning decoy truck chasing after the rest of the convoy.

Not a single round of their precious ammunition had been shot, nor a single man wounded. In the confusion, the loot truck had been completely abandoned and the soldier's machine gun neutralized.

The men gathered at the agreed upon rendezvous.

"I thought we were all dead men," was all Henri Gireau could laugh.

Sid sat back with a bottle of wine and a look of satisfaction on his face.

"It's not how big the blast, but the chaos you create in the minds of your enemy. They did all the work. They panicked, and never realized no one had been seriously hurt - except maybe the driver Jean Pierre clubbed."

"We had to leave at least one body lying on the ground. We have a reputation to think of."

The men all laughed.

"Blowing out the windshields was easy, but gives the illusion of far more damage. The nails - they will leave their scars, but I doubt if we killed any of the soldiers - we simply did not have the firepower to do that. The side explosions, they panicked the drivers so badly they could only see one thing - the open end of the alley and their own freedom. That gave us the opportunity to hit the last truck while the others drove off sacrificing him. As for the soldiers - by the time they reacted, the attack was over. All they could do was try and catch up - and explain to their superior why not a single round of machine gun fire was used to ward off the attack."

"As for the Circle," Henri proclaimed as he raised his bottle high, "we have their truck, their cargo, and that Nazi-loving fool Captain Foucault still has to pay the bribes he promised. All in all, a pretty good day."

Sid knew these men would cooperate with him now. He also knew the Black Circle would be stirred to action by the attack.

Men consumed with thoughts of revenge make mistakes.

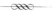

CHAPTER 10

THE CITADEL

*Men are so simple and so much inclined to obey
immediate needs that a deceiver will never lack
victims for his deceptions.*
- Niccolo Machiavelli

Wine flowed that night in the galley of the *Sorcière*.

"Wine is our currency. Everything is rationed, but we stockpiled a large cache at the first news of the German breakthrough in Belgium in 1940. The Circle has also obliged us with much of their own supply over the years. We trade it for much of what we cannot steal."

Henri Gireau and Sid were the last to remain at the table, savoring the victory. The others had wandered off in the dark streets to resume their daily occupations or hide from the ever-present police. Gireau deliberately kept Sid on board the *Sorcière*, and under his control.

"To tell you the truth, my friend, I had fully expected to have to shoot you in the back during this little escapade you planned. But you have proven yourself. So it is time to drop the pretense. You were not sent here to count artillery. A flyover with cameras can do that. What are you really doing here?"

Sid stood at a crossroads. He had precious little time to complete his mission; and these men and their families - they might certainly be killed in the coming air assault unless they were warned. Yes, it was time to lay it all open.

"I need to get to Belle Isle."

"What for?"

"Two things. What I told you about getting the intelligence on artillery capability and the size of the garrison was true. Command is concerned artillery from the island would be hard to neutralize and could disrupt any plans for a sea assault to coincide with an attack on Lorient."

"So there is an assault planned?"

"Yes."

"We have survived air attacks before."

"Not like this one."

Sid left the weight of this warning hang in the air.

"When?"

"I have until the fifteenth to get out of here. It will occur sometime after that."

"Not much time, my friend. For you or us. But you say there are two objectives?"

"Yes. I am looking for an artifact, something apparently of great value to the Church."

At the mention of the Church Henri spit on the floor.

"Collaborators. They kiss the ass of the German regime so they can take their cut of the spoils. I have no reason to help the damn Catholics."

Sid realized he hit a nerve - the schism between the resistance and the Catholic Church that Patton feared.

"Look, I couldn't care less about what the Church wants, but the military is afraid of fueling a rift between the Church and the French forces that might cause trouble in their rear once the assault turns east and north, to Paris."

Henri thought over the explanation carefully.

"Yes, that would be wise. Your feet must stand on hard ground in order to fight. This artifact - what is it?"

"The monsignor called it the Madonna Rosa."

At the mention of the Madonna, Gireau looked up, startled.

"The Madonna Rosa?"

"Yes. You know of it?"

Henri spit on the floor again.

"It is not the property of the Church despite what lies you have been told. The Church has sought the Madonna for several hundred years. It is the symbol of independence for Brittany, not an icon of the Church."

"I don't understand. Monsignor Jacquette personally approached General Patton asking him to help him recover the icon on behalf of the Archdiocese."

"It was taken from the Church when the Duchy of Breton tried to secede from the authority of the Crown, and from the nobility following the Revolution. It has remained in darkness ever since, hidden from the Crown Church by those loyal to Breton independence."

"You said it has remained in darkness ... what do you mean by that?"

"Hidden, and protected by a secret order of women descended from a child blessed by the Breton church when the Madonna was taken back from the nobility. I have heard rumors it has disappeared -

all Brittany knows of this. But no one knows where. Not even La Guardienne."

"La Guardienne?"

"Les Guardiennes follow the matrilineal line of descent from the blessed child. Each Guardienne receives her charge from her mother on her ascendency to womanhood. She in turn passes that on to her daughter, and hers in turn.

"La Guardienne teaches her daughter the traditions and passes the trust forward. But something happened during the fall of France, and the trust was broken. The relic disappeared from its sacred place - probably to keep it free from the Germans. Only God knows where its rests."

"This madonna. Describe it."

"I cannot. No one save Les Guardiennes have actually seen it. It could be hanging in the public square and we would not know of it."

"The monsignor thinks it is held on Belle Isle."

Henri Gireau just shook his head.

"I will not help the Church steal the Madonna."

"Henri, I am not after the artifact. Neither is the American Army. General Patton wants the intelligence to justify sealing off Lorient and bypassing the fortress. The monsignor simply bought him an extra week to make his case. Nothing more."

Henri Gireau gave Sid a long, hard stare.

"And the Madonna Rosa? What if it is on the island, as you believe?"

"I don't want it. Do with it what you will."

Gireau poured himself the last glass of wine from the bottle.

"Then I will get you to Belle Isle. If you are lying, I will slit your throat."

He raised his glass to Sid.

The following morning Sid heard Gireau talking to Marcel from the deck of the *Sorcière* as he poured coffee.

"Tell the mate to expect a passenger. I will follow later when I get the orders."

Gireau came below and poured himself a cup.

"We have a fishing boat to take you to Belle Isle. The captain is not one of us, but has no ties to the Circle. He has agreed to play the fool in our little charade."

"How do I get past the harbor master?"

"You will see, in a moment. I will follow later in the *Sorcière* to bring you out. A call was made for supply craft to work the harbor - that means a submarine will be arriving soon - perhaps the same one we stole from. That will be my ticket into the harbor. I will arrange a place for you to stay where we can meet."

"You will help unload the submarine?"

Gireau just smiled.

"A man has to work to support his family, does he not? But if you find the Madonna Rosa, I will kill to keep it from the priests. I might even have to kill you, my friend."

The two stared at each other for a moment. A knock on the galley door broke the silence.

"Ah, this would be your identity papers ... *entree!*"

A bookish old man opened the door and carefully examined the galley before entering.

"It is okay, Alfonse. This is a friend."

"A friend who speaks perfect German I hear?" He smiled. "I think you will like what I have prepared for him. But you must get him out of Lorient quickly."

"What have you heard?"

"They shot a young officer this morning for allowing a spy to enter Lorient. I presume that was our friend here. The police are searching everywhere."

The old man handed Gireau an envelope, nodded his head, and backed out of the room. Henri looked at the documents and laughed.

"So, he has outdone himself ... fitting, for what I charged you. Your ticket past the harbor master."

He handed Sid the documents.

Sturmbannführer Reiner Schuster
SS Special Intelligence

"What about a uniform?"

Henri smiled.

"It is my pleasure to do business with you ... ."

The cargo boat *Toirette* rounded the breakwater and entered the harbor at Le Palais, the rolling swells of the Atlantic finally subsiding. The commercial quay lay to starboard, beneath the massive gray edifice of Citadel Vauban. Twelve hundred German troops - an odd assortment of U-boat and naval crewmen, ground forces, and crews of the Luftwaffe - were bivouacked on this small island in the Bay of

Biscay. The fortress held four separate radar sites and a Radio Direction Finding (RDF) installation. A dozen strongpoints, ten medium guns, and four howitzers - the largest two being 175s - defended the approaches to Lorient and Saint-Nazaire harbors.

Unknown to the Allies -- and the German OKW - the island kept an assortment of captives, both British and French, in an ancient stone prison. The commander Colonel Helmut Fleischer had been held prisoner here by the French as a young soldier captured in the Great War. He now reveled in the reversal of roles. Rumors of atrocities spoken only in whispers kept the small civilian population fearful and docile.

There was no way to get to Belle Isle except by small private boat - or German submarine. The harbor master dutifully checked each boat as it either entered or departed the harbor of Le Palais. All of the boats except the *Toirette*. The captain tied to the quay without the usual interference and inspection, and walked nonchalantly into the small dockside warehouse office.

"A rough crossing today, eh, Molaisson?"

The clerk of the harbor always tried to strike up a conversation with the *Toirette's* sour-faced captain Raynell Molaisson, but always failed. At best he received a grunt of acknowledgement. On most days he ignored the young clerk completely unless he blurted out orders.

"I want to leave the harbor by 9:00. Have my cargo off the boat and the shipment for Saint-Nazaire readied by 7:00 tonight."

He walked out of the office and through the warehouse, out the back door, and covered the short distance to the entrance of the Citadel. The massive arch seemed to lead directly into the bowels of the earth, an illusion only heightened by the dark gray edifice looming above. The dimly lit passageway led to a maze of underground passages and chambers. The Citadel served as the operations base for the Circle and its black market commerce between Lorient and Saint-Nazaire. Payoffs to the garrison commander guaranteed the Wehrmacht ignored the frequent arrivals of Captain Foucault's small fleet.

Captain Molaisson was in a foul mood. The shipment today was short, and his cut would barely cover the cost of fuel. If the Circle wanted him to sail on to Saint-Nazaire there would have to be an "accommodation." A serious one. He barged into the office of the harbor police prefecture.

"Devere Gagner, my cargo is short! What the hell is going on?"

"Captain, please, it could not be helped."

"Explain yourself. I was promised a full hold. I cannot even make fuel with this load."

"I am so sorry, Captain. But we all have to deal with the problems of supply."

"Yes, but you sit here nice and comfortable in your puny office while I face the British, those damn side swells, and pay for my own fuel."

"The last cargo, it was intercepted by the maquis. They took an entire truck. They have become even more dangerous, and used explosives this time. The shortage could not be helped."

Molaisson was not moved by the harbor master's excuses.

"Lorient is falling apart. The maquis are getting bolder. And now this spy running loose? Foucault had better watch his ass - or he may find himself disappearing one day."

"What is this? A spy, in Lorient?" The harbor master had not heard.

"They executed an officer by firing squad this morning. They say he let a spy bluff his way into Lorient. The city is on high alert looking for him. They run around like chickens, these stupid French police, while my business falls apart in the chaos!"

Molaisson spit on the floor.

"I pay a high price for protection and must accept this nonsense? I expect a full cargo and a decent cut. Unless there is more to this, you can forget the trip to Saint-Nazaire."

At this threat, the harbor master stiffened.

"Captain, there is critical cargo expected in Saint-Nazaire. Foucault will insist you make the run tonight."

"Then you fill my fuel tanks, stock my galley, and pay me extra to compensate me for my trouble."

"I cannot authorize this, Captain. I will have to radio Captain Foucault."

"I don't care what you have to do. See the boat is ready by 7:00. Or you can tell Foucault he can find me at the La Maison with my hands on some sweaty whore."

He stormed out of the Citadel and headed for La Maison Belle, the *plaison soldatenbordell*, or military brothel, operated for the relief of the soldier's "sexual excesses" while stationed in the backwater garrison. A bottle of brandy and a cigar would help settle his anger, and he could charge the visit to the Prefect of Police.

"You will bathe first, you fat smelly pig," Madame Loutran demanded. She delivered the brandy herself, and selected one of her girls who she hoped could handle the excesses of the violent captain.

The previous spring one of her girls was found strangled in his room, her body cut with a sharp razor. Molaisson had already gone to sea. The Prefect had to pay a fee to Madame Loutran for her trouble.

"Monsieur Gagner, an unknown boat is approaching the harbor."

The Harbor Prefect had tried all afternoon to place a telephone call to the Lorient prefect of police to warn him of the now drunken Captain Molaisson and his extortion demand with little results. Even the radio was not working. The lull in Allied air attacks did little to ease communication difficulties.

"What kind of boat?"

"A private cargo boat, monsieur. It is too far out to make out the name."

"Private? I have no authorization for such a trip!"

Devere Gagner left his office and scurried down to the quay to meet the boat before it docked. As a U-boat supply base, no boats were allowed to enter the harbor unexpectedly. So the arrival of the small cargo boat was a cause for great concern. As the boat rounded the breakwater Gagner could finally make out the name - the *Maxine*.

"Captain, remain on your vessel! I demand to see your authorization to enter the harbor!"

The captain shoved the helm over, backed the screws off, and nudged sideways to the quay. He wrapped a dock line on a cleat and looked with disdain at the immaculately dressed Gagner, fussing like an old hen on the dock.

"This is my authorization," he spat.

The door to the cabin opened and an officer stepped on deck, the double "SS" emblem on his tunic sending a chill down the harbor master's spine.

The officer looked around, annoyed.

"Captain, turn off your engines! I do not wish to breathe that foul-smelling exhaust!" he snapped, reaching for a starched white handkerchief from his tunic pocket, covering his mouth and nose. The captain passed him a nasty look and shut off his engines. The officer stepped onto the quay, free of the exhaust, and glanced up at the Citadel looming above the harbor, ignoring the harbor master.

"Impressive architecture. But hardly appropriate for a military base."

He began to strut up the quay casually, Harbor Master Gagner falling in behind him.

"Pardon, monsieur, but your purpose here? This is a restricted area."

"I am here to see Commandant Fleischer. You will tell him Sturmbannführer Reiner Schuster of SS Special Intelligence has arrived and wishes an audience. Immediately."

"But Herr Schuster, I cannot allow you to disembark without orders. This is most unusual."

"What is your name?" The SS officer continued walking, and would not look at Gagner.

"I am Harbor Master Gagner."

"Well, Harbor Master, do as I instruct you. The SS does not explain itself to the French civil authorities."

"But Herr Schuster, your orders?"

"My orders do not concern you. You, however, should be concerned my report may mention your reluctance to assist me, Herr Gagner." The officer stopped, placed the handkerchief back in his breast pocket, but refused to turn around. "Now, I have been most accommodating. You will immediately go and tell Commandant Fleischer I have arrived. In the meantime, I will examine the grounds at my convenience. You may come and approach me once I have been announced."

The officer, a Sturmbannführer in the SS - the equivalent rank of major in the Wehrmacht - strutted off and away up the hill toward the Citadel leaving the flustered harbor master wondering what to do next. He heard the engines of the fishing boat roar to life as the captain cast off and headed up the harbor seeking moorage.

"That crazy Américain has a death wish," the captain muttered to himself.

"Major Schuster, to what do I owe the privilege?"

Colonel Fleischer rose to greet the SS officer cautiously. He outranked the major, but the Wehrmacht had no command authority over the SS. With orders in hand, Major Schuster stepped into Fleischer's office with a cold, calculated look on his face.

Colonel Fleischer had never dealt with the SS directly. This unannounced visit had him desperately searching his memory - what could have gone wrong? What had been left undone? Who had not been paid off? Was he here about the spy in Lorient?

"A routine visit, Colonel. Thank you for seeing me on such short notice."

Colonel Fleischer motioned for him to sit and offered him a cognac.

"I do not drink alcohol," was all he replied, looking around the room, not making eye contact. Major Schuster wanted to put the colonel off his guard. Refusing the obvious social offering seemed like a good start.

The orderly in Fleischer's outer office had examined the orders - customary for an officer from a different arm of the Reich apparatus. Sid hoped the colonel would think better of examining the fake orders himself.

"I am a little surprised the SS has taken an interest in our small garrison, Major."

"Yes. So it would seem."

What does that mean?

"Is there something in particular I can assist you with?"

Major Schuster cocked his head slightly and sighed with a look of complete boredom.

"You receive regular supply shipments by U-boat, do you not, Colonel?"

Colonel Fleischer tried to remain calm. Of course he received supply by submarine. What is he after?

Major Schuster stood and walked to a large map of the island on the wall, turning his back to the colonel.

"We have concerns over the security of these shipments."

"I can assure you, Herr Schuster, we carefully screen everybody arriving on the island. The Lorient spy could not have come to Le Palais."

He turned back to face Fleischer.

"And what spy would that be, Colonel?"

The cold stare Fleischer saw in the major's eyes caught him short.

Shut up, you stupid fool, and wait for him to speak.

"Just rumors, Herr Major."

"Spreading rumors is not becoming of an officer, Colonel. I would be more discrete in the future."

"Yes, of course, Herr Major."

A bead of sweat began to trickle down Fleischer's forehead.

"I am here on other matters." Major Schuster sat back down and lit a cigarette. He did not offer one to the colonel. "Why, for example, has Lorient been bombed repeatedly by Allied aircraft, yet not a single attack has occurred here?"

"This is a very small port, Major. A small target."

"Yet the fighter-bombers routinely hit small targets on the mainland, do they not? A locomotive on a track presents a smaller target than your Citadel, Colonel."

Major Schuster made up his questions as he went, trying to keep Fleischer off balance.

"Even your anti-aircraft batteries would be useless against a flight of fighters coming in low over the island. Have you even been strafed here, Colonel?"

"No, Herr Major."

"Interesting."

What is he fishing for?

Just as the colonel reached for a handkerchief to wipe his sweaty brow, Major Schuster smiled.

"Perhaps it is just coincidence ... or good luck. In any event, I would appreciate a tour of Citadel Vauban, Colonel. For my security assessment." Sid suddenly had an idea. "This may just be the correct location after all."

"Location, Herr Major? May I ask for what?"

"No, Colonel, it would be premature for me to say. Let me just say the remoteness of your location and the lack of air attacks may prove valuable to the Reich. But I need to see the entire complex."

"Of course, Herr Major!"

Suddenly Colonel Fleischer realized this may be just the opportunity he had always wanted - to turn this backwater garrison into something of importance. He relished the thought of some new V-weapon, or some important assignment - something to rescue his flagging career. Perhaps even an appointment to the SS for him. Anything to get out of this pitiful hole.

"And Colonel ... do not alert your unit sub-commanders I am here. I wish my visit to remain ... discrete. You understand?"

"Of course, Herr Major!"

Major Schuster walked through the complex with the doting Colonel Fleischer leading the way pointing out the "by the book" operations the Germans melded into the old pirate-age Citadel. Sid carefully examined the facility, making mental notes.

This is totally ridiculous from a military perspective. The earthen works protecting the explosive storage could easily be penetrated. The walls would crumble at the first explosions. Why hadn't the RAF bombed this place?

"Very impressive, Herr Oberst. Very impressive, indeed."

Colonel Fleischer beamed at the praise.

"Our reaction time is precise. The garrison trains every day. And our coastal gun accuracy is unmatched."

Sid knew from his briefing the Admiralty remained cautious when operating within range of the Belle Isle guns, but had never suffered significant damage. Still, in a firefight, land-based heavy guns held a significant advantage, poorly manned or not.

He knew the Achilles heel of the artillery garrison was its support and fire-supply operations. A single low-level B17 run or a series of air-to-ground attacks by fighter-bombers could render the garrison incapable of sustaining an artillery attack. However, Belle Isle's aircraft and ship detection capabilities gave the Germans ample warning of high altitude raids anywhere in the Bay of Biscay. The island was mostly flat and any approaching aircraft at attack altitude would be visible by radar from a great distance.

The Citadel was only vulnerable to low-level fighter attacks, below effective radar. But at such a low altitude and high speed the target was vulnerable for only a few seconds.

RAF command listed Belle Island only as a Target of Opportunity - military jargon for when a primary target or objective cannot be met, and at the discretion of the flight commander.

"Colonel, I am curious. The labyrinths beneath the Citadel ... what condition are they in?"

"I am afraid most are in poor repair."

"How many openings are there into the lower tunnels?"

"This is the only serviceable entrance, Major. The others have been sealed off for security purposes. We had some attempts at sabotage among the population, but these have been neutralized."

"Yet you have little security at this entrance."

"We store perishables down the first corridor, and wine, of course - the temperature remains fairly constant. Other foodstuffs and regular supplies comprise the rest of the storage. Beyond that, the corridors house the island garrison, operations, and provide some limited accommodations for guests. The remainder of the labyrinth is sealed off from this end."

Sid was not certain he believed the major's description and decided to press the point.

"Ordinance is not stored below? Are you saying I cannot recommend the Citadel for a very ... discrete operation? There are no other places where such discretion could be utilized?"

Colonel Fleischer began to panic a moment sensing his opportunity slipping away.

"Here, at the main complex, no I am afraid not. Ordnance is stored away from the harbor. However … ," and the Colonel began to stretch to seize the opportunity, "there is the prison complex. It is much more recent, and the walls have been reinforced."

"Yes, the prison. I will take a look." Major Schuster tried to appear nonchalant.

Does the SS already know about the prison?

CHAPTER 11

THE PRISONER

The degree of civilization in a society
can be judged by entering its prisons.
- Fyodor Dostoyevsky

"Colonel, my briefing did not indicate the command authority over these prisoners," Major Schuster vamped as they walked to the northern edge of the Citadel complex along a gravel road.

They already know! Foucault convinced me this was all very secret.

"More to the point, Colonel ... who must I approach when I remove these prisoners for my ... project?"

His project? He thinks this part of the facility will work? Work for what?

"The Lorient Prefect has requested the containment of certain prisoners, especially now with the routine bombing of the city. We have twenty-two in all - a few British air officers, some French officers that Vichy authorities would rather keep hidden away, and of course key resistance members. Captain Foucault uses the prison to interrogate members of the maquis, Major. You might find that interesting."

A private prison, operating outside of military control? Yes, Colonel, I find that very interesting.

"What do you mean, the SS is there?" The harbor master finally managed to get a call through to Captain Foucault at the prefect headquarters at Lorient. "Why do they even know about it?"

Foucault's aide only heard one side of the conversation through the frosted glass window at his office - one of the few amenities that had so far survived the incessant Allied air attacks. What he heard had the captain incensed.

"How could you have let him just walk in to Fleischer's office? Did you check with his superiors? Does he have orders?" Foucault waited for the reply, his right hand twitching. "... then get Fleischer on the phone as soon as you can!"

He slammed the received down. The harbor master never got the chance to warn him about Captain Molaisson.

They stepped through the north gate where an inclined ramp led down into a small courtyard. The small walled-off building below looked more like a warehouse than a prison. A single guard stood outside the small entrance. Sid looked toward the coast - the walled terrace that held the Citadel was lower here, and a back entrance road led to a gate. The shoreline was just a few meters away. He did not see any obvious presence of towers or additional guards.

Not the most secure place to hold prisoners. Plenty of walls to hide behind, lots of obstructed views. And the shore right close.

The colonel led him down the ramp and over to the main entry where the guard snapped to attention. Sid, dressed in his SS officer's uniform, stopped to glare at him, slowly scrutinizing every fold in his tunic, every hair out of place - a tactic he had seen General Patton use. It froze both the guard and Colonel Fleischer in place.

He turned without speaking and stepped past Fleischer through the prison door. A clerk sitting at the table just inside nonchalantly looked up, then jumped to attention, his papers falling into a heap upon the floor. Sid ignored him.

"Tell me, Colonel. The security seems a little informal?"

"The prisoners are in secure cells most of the day, Major. We run a very tight schedule here. Each prisoner gets ten minutes for ... personal hygiene matters ... in the morning, followed by fifteen minutes in the yard. We use soldiers from the garrison to augment the security when prisoners are allowed outside."

And no official command authority? Definitely not standard German protocol.

"I see. And where do their take their meals?"

"In their cells, followed by a thirty-minute exercise in the yard - again, watched over by the garrison. We have had no security problems, Major. We run a very organized routine here."

"I would like to see the prisoners. If we select this location, we will have to consider what to do with them."

I wish he would tell me what he wants to use the Citadel for. Captain Foucault may have to be disposed of.

"I am certain you will find us most accommodating, Major. If you will follow me ... ."

He stepped through a large steel door and was met by another guard brandishing a light machine pistol. The musty corridor was only dimly lit by a line of bare light bulbs, the air cold and hanging heavy and damp. The smell made Sid gasp momentarily. He reached for his handkerchief and struggled to keep his composure.

A central corridor was flanked on both sides by small cells. The door to one of the empty cells was open. The cell measured about two meters wide by less than four meters long. A rough wooden bench against the wall served as a bed - a small opening above the door and an even smaller slit on the far wall let in what little light penetrated the gloom, and a little air. There was no heat. A small drain in the corner reeked of human excrement.

"Really, Colonel. Something must be done with this smell if we are to approve this facility."

"I understand, Herr Major. That will not be an issue, I assure you," he confidently shot back.

Sid continued to walk down the corridor. The next stall held a thin figure dressed in a tattered RAF uniform lying asleep on the wooden bench. Sid simply glanced at him, feigning boredom. The next three cells held other prisoners ... "Mostly from the resistance, arrested by the police. These are particularly dangerous, so we keep them here. We fear they may escape in the confusion of an air raid if kept in Lorient."

In the next cell a French voice, defiant but weak, barked out, "Wine! I want wine. And women! You dirty Boche bastard, you may as well kill me. I spit in your mother's face."

"Another of the dirty French," the Colonel grimaced. "A most uncouth lot. I prefer the British prisoners."

"That first prisoner. A RAF officer?"

"Shot down over Belle Isle during a raid on Lorient."

"And why has this prisoner not been turned over to the Luftwaffe?"

"There is no organized air command in Lorient. Our garrison contains many Luftwaffe ground crews caught in the general retreat ... ,"

"Retreat?"

The major stopped and turned, glaring at Colonel Fleischer.

"And who has informed you the German army is in retreat? A strategic reorganization to contain the Allies is not a retreat, Colonel. Be careful with your loose tongue - you might find it missing one day."

"My sincerest apologies, Herr Major." Colonel Fleischer began to backtrack. "The pilot was aided by members of the island resistance. He is being kept here and interrogated. When he reveals what he knows, he will be turned over to the regular authorities."

"I will mention in my report there are prisoners of war that may need to be evacuated by submarine and taken to more efficient interrogation facilities."

"Yes, Herr Major. I can understand that. And the French?"

"The French are a defeated people. Do with them what you wish."

The next room was slightly larger. A single chain hung in the center, a set of manacles on chains attached to the wall. Sid knew exactly what happens in this room. He dismissed the "special activity" room and stopped in the adjacent hallway. A door opened to the outside.

"And this door?"

"To the inner courtyard, Herr Major. It is the only way a prisoner can leave the cell compound."

"Open it."

"There is a prisoner on the grounds, Herr Major."

"Are you telling me I have something to fear from a prisoner under your careful observation, Colonel?"

"No, no, Major, not at all. I was just thinking ... ,"

"Then I wish to see the courtyard."

Sid stood waiting for Colonel Fleischer to react. Clearly, he had him back on his heels and wanted to exploit his advantage. Fleischer stepped past him and opened the door. The bright light of the courtyard flooded into the corridor, the wave of fresh air a relief from the foul mustiness of the prison. Sid stepped through the doorway.

A high wall surrounded the central cell block, clearly an afterthought in the construction. What the colonel called the courtyard was a small width of bare ground surrounding the building. When it rained the ground turned into a muddy morass, the grass long since trod into oblivion. He could only see a small part of the open space. He began to walk up the long side of the building to where he could get a good look at the exterior compound wall, along the shore side. If he were to organize a breach of the prison, this was the most vulnerable spot.

He saw the guard first, a large burley soldier standing with a look of complete boredom on his face holding a light machine pistol. As Sid approached, the guard straightened and feigned interest in the prisoner he guarded - a lone figure who shuffled slowly along the ground. The prisoner was dressed in rude hanging pants and a dirty shirt. A mess of shabby hair where cut by a crude blade masked any features from behind. The prisoner stopped but did not bother to turn around when the guard cried out, "Halt!"

"As you can see, Major, we have very close observation here. Now, if we could return to my office and discuss your plans ... ,"

Why does he not want me to see this prisoner?

"I wish to address the prisoner."

"I cannot allow that, Major. It would be far too dangerous."

Sid drew his breath short, stopped, and refused to look at the Colonel.

"Colonel Fleischer, are you refusing to submit to my request?"

"But Major ... ,"

"Is your security adequate or not? You think I am threatened by a single skinny prisoner under guard? Perhaps your security is an illusion, Colonel?"

"No, Major. I simply meant ... ,"

"I will repeat myself once more. I wish to address the prisoner."

Colonel Fleischer nervously looked around, considering his options. To outright defy an officer of the SS, even one below his rank, could be career suicide ... or worse. But this prisoner ... it was his bad luck this particular prisoner was in the courtyard at this precise moment.

"Very well, but I must ask you keep your conversation short. This prisoner is extremely violent."

"I think I can deport myself adequately, Colonel," Sid replied sarcastically, and stepped toward the guard. Colonel Fleischer frantically caught up with him as he stepped close to the prisoner.

"You will turn around and face this officer, and not speak unless requested," the colonel barked.

The prisoner turned slowly in place, eyes cast downward. To Sid's surprise, it was a young woman. He kept up the charade.

"This is your idea of a dangerous prisoner?"

The woman looked in her mid-twenties, although the harsh treatment she received in the prison had left its mark. Her hair was shabby and matted, and carelessly sheared leaving large splotches of scalp exposed. Her clothing was filthy, the smell overpowering even at this distance. She kept her gaze on the ground.

"Look at me," he barked, striking his crop against his thigh. The guard struck her with the butt of his gun, knocking her to the ground.

"You will answer the officer!"

"Enough!" Major Schuster barked at him. "I cannot interrogate the prisoner if she is injured!"

Colonel Fletcher shot him an anxious look, and the guard grabbed her by the arm and lifted her roughly to her feet.

She slowly looked up, her eyes dulled, her reaction slurred.

"And who is this prisoner?" the major demanded.

"Just a criminal, Herr Major."

"We shoot criminals, Colonel. I ask you again, and I will not repeat my instructions to you. Who is this prisoner?"

Colonel Fleischer knew he was out of options. Foucault would be furious with him over this, but it cannot be helped.

"A leader of the resistance, Herr Major."

"The resistance? This tiny girl? Why, a single slap with my crop would drop her to the ground with ease. How can she be a leader of the maquis?"

Colonel Fleischer started at the use of the French word. He had never heard a German officer refer to the resistance that way.

"She has information on the resistance cells we have tried to get from her. Valuable information. The bombing in Lorient made it too dangerous for her to remain there."

Suddenly Sid knew he had stumbled upon something important, perhaps something at the heart of his mission.

"Your name?"

The woman simply stared ahead.

"Her name is ... ,"

"I did not ask you for her name, Colonel!"

He looked deeply into her eyes. They flashed for a brief moment, belying the fierceness she kept safely hidden away.

"Your name, madame."

This officer. He dresses like the SS. He walks like the SS. But he asks questions. The SS never ask questions. Who is he?

"Anisette. Anisette Durande."

"And where are you from?"

"The commune of Redon."

"And you are a criminal? Perhaps you kill German soldiers? Perhaps you sell information ... maybe to the resistance? Maybe that is why they keep you here? To keep you away from your own people? Tell me, madame, are you a criminal?"

She looked at him, curiously. Something about this man is very different. What is he fishing for?

"I am a woman of the church."

"Ah," Sid droned, sizing up the woman's defiant voice. "Once again, the specter of the Catholic Church rises up through the stinking muck of the French countryside. The Church promises cooperation, yet breeds gutter rats like this to do their dirty business."

Anisette Durande. I need to find out about this one.

"I have seen enough, Colonel."

Sid turned and abruptly walked away, back toward the side door. Colonel Fleischer tried to keep up with him.

Once back inside the colonel's office, Sid sat and looked completely bored.

"I will take that cognac now, Colonel."

The request caught Colonel Fleischer by surprise.

"Certainly, Herr Major. Certainly."

Fleischer reached behind him to a small side table, took the top off a decanter, and poured two small snifters of brandy.

"Perhaps the best reason to occupy France," Sid smiled, and took a long, slow draw of the cognac. "Now, one last question, Colonel."

He stopped and let the anticipation sink in for a moment, what felt like an eternity to Colonel Fleischer.

"I have been following shipments of ... shall we say, certain property of the Reich. The Americans are notorious for destroying the great artworks in their path, and many fine pieces have disappeared where they have made their modest advances through France. Reichsführer Himmler shares the Führer's concern that the valuable artwork, and especially religious icons, will simply disappear in the current situation."

The Colonel looked oddly unconcerned by this line of questioning.

"If I may be blunt."

"Of course, Herr Major."

Fleischer put his snifter of cognac on the side table.

"I have a report, Colonel, that details the shipment of certain of these art treasures to places along the Bretagne coast. There is concern - at the highest levels - some may be stored here, at Citadel Vauban, in violation of the strict orders of the Reichsführer himself."

Sid watch in amusement as Colonel Fleischer turned a deep shade of red, leaped from his chair, and exploded in an uncharacteristic flood of emotions.

"Herr Major, I can assure you! There is no such activity going on here at the Citadel. Why, I have personally shown you the entire complex. Who could have made such a fantastic claim?"

"It matters not who. What matters," he continued in a carefully controlled voice, "is my inspection has been most thorough. My report on this matter may just settle the entire question."

"On my word as a German officer, Major, I have shown you the entire complex. You may interrogate any of my staff, any of the garrison, at your convenience. We will cooperate fully to clear this insidious claim, Major."

Sid had not expected this reaction. This fortress, it holds secrets, but not what I thought. Yes, Colonel, there is no artwork hiding here. No icons, either. But something is wrong. Perhaps I can turn this to my advantage.

He stood, adjusted his uniform, and snapped dutifully to attention to the ranking officer, just to make a point.

"I believe you are telling me the truth, Colonel. I must apologize for my slight deception, but I have acted under orders. You have been most accommodating to me in my inspection. I do not believe you are hiding anything here."

Except at the prison. That was where you were nervous.

"Thank you, Major. I cannot think of who would want to make such an accusation."

Sid caught the moment, and replied, "I believe it was an official in Lorient, if my memory serves me."

Colonel Fleischer's eyes dilated.

"I believe the name was Foucault."

Captain Foucault sat back, a worried look on his face. Who is this officer? Why did no one in Paris know of him? The SS - they take their orders from Paris in the West ... unless he is operating with separate orders, from Berlin, perhaps.

I must try and undermine this man's credibility ... and stall him off until I can reach Le Palais and see for myself.

"I will take my leave of you, Colonel. Again, let me assure you I have the utmost confidence in your administration of this island. My report will eliminate any confusion in this matter."

"Thank you, Major. May I offer you accommodations here in the command headquarters? Our facilities are probably more spartan than you are accustomed to, but the food and the cognac are excellent."

"Thank you, no, Colonel. I have made arrangements in the town already. And I have some additional investigation to do on an unrelated matter that requires my presence in the port."

"And your transport back to Lorient?"

"My boat will convey me back to Lorient tomorrow. I appreciate your consideration, Colonel, but my arrangements have been most thorough. Good day to you. Heil Hitler."

"Heil Hitler."

Colonel Fleischer killed off his cognac, thankful the SS major had finally left the Citadel.

Henri Gireau had arranged for Sid to stay at Le Grande Hotel Bretagne overlooking the harbor entrance - convenient to monitor boat traffic and to make a quick escape if needed. The manager of the hotel knew Henri Gireau well.

"You are Monsieur Deveau?"

"Yes, Major."

"You will prepare me a room."

"I was not informed of your visit, Major."

"And that concerns me, why? Some wine and cheese while I wait. Do you have Cantal?"

"No, monsieur. Only local cheese."

"I suppose it will have to do."

"Do You Have Cantal" - that was the code phrase Gireau told him to use to identify himself. As he waited for his wine, Sid sized up the few patrons in the room. Madame Deveau brought his wine and a tray of cheeses and breads.

"You are not safe here. Be careful," she whispered under her breath.

The other patrons looked at him nervously as he mounted the stairs. He knew this was a haven for the maquis, being just across the road from the breakwater. Tomorrow he would have to maintain his charade long enough to contact Henri Gireau. He knew he was dancing on a thin edge. Tomorrow he must make his way back to the mainland and through to the American lines or he might not return at all.

The prostitute fell off the bed and collapsed on the floor. The girl gasped for breath, holding her throat where Captain Molaisson had gripped her so violently she kicked over a lamp and sent it crashing through the window, alerting the madame. Madame Loutran opened the door and stepped between them just as Molaisson staggered back against the wall.

"Captain, enough!"

Two of her other girls rushed in and grabbed the dazed naked woman and dragged her from the room. Raynell Molaisson knew better than to confront the brothel's madame. She served at the discretion of the Circle, but enjoyed their protection as well.

"The bitch says there is a spy," he slurred in his drunken stupor and he braced himself against the wall.

The woman he strangled had serviced the captain of the *Maxine* from Lorient earlier in the evening. Too much brandy had loosened his tongue, and he wanted to impress the woman with his importance. He told her of an officer - a spy. In his rage, Molaisson had tried to strangle the information out of her.

"*Capitaine*, there is no need to worry tonight," she calmly approached him, gently waving yet another bottle of brandy before her. "I have someone special for you tonight."

A tall fierce-looking woman entered the room dressed in tight leather, with black fishnet stockings and wearing a black mask. She slapped the bed rail with a short riding crop.

"You have been very bad, *mon capitaine*," she barked, and slapped the bed rail again. "You need to be punished."

Molaisson grabbed the bottle from Madame Loutran, bit off the cork, and took a long swig. He slammed it on the table. As he staggered forward, Madame Loutran turned and left the room.

Captain Raynell Molaisson forgot about the spy.

⸙

CHAPTER 12

PLAYING THE ACE

The cause of violence is not ignorance.
It is self-interest.
-William Sloan Coffin

From the window on the hotel's third floor the next morning Sid could see a flurry of activity in the harbor. Small open boats manned by uniformed Germans sortied in the harbor weaving in and amongst a small fleet of fishing and cargo boats. A small coastal patrol boat with a heavy gun on the foredeck cruised back and forth within the harbor. He looked closely and recognized the familiar face of Colonel Fleischer on the deck. Sid noticed none of the local fleet of fishing or cargo boats left their moorages.

He donned his uniform, walked downstairs to the restaurant, and casually strolled through to the outside café tables and sat down.

"A coffee."

When Mme Deveau arrived with the drink, he quietly asked under his breath, "What is happening?"

"A U-boat has anchored outside the harbor. One of the supply ships. The small boats transport the cargo to the quay." And she quickly left.

This was probably the same U-boat Henri and the maquis had robbed two days before. It would be offloading supplies for the artillery garrison, supplies not left at the Scorff submarine pen. I need to get a closer look.

Sid sat for a moment and devised a plan. He left and walked quickly up the harbor to the commercial dock and approached a small launch tied dockside.

"You. You will take me to the submarine. I wish to leave now."

"I have no authorization to leave harbor," he protested.

"I am the only authorization you need. Cast off," and he stepped aboard.

It wasn't a request. The launch operator looked at him suspiciously, but fearing arrest - or worse - he complied.

"Welcome aboard," he grumbled, and fired up the small diesel engine. He motored away from the dock as one of the patrol boats peeled away from its patrol route and gained speed to intercept them. Sid stood in the bow conspicuously.

"Stand down there!"

The order came from a megaphone held by the command officer. Sid turned and faced him, an indignant look on his face.

"You will not interfere. I am on official business!" He turned to the launch operator. "Maintain your course and speed."

"You are commanded to stand down, immediately, and prepare to be boarded!"

The patrol officer was not going to back down. Sid turned to the launch man and whispered under his breath, "Do as he asks, then pull away quickly," in broken French, with an odd accent.

The American! The one Deveau warned me about!

He nodded, and throttled back. As the patrol craft pulled alongside, Sid jumped across to the boat, pulling his service pistol.

Before the command officer could react, Sid pressed the Luger to the side of his head, freezing the crew in its place.

"How dare you interfere with me! I am Sturmbannführer Reiner Schuster of SS Special Intelligence on a special assignment from Berlin! You are under arrest!"

Sid pushed the pistol into the side of his head, forcing him back toward the gunwale as the officer tried to regain his footing. At the last moment Sid gave him a hefty shove and he plunged over the side into the harbor.

Sid immediately turned to the young enlisted soldier at the helm.

"Unless you wish to be shot, you will convey me immediately to the U-boat. Do you understand?"

"Yes, Herr Major. Immediately," he stammered.

"Good. Your name?"

"Corporal Helmut Schaefer, Herr Major."

"I will mention you favorably in my report, Schaefer. At least I have found one soldier who knows how to follow orders!"

"Yes, Herr Major. Thank you, Herr Major."

The launch turned and headed out past the patrols into the open bay.

The captain of U-227 met the SS major on the deck.

"I am Captain Dietrich. What is your business here, Major?"

Sid snapped to attention and saluted.

"Captain. Forgive my imprudent boarding, but I am on an important assignment, and acting upon a recent tip made the decision to board without your permission. I assure you it was necessary. I am Sturmbannführer Reiner Schuster of SS Special Intelligence."

Captain Dietrich looked suspiciously at the major, but was cautious in his approach. The U-boat service enjoyed a considerable degree of independence from the other services, but it was not good policy to directly confront an officer of the SS.

"Walk with me, Major. I assume you wish to talk in private."

"Thank you, Captain."

The two officers strolled casually down the deck toward the bow of the U-boat.

"I am expecting the arrival of a small boat from Lorient, one of the regular cargo carriers that operate between here and the mainland ports. I have just received a suggestion it may be carrying weapons for the maquis here in Le Palais. I cannot request orders from Paris on such short notice, so must rely on your cooperation to investigate, Captain."

"Of course, but without orders, Major, I cannot allow you below decks."

"I understand completely, Captain. I will wait for the boat's arrival here, with your permission, and search the boat when it comes alongside."

"Certainly, Major. I must attend to other matters, but I will inform my officers to assist you in any way they can."

Anything to make sure you remain topside.

"Thank you, Captain. I will remain as unobtrusive as I can. I thank you for your cooperation."

"My pleasure, Major."

Captain Dietrich gave a small formal bow and walked off, stopping to talk to one of the deck officers who turned, looked at Sid, and nodded his head in compliance.

The captain of the cargo boat *Sorcière* heaved to and threw the U-boat crew its mooring lines. Henri Gireau began to clear the loading crane when an armed sailor appeared overhead and cocked his rifle.

"You will stand aside and be boarded."

He pointed the rifle at Gireau who looked back with alarm. The sun directly behind the soldier masked his features in a dazzling haze. A second voice called out with authority.

"You will consider yourself under arrest, monsieur, until I inspect your boat."

Henri Gireau could not see this one's face, but recognized the voice.

"What do you want? I am here to unload cargo."

"You will comply with my request to inspect your vessel, Captain. Move away from the crane."

Sid clamored aboard and hastily strode around the deck.

"You will follow me below, Captain." He turned and spoke to the soldier. "You are no longer needed."

Once safely below decks, Sid and Henri Gireau slid into the small galley table. Gireau reached for a bottle of wine.

"You certainly have made yourself at home here," he groused. "I hardly expected to see you aboard the U-boat."

"It is easier to believe a big lie, Captain, than a series of little ones. The regular German services fear this uniform."

"And so they should. Now, what's all this about?"

"What can you tell me about the woman you called the Guardian? The one that went missing during the evacuation of the British."

"She was in, oh, her early twenties. I don't know exactly. There were stories her grandmother is still alive, representing the Guardians, but her mother was killed. I don't know her name. Few do, exactly. But there were a lot of stories. Hard to determine what is the truth."

"I think I may have found her."

"Here? In Le Palais?"

"There is a small prison here, on the north side of the Citadel. It is surrounded by low walls, and the compound itself is walled, but hardly secure. There is a small guard presence most of the time."

"Why do you think The Guardian is here?"

"I saw a young woman ... one the garrison commander was reluctant to let me see. She is being held in isolation, and only let out alone and under guard. Early- to mid-twenties. Hard to tell much more about her. She was very thin and looks like she has been mistreated badly. Her hair ... it has been chopped away by a crude instrument of some sort - blotchy and uneven. She was dirty, and malnourished. But she stood defiantly in front of me, thinking I was SS."

Henri looked down at the ground and a deep frown crossed his face.

"The hair ... that may be significant. Les Guardiennes do not cut their hair. Only when she passes the icon to the next generation may she do so. Her mother, her grandmother - they all wore their hair long and untouched by razors until they relinquished control to the next generation. If she is La Guardienne, cutting the hair would be a form of punishment in itself. It would be like rape - and an affront to God."

"Part of the process of breaking her down."

"How many in this prison?"

"Not a lot - twenty or so. And, Henri, it is outside of normal military control."

"What?"

"It's a private prison. Colonel Fleischer says it is run by Foucault."

"Foucault? The snake. The occupation is just one big opportunity for him to get rich. He would sell out his mother if there were a profit."

"My question - why is he running this prison?"

"Did you see any other prisoners?"

"A British pilot shot down over Belle Isle. A few French civilians. Probably maquis."

"Or more likely, '*nacht und nebel.*'"

"Night and fog?"

"A term used to describe those who simply disappear at night - into the night and fog of France. These people are arrested with no charges, no trials, nothing. They simply disappear. If you cross Foucault, that is your fate. That is why they do not want the authorities watching."

"But the garrison commander. Surely he has to report this activity?"

"Not if he is part of The Circle. Think of it - stuck out here, away from the glory and action of the war. A dead-end post for an officer, so why not use it to get rich? Especially if you can easily move your money to Spain or Portugal by boat. A sweet set up."

"And the girl, the Guardian?"

"She knows where the Madonna is - or at least, where it was in 1940. The Church wants it, the SS wants it, so does Foucault ... and of course, Les Boucliers. A valuable piece of hardware."

"Les Boucliers?"

"A private guard of sorts for La Guardienne. The word bouclier - it means 'shield.' Les Boucliers and the Church are sworn enemies, and have been for centuries."

Sid thought back to Patton's worry about a local religious war erupting in his rear guard.

"So she has been tortured, and obviously has not given them the information they want."

"If you believed that by telling them you would be damned, what would you do? Give in, and burn in the fires of Hell, or resist - despite the pain - and join God as He promised?"

"I don't believe in all that Heaven and Hell stuff."

"Neither do I. But she does, as do those she gathers around her. There are men - hundreds of them, may thousands - who are not FFI or maquis. These men would rise up to destroy anything German or Vichy only if she were to command them. That is the power she holds."

"Wait a minute. You said there was an older woman - the grandmother - still alive. She cannot summon the maquis like this?"

"She has influence, yes. But she has passed protection of the icon to her granddaughter, and so passes the power as well. The girl represents the independence of Bretagne. With her gone, the enemy still have the power - despite the ragtag groups that fight as the FFI and the maquis. But if she were to rise from the dead - like so many would think - and call for a general uprising in the name of God, with the Madonna held before her, Bretagne would erupt in flames. There would be no safe place for any German, or collaborator, anywhere in Brittany. And they would chase the German dog all the way to Hell if she directed them."

"She holds that much power?"

"Yes, my friend. If you have discovered La Guardienne, you are a marked man. Foucault will hunt you down and kill you to protect his secret."

"Then we will have to act fast."

"What do you mean? To do what?"

"To free this woman, and set Brittany ablaze."

Henri looked at him like he was insane.

The telephone on Colonel Fleischer's desk rang incessantly off and on for several hours. With the submarine anchored offshore unloading cargo, the Colonel was aboard the gunboat supervising the unloading. He personally directed all such visits, and made certain the "correct" goods were stored in the special warehouse. He did not return to his office until midday for a glass of cognac with his lunch, and arrived in time for yet another of the incessant phone calls.

"Foucault ... you are not to call here. One cannot trust the security of this line."

"It cannot be helped, Colonel. The harbor master told me you were paid a visit by the SS. A Major Schuster?"

"Yes. A somewhat routine inspection."

Fleischer was careful not to reveal the true purpose of Schuster's visit. The major's suggestion Captain Foucault may have tried to implicate the colonel in the alleged art thefts had left him guarded and concerned.

"I checked on this, Colonel. The Paris SS commander has no knowledge of an agent assigned to inspect Belle Isle and did not recognize the name Schuster."

"That is interesting, Captain. And just who would this be? He had the appropriate orders."

Are you lying to me? Trying to discredit the major and save your sorry ass?

"What did he want of you?"

"Just routine. I gave him a tour of the Citadel, and we talked about problems ... with supply."

"Did he see the prison?"

Now why are you so concerned about that? Somewhat sensitive, are we not?

"Of course not," he lied.

"Is he still in Le Palais?"

"Yes, I believe so. He mentioned catching a boat back to the mainland, but we are unloading a U-boat, and nothing is allowed to leave the harbor. He will probably remain the night on the island."

"Do not let him leave. I will arrive this afternoon to deal with him."

"As you wish, Captain. But I believe you are concerned about nothing."

He hung up the phone.

No record at Paris SS headquarters? One of these men is lying.

"How many men can we raise here on the island?"

"Maybe a dozen. On short notice, it will not be easy. These men do not trust outsiders."

"They trust you?"

"Only because I steal from the Germans. But La Guardienne - she gives us the edge we need. But how can we prove who she is - we don't know for certain ourselves."

"I know her name. Anisette Durande."

"That will not help. No one knows the name of La Guardienne. At least not anyone outside of her select circle of protectors. And if she was captured they certainly have all been killed or at least scattered throughout the peninsula. And then there is a problem of weapons and ammunition."

Sid looked out the galley window toward the Citadel.

"Then perhaps there is another way. Can you leave the harbor?"

"As soon as the unloading is completed. The U-boat will not remain exposed on the surface longer than necessary."

"Can you get a small crew? Maybe three?"

"That would be easy. But to break the woman out of the prison ... ."

"We might not have to. Where do you lay to when you are in harbor?"

"The port dock, just inside the breakwater."

"That will do. It is close to my hotel - that makes it a convenient and plausible spot to wait."

Sid rose from the galley table and straightened his uniform.

"I will direct the U-boat commander to release you from the detail. You drop me off on the Citadel wharf and tie up below the hotel. Wait for me there, but appear to be tied up for the night."

"What are you going to do?"

Sid's eyes narrowed to small slits of black as he thought through the details.

"Be ready to make way ... at 0700."

"Major, you cannot just barge into the office like ... ."

Colonel Fleischer heard the frantic voice of his aide a split second before Major Schuster threw open the door and burst into his office.

"Tell your aide to return to his desk. And you will follow me, Colonel. Now!"

Major Schuster turned abruptly and strode haughtily out the door. Colonel Fleischer rose shakily from his seat, grabbed his hat, and slipped out the door as quickly as he could to catch up with the major as he briskly strode down the hallway to the outer courtyard.

"Major, what is the matter? I am certain we can clear this up, no matter what it is."

Major Schuster ignored him. Once outside he turned and walked defiantly toward the main door of the prison building.

"Open the door!" the colonel screamed at the guard as the major refused to slow down. He did not stop until he was deep inside the building, near the interrogation room.

"How dare you!"

He turned and slapped his thigh with his crop.

"What is it, Major? I am certain there is a misunderstanding. If you would just let me know."

Despite the difference in their ranks, the colonel was sweating profusely, his hands shaking.

"This!" And he pointed with his crop at the interrogation room. "This is a disgrace! You have had her for four years and you still have not broken her? And you have kept this woman secret from the SS all this time? She is a Guardian! Did you not think the SS would want to know of this?"

"A Guardian? But how did you know?"

I was right!

"When I spoke with Reichsführer Himmler, and he asked me the woman's name, he flew into an uncontrollable rage! How do you think that made me look! I'll tell you what - like a complete fool! Consider yourself lucky Herr Himmler did not order you shot!"

"You spoke to the Reichsführer, Herr Major?"

"Who do you think ordered me to Belle Isle, you fool? No one else knows I am here - not Paris, not Lorient - no one! You think if they knew I was coming the treasures we are seeking would still be here?"

"But there are no treasures, Herr Major."

"No treasures! Are you deaf, man? The Reichsführer shared with me only a few minutes ago that the treasure he suspected was kept here was not stolen art, but the Guardian the SS has been seeking for over four years! He feared if anyone knew what he was looking for he would be betrayed - there are liars and conspirators everywhere, Colonel. I found what he was seeking only because I did not know what to look for. Only when he heard my report did his superior intellect discern what I had discovered."

"He was looking for the woman?"

"My god, man, how did you earn the rank of colonel? Of course that is what he was after!"

"Why, Major?"

"Perhaps you should call and ask him that question yourself! I do not care why. I am an officer of the SS. I follow my orders. And my orders are to deliver the woman to Berlin, immediately."

"How will you do this, major?"

"That is my responsibility to determine. Yours is to get this woman ready to travel. We leave before it gets dark. Those are my orders from Herr Himmler. You are to tell no one of this. The last thing I need is for some drunken soldier to brag to his whore in the brothel what is happening, and alert the resistance. No, Colonel, you will clean her up, find her suitable clothing, and present her to me at my hotel - 7:00 sharp! Do you understand?"

"Yes, Major. I will do as you order."

"These are not my orders, Colonel. A major does not give orders to a colonel. These are orders directly from Reichsführer Himmler!"

"Yes, Herr Major. I understand completely!"

"Do this, Fleischer, and I will include in my report you were most cooperative, and that this Lorient policeman ... what was his name?"

"Foucault, Herr Major."

"Yes, Foucault. I will include in my report he was responsible for this absurdity. You can do with him whatever you wish."

"Yes, Major. Thank you, Major. I will make this happen as you wish."

"See that you do, Fleischer. And remember, no one is to know. No one!"

"Yes, Herr Major."

Sid turned and strode out of the Citadel. Fleischer hurried back to his office, his hands shaking as he penned an order for his aide.

Orders directly from Berlin. That explains why Foucault failed to confirm the major's presence in Paris.

He barked out.

"Get the woman and clean her up! She is leaving."

"What about Captain Foucault? Should he not be informed?"

"My orders come directly from Reichsführer Himmler. I do not wish to cross the SS. That snake Foucault, he is setting me up. I will deal with him."

"Cobra 1 this is Cobra 3. They just aren't here, Commander."

"Yeah, Smitty. I can see that."

Commander Hughes led his fifteen British Spitfires on a mission to rendezvous with a small fleet of Lancasters for a raid over the submarine pens at La Pallice, southeast of Lorient. They had arrived at the designated coordinates five minutes ahead of schedule, but Lancasters were nowhere to be seen.

"We can't wait much longer. What do you want to do?"

The fighter escort commander reviewed his list of secondary targets. His operation orders required him to break away and seek "targets-of-opportunity" if the bomber fleet did not show by 1800 hours. It was now 18:05.

"Cobra squadron, this is Cobra 1. They aren't coming, lads. Let's head toward Belle Isle and see what's cooking. Maybe we can take out a radar tower or two."

"Radar? Where's the fun in that?"

"Shut up, Smitty. Change course, 145 degrees, and follow me. Cobra 4, radio base and tell them TOA - Belle Isle. Then radio silence all the way to target."

Fourteen Lancasters of the 617th Squadron known as the "Dambusters" lifted off from their base at Lossiemouth in Scotland heading for the submarine pens at La Pallice. Major Hampton had scraped together six of the 12,000 pound "Tallboy" dam buster bombs and an equal number of 2,000 pounders. He was convinced the Lancasters would finally destroy the La Pallice base.

The Lancasters arrived at their rendezvous twenty minutes late. Their fighter escort was nowhere to be seen.

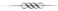

CHAPTER 13

THE SPITFIRES

Which death is preferably to every other?
The unexpected.
- Julius Caesar

Colonel Fleischer's staff car rounded the head of the harbor and drove along the frontage road toward the Grande Hotel Bretagne at 7:00 as ordered. Sid, dressed as Major Schuster, stood waiting on the curb and stepped forward to meet the colonel.

"Excellent, Colonel."

He stopped to examine the woman who looked around, dazed and disoriented.

"She was uncooperative, Herr Major, so we had to drug her. I assure you we used only a minimal amount of serum."

"I hope she was not injured."

"Absolutely not, Herr Major. I oversaw her preparations myself."

"Good. That will be reflected favorably in my report. I spoke with the Reichsführer about an hour ago and he was most appreciative of your efforts to resolve this ... unfortunate misunderstanding."

Colonel Fleischer bristled with excitement at hearing he had been mentioned to Himmler.

"Perhaps, Major, you could suggest an appointment from the Wehrmacht to the SS, that is, if it would not be asking too much."

"Colonel, your cooperation has been noted. I think it entirely appropriate for me to recommend you for a position in the SS. The SS always needs good officers, ones who know how to follow orders and work only for the glory of the Reich. I will make a point of it, you can be assured."

"Thank you, Major Schuster. Now, where can my men take the woman."

"That boat there ... ," and Sid pointed with his baton at the *Sorcière* tied to the dock nearby. "I have commandeered it for passage."

"Will you require the assistance of one of my men for the passage, Herr Major?"

Sid hadn't anticipated this development, but quickly improvised a plan.

"That would be most appreciated, Colonel. This one ... I think he will do fine."

Sid pointed to the broad-chested soldier that had struck the woman in the courtyard.

"Corporal, you will accompany Major Schuster until you are no longer needed."

The soldier saluted, grabbed the woman by the arm, and led her - dragged her - down the gang walk as Gireau shot Sid a questioning look. Sid turned to Colonel Fleischer.

"One last detail, Colonel. This man, Foucault ... ,"

"Leave Captain Foucault to me, Major. I will send you my report."

"Good. Send it to SS headquarters in Berlin, to me personally. I will see that Herr Himmler reviews it as well. And now, Colonel, I will take my leave. Heil Hitler!"

"Heil Hitler!"

The colonel watched with satisfaction as his future marched haughtily away, down the gang walk, and stepped aboard the *Sorcière*. With a wave of his baton, the boat slipped its mooring lines.

"Why the German?" Gireau whispered hoarsely under his breath as he gunned the engines.

"Insurance. Pass close by the U-boat as you leave the harbor."

"Captain, a small boat is approaching from the starboard quarter."

Captain Dietrich of the U-227 mounted the ladder to the conning tower.

"There, Captain."

The crewman pointed toward the *Sorcière* as it made its way to pass the U-boat. Captain Dietrich raised a pair of binoculars and examined the small craft.

"Hah! It's that arrogant SS major, standing on the aft deck like some strutting rooster. Radio the Citadel and check his clearance."

It took just a few minutes for the crewman to return.

"He is escorting a prisoner, Captain."

"Yes, so I see. There is an armed guard on board as well. I hope they both enjoy the trip across the strait - what I would not give to see how green his face looks as he crosses through that slop!"

The crewman laughed as Captain Dietrich scanned the approach to Le Palais in the late afternoon glare.

"Continue to make preparations. I want to raise anchor within the hour."

"Captain Carlisle, you wanted an immediate report of any activity in and around Belle Island?"

"That's right, corporal. What do you have?"

"I just received a communique from a Spitfire squadron southeast of Brest. They failed to meet their bomber rendezvous and radioed a TOA. Belle Isle."

Carlisle snatched the report from her hand.

"They'll be over the target within the hour." She stopped reading the dispatch and stared up at the clock on the wall. "Any way to radio them - I need to call this off."

"No, Captain. They would have gone silent by now."

Captain Carlisle sat back in her chair and stared ahead, lost in thought.

"I hope to God he keeps his damn head down."

"Set course 5 degrees, east. Quiberon."

Captain Gireau cleared the harbor mouth and changed course putting the collection of boats buzzing around the submarine behind. He immediately went below decks and pulled down a chart, spreading it out on the galley table. The Quiberon Peninsula was the shortest route across the straight from Le Palais. Quiberon was still in German hands, and patrol boats could be expected. At the moment, with the German soldier still aboard and the *Sorcière* still visible on radar, there was no alternative. The woman was safely stashed away in a forward berth, now unconscious from the effects of her drugging. Major Schuster remained conspicuously on deck, the German corporal nervously standing guard.

Captain Foucault anxiously waited for the small launch to reach the harbor at Le Palais. He had commandeered a German staff car and rushed from Lorient along the length of the unstable German lines down to the Quiberon Peninsula where he boarded the small boat for the short run across the strait.

A submarine anchored just to the right of the harbor mouth as Foucault's boat approached. A small flotilla of support craft busied themselves offloading cargo to the quay.

"Make course to the submarine," he called to the helmsman. Foucault knew Colonel Fleischer would be aboard the gun boat - always near the submarine.

Raynell Molaisson stumbled out of La Maison Belle and winced at the bright sunlight reflecting off the harbor. He had slept late, his senses dulled by the excessive brandy and late night excesses. He walked favoring his right hip to try and avoid the welts raised up along his leg from the night before.

He looked out at the busy activity in the harbor. He never participated in the unloading. His private load would be brought aboard once the submarine and the fleet of small craft dispersed. Fleischer wanted no prying eyes.

Through the alcohol haze he struggled to remember.

What did that little whore tell me? Something about a spy ... an American?

He struggled up the hill and pushed his way into the prefect's office at the Citadel.

"Where is the harbor master?" he demanded, his voice hoarse and rough.

"He has gone to meet Captain Foucault."

The clerk was nervous with the hung-over Molaisson standing there smelling up his little office.

"Foucault? What the hell is he doing here?"

"I do not know, monsieur. M. Gagner is meeting his launch at the submarine."

He turned around and slammed his fist against the door and stomped his way down to the *Toirette*.

Colonel Fleischer could not believe his eyes when he saw the small boat approaching the side of the U-227 where he lay tied, with Captain Foucault on deck.

"What the hell is he doing out here?"

One of the small patrol boats intercepted Foucault who Fleischer could see waving his arms frantically, screaming over the voice of the engines. The patrol boat peeled away and Foucault made course straight toward him.

As his boat pulled up along side Foucault paced nervously back and forth.

"Colonel, I need to speak to you ... in private. Immediately!"

"Can it wait, Captain? We are still unloading."

"No, Colonel. It cannot."

"If we must ... tell the captain to cut his engines and come aboard. We can meet in his cabin."

As Captain Foucault turned and began to bark instructions to the captain of the small boat, Fleischer was distracted by the ship's horn of the *Toirette* bearing down on them both.

"Now what?"

"All right, lads, hit the deck."

The Spitfires rolled over and dove to just above the wave tops and sped onward toward the windward coast of Belle Isle. The fighters hugged the flat coastal land of the island in what the pilots called a "daisy cutter" to confuse the German radar. At that speed it would be impossible to hit any of the fighters with anti-aircraft or small arms fire.

"Harbor in sight."

"Look at that, commander. Straight ahead!"

Commander Hughes couldn't believe their luck. Directly ahead he could see a U-boat, still at anchor - its crew scrambling frantically to train its machine gun toward the screaming Spitfires.

"Duck in behind that old fortress, then drop on top of them. You won't have much time to fire, lads, so make it count."

One by one the speeding Spitfires swooped up and over the Citadel and pounced on the U-227 with their machine guns blazing. Deck crews frantically dove overboard to escape the fire that tore through the conning tower. The five Spitfires carrying rockets blasted the collection of boats tied alongside, sending scraps of wood and metal flying in all directions.

The last fighter carried two 250 pound bombs, and dropped them at near conning-tower height as the other fighters peeled off to get clear of the explosions. The bombs missed the submarine's hull itself, but detonated on the shallow sea floor beneath. Two quick explosions lifted the submarine directly amidships with a terrific rush of water, and the hull cracked in two before slamming back to the sea. The starboard side explosion ripped a small gunboat and several other private craft to shreds.

The raid lasted just a few frightening moments.

"Scratch one U-boat!" came the jubilant radio call.

The Spitfires turned North and headed for their base.

As the wind freshened from the West, the waves abeam rolling the boat uncomfortably, the burly German soldier shouldered his rifle and held tight to the rigging. Major Schuster stood stoically, watching the soldier, deliberately adding to his discomfort.

The routine humdrum of the harbor suddenly was shattered by the scream of powerful fighter engines. They all stood dumfounded as a flight of Spitfires first rose from behind the Citadel then pounced with guns blazing on the harbor below. The guard braced himself awkwardly while he freed his hand and tried to get the rifle off his shoulder. In the awkward rolling of the boat, he fell against the gunwale. As the boat rolled back, he grabbed the rigging again for balance and his rifle fell to the deck.

Suddenly two explosions rocked the bay as Sid watched the submarine rise and split in two before crashing back to the sea.

The *Sorcière* settled into a trough, the bow ploughing deep into the forward swell, then pitched violently to port, water splashing over the gunwale and onto the soldier. As he turned to brace himself against the roll, he looked into the drawn pistol held by Major Schuster.

BLAM!

The soldier disappeared over the side as the boat rolled further and righted itself in the following wave. Sid braced himself against the crane, holstered his pistol, and reached for the rail leading down to the galley. Henri Gireau looked up from watching the carnage in the harbor through a porthole.

"Where is the German?"

"What German?"

CHAPTER 14

THE RED ROSE

A thorn defends the rose, harming only
those who would steal the blossom.
- Chinese Proverb

"Captain! Contact ahead! Five hundred meters!"

The forward tank observer of an advance element of 4th Armored Division radioed in a panic. The contact appeared through the low mists of the early evening, solid grey shadows - possibly Tiger tanks. The 4th had been chasing a retreating column of German panzers and the tracks led right over this ground.

"Fall back, and take cover. Charlie 2, cover Charlie 1. Get air-ops on the radio. Now!"

The tanks arrayed themselves along a line in the firm scrub ground and prepared for a firefight. Their commander radioed for air support - P51s supporting their ground assault would attack within the half-hour from airfields near Rennes and disrupt communications and supply. The 4th would charge through the center into the rear in the immediate chaos - a tactic that had driven the once mighty Wehrmacht into a chaotic retreat.

Twenty minutes to go. The waiting was worse than the combat.

Corporal Walker who ran the radio called out.

"Captain! Frenchie needs to talk to you."

The forward observer from the Free French Armored Support hurried up to the temporary command post.

"Capitaine! Wait! You must call off the air attack!"

"Are you crazy, Frenchie? We've got a line of German tanks ahead!"

"No, Capitaine. It is an illusion - because of the fog. We are at Carnac. They are not tanks."

"Carnac? What the hell is that?"

"Stones, Capitaine. Ancient standing stones. This is sacred ground. The stones have been here since before written history. You must not let the fighters destroy them."

"You telling me we are gettin' ready to attack a bunch of rocks?"

Not rocks, you stupid Américain.

"The Standing Stones of Carnac, Capitaine. The prehistoric stones are a national treasure of France. I beg you."

"Pre-historic, Captain? You mean, like dinosaurs and shit?"

Frenchie turned and just glared at the corporal.

The captain thought for a moment.

"Walker!" he barked out to a private sitting on the rear of his tank. "Go with Frenchie and check this out. Then radio back. You got five minutes."

"Gotcha, Captain."

The five minutes dragged on, but finally the radio crackled with Walker's report.

"Rocks, Captain. Frenchie was right. The Germans drove right through this spot ... nuthin' but rocks."

"Cooper - get air ops back. Right away!"

The air assault was called off in time, but two P51s dived low and fast overhead to ascertain just where the German tanks had gone.

"Captain - HQ on the radio."

The corporal heard just one side of the conversation, but knew his commander was not happy.

"Pass the word, Coop. Set up a defensive wall. The Germans have regrouped along a line five clicks ahead. We've been ordered to stand here and wait."

"Wait for what, Captain?"

"Hell if I know."

The captain jumped down from his tank and peed against the side of the tank. As he turned to stretch his legs he could smell the sweet aroma of wild roses.

As the 4th Armored Division was setting up their holding position, just off the coast the *Sorcière* continued shoreward through the darkening twilight.

"Now, to get you to the American lines. It is too dangerous to go to Lorient. Your little escapade on Belle Isle surely has caught the attention of Captain Foucault by now. I can only imagine what that snake is doing if he thinks the SS is crawling up his ass."

"In my briefing, I was told the 4th Armored Division would push to the Quiberon Peninsula and seal off the peninsula."

"German boats are still leaving the port of Quiberon. If your Americans are driving on the peninsula, they have not reached it yet."

"What about west of Lorient?"

"The coast is no-man's land right now. German boats patrol the coastline looking for isolated German units trying to escape, and anything not authorized is stopped. If the Allies are coordinating an assault, we can expect British gun boats as well. Going west would be suicide. The BBC says they have driven the Germans back into pockets at Lorient and Saint-Nazaire. That would imply there are Allied forces in between - perhaps at Vannes."

"Can we get there by sea?"

"It is up a long river estuary. There is no guarantee the Americans hold either side of the river."

Sid sat down and studied the chart.

"My guess is that most of the coastline west of this large bay has been deserted by the Germans even if it is not yet under Allied control."

"That is called Carnac. It is open ground. I pray they do not fight there."

"You say Quiberon is still in German hands? They would have to protect the road south from Plouharnel. Too far east and they open the road to a sweep north. I would defend here ... ," And Sid pointed at a line slightly east of the town, facing Carnac. "That would seal off the narrow ground leading to the peninsula and allow me to concentrate my forces against an attack. If the reports of pockets forming in Lorient and Saint-Nazaire are accurate, this is where I would expect the Germans to stand their ground. That would make the coast east of there safe to go ashore."

"I hope you are right. We need to get off the bay as quickly as possible. We can disappear into the countryside easier than hide on the open water, that is certain. I suggest La Trinité," and Gireau pointed to a commune up a narrow bay east of Carnac. "It is a protected harbor. We can go ashore along any of these beaches if we need to without fear of a high surf. If the port is clear, we can easily contact resistance forces to make your escape."

"La Trinité it is then."

"Now, my friend. What to do about that uniform."

Sid stood and adjusted his tunic.

"I happen to look good in this. If we get stopped by Germans, I will go into my Major Schuster tirade."

"And if we are stopped by the Americans or the British?"

"Well, you get the pleasure of turning over a German SS officer to them. I have a unique history of being arrested in uniform."

Henri laughed.

"Pray we do not meet the FFI. They will simply slit your throat before listening to your bull-shit."

Once inside the lee of the Quiberon Peninsula the rolling swells subsided, the seas calmed. The *Socière's* mate broke out coffee, a brick of cheese, and a loaf of bread. The men sat in silence, the drone of the boat's engines lulling them into near sleep.

Sid heard a soft whimper coming from the forward berth.

"The woman ... I think she is awake."

Gireau rose and slipped through the narrow passageway forward. In a moment, the woman from the prison stood shakily in the doorway, held up by Gireau. When she saw Sid dressed in his SS uniform, she suddenly panicked, and pushed back away from the galley against Gireau.

"It is all right, mademoiselle. He is not SS. He is an American agent. He is the one who released you. Now, please, do not be afraid. Sit, and eat."

He guided her to the galley table, but her eyes never left Sid's. It was the same fiery gaze he saw when he confronted her at the Citadel prison.

"You must have something to drink, mademoiselle. And some bread and cheese. You are very weak."

The Citadel commander's private guard had cleaned her up and dressed her in a soldier's work shirt and pants, and a pair of rude slippers. The mate poured her a glass of water and cut off some bread and cheese. She carefully tasted the cheese, and sipped some of the water, still staring at Sid.

"Slowly, mademoiselle. You must eat, but slowly." Gireau doted over her, brushing her hair back from her eyes. Sid looked a little suspiciously at him.

"She is the same age as my daughter when the Germans came and took her. She died in one of their brothels." He could hear the pain in his voice, and knew it fueled his violent rage against the Germans occupiers. "These men, they are unfit to live even as dogs."

The woman looked up, and spoke quietly.

"Who are you? Where am I?"

"Mademoiselle, I am Henri Gireau, captain of the *Sorcière*. This is an American agent, his name is Woodard. He was sent to the Citadel to determine its strategic importance. It was there he discovered the prison, and you, mademoiselle."

"Why did you release me? What am I to you?" She continued to look uneasily at Sid in his SS uniform.

Sid rose and turned to leave the galley. Gireau sat in his seat.

"Eat first, and when you feel better, we will talk. We are still at least an hour from our destination."

"Which is where?"

"The Allied lines, mademoiselle. To liberated Brittany."

She looked at Gireau, bewildered.

"*Bretagne, libre?*"

"Oui, mademoiselle. The liberation of France has begun."

A tear rolled down her cheek as she tried to take another bite.

"Stay to starboard, Luis. The port side is very shallow. The Germans have removed the navigation buoys and only the main channel can support any patrol boats at low tide."

The musty smell of the estuary mud to men of the land meant the sea, but to sailors told of a near shore. Henri looked over his chart and gave direction to his crew.

"La Trinité has a good harbor, but we do not know where the Allied forces are. Look for a small dock along the starboard shore where we can safely land. I don't want to chance getting stuck in the shallow water."

The *Sorcière* motored at half-throttle up the small inlet toward the port of La Trinité-sur-Mer. All eyes remained alert for patrol craft, and the helmsman strained to see in the dark without the aid of any lights, save for the quarter moon. The flat terrain offered few silhouettes against the near-dark sky.

"There! Captain, a dock. You can just see it through the moonlight."

Gireau clamored back on deck and strained to adjust his eyes to the near-pitch blackness. The quarter moon, slipping into and out of a broken cloud cover, only occasionally gave him enough light to see the shore. But there it was - a fishing dock, with the dark silhouette of a small loafing shed in the background. He went below and checked the chart.

"The depth is good. We are about a half-kilometer from Les Presses. There is a frontage road, so we can move easily up the bay to the town of Kermouroux." He called back to the helmsman, "Make for the dock."

Sid stepped out on deck as the helmsman throttled back to a near idle, guiding the *Sorcière* slowly forward. A crewman jumped off with a mooring line and tied the stern to a cleat, then secured the bow and spring lines. Sid scanned the shoreline for any signs of movement. In the cabin, Gireau made the woman ready for travel.

"Mademoiselle, we must hurry and find a safe place to remain until daylight. Do you feel strong enough to walk?"

Anisette slid out of the galley bench and braced herself as she stood, her legs still shaky.

"Yes, I can walk," she mostly whispered, leaning on Henri for support as they stepped up and onto the deck. Sid reached for her arm as the three men half-lifted her to the dock. The solid surface helped her regain her balance.

"Major, you need to do something about that uniform, at least until we know whose lines we are behind. Cover your tunic with a rain coat. If we encounter Germans, you can play your crazy major act. If not, I don't want to be shot at."

"It might help if you stopped calling me 'Major.'"

Gireau gave a slight laugh as the helmsman cut the engines, and silence enveloped them once more. Once off the dock some overturned row boats gave them a bit of cover from prying eyes. Gireau whispered to his crewman.

"Check out the shed, and see if we can hide in there."

The man slipped quietly across the open boatyard and tried the small door. It was not locked. He carefully opened the door, stopped to hear if there were any sound from inside, and disappeared into the darkness. A moment later he appeared, and waved the small group to join him.

They dared not light the small lamp hanging just inside the doorway, but settled into a corner of the shed. Despite the warm night air, the shed was still cold. Sid removed the rain coat covering his uniform and placed it over the woman to warm her. In a few moments she was lost in the safety of sleep.

Sid checked his sidearm.

"I'll stand watch."

At first light Gireau woke the sleeping Anisette. She stirred, the aches of her tormenting amplified by the night on the cold dirt floor. As she lay collecting herself, she could hear Gireau and Sid talking.

"Luis has not returned. I am concerned about that."

The man Sid knew only as Luis, the helmsman, left two hours before dawn to make discrete inquiries among the nearby cottages to find out the location of the enemy forces. He had not returned. Sid carefully opened the door, surveyed the surroundings, and slipped around the side of the shed to look around. He immediately returned and shut the door.

"A truck is coming. Down the frontage road."

Gireau pulled Anisette to her feet and whispered hoarsely, "We must find cover in case it stops." He checked his weapon, and moved some boxes to make a better defensive position, placing Anisette behind him. Sid took up a position to the left with a clear look at the door and an open path for escape behind him, and waited.

The truck stopped outside.

Luis burst through the door, followed by three men carrying American-supplied machine pistols.

"Captain, it is Luis. Do not shoot."

"Silence!" one the men bellowed. "I have your man. Come out, or I will shoot him without giving you the chance to explain."

No one moved.

After a dangerous silent moment, Gireau heard Sid's voice, speaking in perfect German.

"I am coming out. I am an officer in the SS, and I command you to lower your weapons!"

Sid stepped out from behind his hiding place showing his SS uniform, and to the amazement and surprise of the three men he pointed his pistol at them.

"I am Sturmbannführer Reiner Schuster, SS Intelligence. And who are you?"

The three turned to face him, raising their weapons.

"You are our prisoner. You really think that little pistol will protect you?"

Before Sid could answer, Gireau had sized up the situation and sprung from his hiding place, striking one of the men in the head with the butt of his pistol and jamming the barrel into the back of the neck of the man who appeared to be their leader.

"Put down you weapons, now!"

The other Frenchman froze, and with a nod of the head from the other, he dropped his machine pistol to the ground. The man on the floor lay still, groaning from the blow.

"And now you, monsieur." The leader of the three handed his weapon to Luis who quickly gathered them together and took them a discrete distance.

"OK," Gireau started. "That is better. We will talk."

"I will not speak to a collaborator!" the man spat at Gireau.

"I am not German," Sid spoke, to the surprise of the Frenchmen. "I am an American agent. OSS."

"You are dressed in an SS uniform. And speak perfect German."

"Which is why I am dressed in a German uniform."

Sid put his pistol in his holster.

"Stand down, Henri. We will tell these men the truth. Help your man up. Then we will talk."

"Derrall ... ." The second man stooped to help the dazed man from the floor.

"OK, who are you?"

"I am Sid Woodard, OSS. We have come from Belle Isle where I was assigned to return intelligence on the artillery batteries and radar installations. These men are with the Lorient maquis, and were my transport."

"If you are American, why are you sneaking into the country. The Americans control this sector."

At that news, Sid breathed a sigh of relief. All he had to do was control the emotions in the room, and he should be able to get back to command headquarters soon.

"We did not know the positions of the forces here. We had to assume this was still in German hands. And from the look of your weapons, you are FFI. Correct?"

"Yes."

"And you are called?"

"I am Albert."

"Who is your contact at OSS?"

"We have no contact. Our materials are dropped in zones relayed to us by the FFI in Redon by radio."

"And how do you get your orders?"

"Again, by radio."

"From who?"

"A colonel in the FFI. Luis Verbon."

The men were startled by a sound from behind them, and even more surprised to see Anisette walk out from her hiding place.

"You know Colonel Verbon?" she asked, quietly.

"Who is this?" Albert demanded.

"A prisoner we helped escape from the prison on Belle Isle."

Albert looked at her suspiciously.

"No one escapes the Citadel prison." He looked back at Sid, especially at his uniform.

"Not until now," Sid replied sarcastically.

"What is your name?"

"I am Anisette Durande. And I must get to Colonel Verbon."

"What for?"

She stepped defiantly in front of Albert.

"You will take me to Colonel Verbon."

"I do not take orders from a woman, especially a skinny one!"

His two comrades laughed. Anisette continued in a calm assured voice.

"You will take me today."

"And why will I do that?"

"Because I am La Guardienne."

The men stopped laughing, and all but Albert took a step back and gasped.

A strange reaction, Sid thought.

"La Guardienne is dead. The chain is broken. And you are a liar."

"Albert ... ," the man named Derrall started.

"Shut up!" He turned back to Anisette and stared in her eyes. He then reached forward, grabbed the front of her shirt, and ripped the buttons apart, exposing her bosom.

Anisette stood defiant.

On the inside of her right breast Sid could see a small tattoo, a red rose. Albert saw it too, and took a frightened step back. He fell to his knees and made the sign of the cross.

"Guardienne, I beg your forgiveness, please," and his men fell to their knees as well. No one dared look her in the eyes.

Henri Gireau removed his light coat and Anisette put it over her torn shirt. She bent down on her knees and took Albert's hands in hers. She looked at his right hand, and gently stroked the tattoo of a small rose between his thumb and index finger.

"You were right to question me. To demand proof. Now, please, rise. There is much to be done."

"Oui, mademoiselle. I am your servant."

CHAPTER 15

A MAZE OF INTRIGUES

Society bristles with enigmas which look hard to solve.
It is a perfect maze of intrigue.
- Honore De Balzac

Gireau and his crew prepared to return to the *Sorcière* to make way back to Lorient.

"I will take my boy and make to sea until the bombing has stopped," he told Sid, and the two shook hands as Sid and Anisette prepared to leave by truck. The man called Derrall climbed behind the wheel and they drove away from the shed.

The truck stopped at a barn on the outskirts of Saint-Philibert where they were ushered into a room built out of a root cellar. The entrance was cleverly disguised and the room had lasted four long years of the occupation without being discovered. With the Germans routed from the peninsula Sid had to wonder why the FFI maintained such a heightened level of security.

"Tell my wife to bring La Guardienne something to eat, and a bottle of wine. The rest of you - we have very little. You will have to fend for yourselves."

Years of strict rationing had reduced the population to near starvation. With the threat of German patrols gone, and the Americans ordered to maintain a low profile with the civilian population, the black market exploded. Prices skyrocketed, and crimes against anyone hoarding food of any kind were common. If this FFI faction had any reserves they would be careful not to expose them.

Albert sat at a small table directly across from Sid.

"OK. You need to get to Redon. This I can arrange. But you - with that uniform. How do you plan to get through the American lines? That will be difficult. Your army has abandoned Rennes and moved east and north. They have left a division here to seal off the port fortresses. The front has moved toward Falais."

"Then a local command? There has to be a static headquarters if they are simply going to sit on the ports."

"What kind of identification do you have?"

"I have no identification except my German papers."

"*Jouir d'une vie courte.*" With that Derrall left the room and went back outside to check the truck. Sid turned to Albert.

"What did he say?"

"Enjoy a short life."

The truck rolled on to Redon with the small party safely inside the tarped truck bed.

"So mister SS man ... ,"

"OSS, mademoiselle," Sid smiled.

"I am corrected. Did you find what you were seeking on Belle Isle?"

The color in Anisette's face slowly began to return after a meal of bread and cheese. It was more food than the family of Albert Moragne had eaten in several days.

"Call me Sid. And yes, I think so. I found you."

"Me? I thought you were looking at the German guns."

"In part. Belle Isle holds many secrets."

Sid relished the chance to finally talk with La Guardienne. He could feel her caution, so decided to be blunt.

"You are the Guardian of the Madonna Rosa, so I am told. There is a Catholic leader who says the Madonna is the property of the Church."

"Jacquette." Her matter-of-fact reply surprised Sid.

"Yes. Monsignor Jacquette asked General Patton to help him recover it."

"So, he has contrived to raise himself to a monsignor. He has sought the Madonna for a long time. And now, M. Sid, you are the one sent to find it?"

"The army has no interest in the relic itself. Standing orders are to avoid conflict over sacred and historic objects. We realize there is a dispute between the FFI in Bretagne and the Church. The general wants only to make certain a civil war does not erupt in his rear that might keep his forces tied down."

"I see. And if the relic is found, what are your orders?"

"To make certain it does not leave France in the knapsack of some Allied soldier." Sid watched carefully as Anisette's eyes dilated for just a moment.

I hit a nerve.

"Beyond that, to make certain its fate is controlled by the French."

"And why would the American army be concerned over the FFI and the Madonna?"

"We need the FFI to clear the remaining pockets of resistance from Brittany, leaving the armored units in place to seal off the ports. This stabilizes our rear, and allows Third Army to sweep toward Germany."

"And the French bureaucracy? You will need them, too."

"General Bradley and Ike may need them in the long run. In the short run, Patton needs only a justification to move east."

"And how do I give him that justification?"

"I was told the FFI will rally around the Madonna. They believe an army carrying the icon before it has great power."

"And you think I will lead such an army?"

A subtle shift in her voice left Sid with a sudden sinking feeling in his stomach. This was not coming together as neatly as he imagined. Anisette lowered her eyes.

"Intrigues surround the long story of the Madonna. The Church excommunicated all those who protected it, forever binding the Madonna with a fear of eternal damnation. Fear imparts power and leads men to make rash judgements.

"The Madonna is not about fear, or power. Many armies have carried the Madonna Rosa before them, only to be defeated in battle. The Blessed Virgin does not help men kill one another."

Sid looked at her in amazement. The passive countenance, yet the power in her words, confused him. This was not a warrior among men. There was something entirely different about the power of the Madonna Rosa and this frail girl.

"Forgive me, Mlle Durande. At this moment, I am a little confused."

The truck passed several checkpoints, but these were manned by FFI and Albert had no difficulty in passing through without inspection. Redon and Colonel Verbon lay directly ahead.

"The Madonna. Can you tell me what has happened to it?"

"No, I cannot."

"You mean, you will not?"

"M. Sid, I am a woman of the church, sworn to serve God. I do not lie, or play political games. I do not know what has happened to the Madonna Rosa."

Sid knew by the soft dropping of her voice she was telling the truth.

"The colonel is not seeing anyone today."

That was how Sid translated the French. They had stopped outside a nondescript warehouse fronting the narrow harbor created by the locks on the River La Vilaine. The quay allowed the easy movement of supplies up the river from the bay, but exposed them to almost an unlimited view from the west side of the port. Not the best place to allow an easy escape Sid mused as he stepped from the truck, surveying the area.

The warehouse served as the headquarters of the Bretagne FFI forces. He heard Albert talking in low whispers for a moment before the large door opened and the truck passed through to the inside loading dock. The back tarp was flung aside and two men holding guns pointed them at Sid and motioned him outside. Albert stood on the loading dock, a grim look on his face.

"Take the SS pig inside. To Verbon."

One of the men prodded Sid with the butt of his rifle. Sid shot a glance at Albert who simply managed a slight smirk. Before he stepped into the warehouse he turned back to see Anisette being helped from the truck, a woven shawl given her by Albert's wife over her head, disguising her face.

The guard shoved the barrel of his rifle into Sid's back and pushed him inside. The building was largely empty. There was a large coal cast-iron stove in the far corner with a stash of firewood against the wall. Coal was practically nonexistent in Brittany. Next to the stove was a table, with a single man seated examining maps.

Rennes

The cathedral at Rennes lay in partial ruin following Allied bombing and the retreat of the German army. Despite the destruction, a makeshift office for Monsignor Jacquette had been hastily furnished and business-as-usual returned quickly. Monsignor Jacquette prepared for several visits from key French administrators when his morning routine was interrupted by one of the subordinate priests.

"Brother Petrin, I wish not to be bothered at this time."

"Pardon my interruption, Monsignor, but a matter of utmost concern compels me to interrupt."

Brother Petrin motioned for a rough-looking peasant to enter who from even a distance Monsignor Jacquette could tell had not bathed in weeks. The man held his cap in hand and bowed his head.

"Very well, what is it?"

"This man has news, Monsignor. News of the Madonna."

Monsignor Jacquette immediately felt a sharp pain in his chest, but held his composure.

"Approach."

The man came closer to the desk and stopped to cross himself. Monsignor Jacquette did not bother to rise.

"Tell Monsignor what you told me."

Brother Petrin stood immediately beside the man to prod him to speak. He was shaking, and spoke in a fast, nervous rant.

"La Guardienne. She has been found. She is in Redon."

Impossible! La Guardienne is dead!

Monsignor Jacquette feigned an air of ambivalence while his heart began to race.

"And how do you know of this?"

"My cousin Derrall, Monsignor ... he told me this."

"Tell him the rest," Brother Petrin snapped.

"There was a German with them. He wears the uniform of the SS."

The SS? What kind of nonsense is this? These ignorant peasants. The word of a cousin? How can I know for certain? Foucault assured me the woman was killed, along with her mother.

"And this news ... is there talk of an artifact?"

"No, Monsignor. I am sorry."

"Redon, you say?"

"The headquarters of the FFI under Colonel Verbon," Brother Petrin added.

"Tell me, how did your cousin come by this news?"

"He drives a truck for the FFI. He told me he took them to see Verbon."

The monsignor struggled to maintain his composure.

"I see. Very well, thank you, my son."

Jacquette dismissed him and turned slightly, indicating to Brother Petrin he was to remove the unsightly peasant from his office.

"Leave me, Brother Petrin."

Verbon and La Guardienne? Do they have the Madonna? The German - did he steal it from the Citadel? Perhaps to bargain his way to freedom? If La Guardienne is alive, she will know where the Madonna is. Les Boucliers must have it by now. I cannot allow this to be.

How could I have been so stupid - to believe that snake Foucault that the woman was dead? Did he hold her at the Citadel all this time?

He sat back and closed his eyes, his head spinning with possibilities and questions.

He understood one thing very clearly - Anisette Durande cannot be allowed to appear back from the dead.

Verbon sat at a table looking over a map of the Lorient pocket when he looked up to see a man dressed in an SS officer's uniform walk through the door, followed by two of his men. He instinctively pulled his sidearm.

"What is this? You brought a prisoner here?"

"Albert Moragne arrived with a truck, and this piece of shit was inside," the guard spat on the floor.

"I see. Albert Moragne has caught a big fish in his lousy net. I think we will have some fun with this."

"No. You will not. He is under my protection."

The soft voice, barely audible in the vastness of the warehouse, nonetheless filled the void as sharp as a thunderclap. Verbon looked up, startled. The silhouette of a slight woman appeared backlit by the harsh sunlight outside. He could not yet make out her face, but she walked like a ghost toward him and lowered her shawl.

Colonel Verbon looked up defiantly, then fell to the ground in tears. The men in the room stared in disbelief.

Anisette walked quietly over to the crouching figure of Colonel Verbon and knelt before him.

"I am not a ghost. I am back from the very gates of Hell. God has rescued me, in the form of this man."

Verbon could not raise his head.

"He is SS?"

"No, Luis, he is an American. And he rescued me. We all have a story to tell you. But first, you must rise and embrace me - not as La Guardienne, but as your sister."

Sister? Anisette Durande and the infamous Colonel Verbon - brother and sister?

Verbon rose, and with disbelief still coloring his face, now red and awash with tears, threw his arms around Anisette and held her tightly, crying even harder.

"*Ma soeur, ma soeur.* Where have you been? My God, my gracious God, thank you for bringing her back from the dead."

You are welcome, Sid thought.

Rennes

The morning air hung sweetly in the café garden where Captain Kennedy waited. He thought better of ordering wine, and opted instead for strong coffee and cakes. He hated the French coffee.

Precisely at one o'clock he saw a man approach him, dressed in the brown frock coat of a priest of Cathedral Rennes. Kennedy did not rise to greet him.

"Captain Kennedy?"

The priest carefully looked around the garden as he approached.

"Yes."

"I have a message for you. From the monsignor. May I sit down?"

"Please. I have been expecting you."

"You told no one of our meeting?"

"No. I received a note asking for a private meeting. Very private."

"Very good. The monsignor wishes the utmost discretion in this matter."

The priest looked up for the waiter and motioned for coffee then turned back to Kennedy.

"We have information regarding the Madonna. One of the thieves who has kept the relic hidden had been arrested and held by the occupation authorities. She has escaped with the help of renegade accomplices and, we are told, a German SS officer."

This information caught the captain by surprise.

"An SS officer? Loose in Allied territory?"

"Yes. He travels with a band of criminals - collaborators who seek to undermine the stability of Brittany with the German retreat. This officer helped her escape - he is a criminal to the German command,

and a dangerous man. He traded this help for safe passage to Spain. The woman knows the location of the Madonna and will use it to pay for their escape."

"That is a lot of information."

"We have a man, a loyal servant of God, who has infiltrated this group and drives their truck. He has sent word they are in Redon."

"Very convenient. But what to you want from me?"

"They move quickly, too quickly for us to intercept them. But your army is in contact through radios with the various units throughout the peninsula. The monsignor is asking the army to arrest the officer, and let us retrieve the Madonna in the process - once we know she has taken possession of it."

"I see. We arrest the German, and it just so happens this artifact surfaces."

"Your Army need not concern itself with the relic. It would help avoid certain ... complications."

"Yes. We are ordered to stay out of partisan squabbles."

Kennedy thought for a moment. So far he had been relegated to processing routine intelligence paperwork. This was not the exciting job he imagined when he joined the OSS. But this - arresting a Nazi officer, especially an SS officer. He smelled a promotion lurking in this intrigue.

"I will have to get permission from my commanding officer, of course," Kennedy hesitated, waiting for a reaction, "but that would just be a formality. What do you need from me?"

The waiter brought the priest's coffee.

"So, you say you bluffed your way past the commander on Belle Isle. You understand I do not believe a word of your story, *Américain*."

"Sid. Private Sid Woodard."

"And what is a lowly private doing masquerading as an SS officer?"

God, I hate that word ... lowly.

"What difference is that to you? I have a job to do. Nothing more."

"And your job was to rescue La Guardienne? How do you know of her?"

This is a trap.

"Monsignor Jacquette asked Third Army to help him recover what he called a stolen relic belonging to the Church."

"The Madonna Rosa."

"That's right. He told quite a story - one that none of us believed, I might add. But General Patton was concerned with infighting behind his lines here in Brittany, so asked me to do some investigating. To see what was really going on."

"And just what did you discover, Private Sid Woodard?" Verbon drew out his name in an obvious slur.

"The Madonna was not stolen from the Church, at least not in the time frame the monsignor implied."

"It was never stolen from the Church!"

"Look, Colonel. I don't care about your ancient history. I really don't. That's for you and the Church to settle. But I don't like being played - which is what the Monsignor did. And your sister ... what they did to her. I can't stand for that."

"And what if I told you the colonel at Belle Isle was in league with the monsignor, and the police captain in Lorient? Would you believe that?"

"I don't disbelieve anything, not in this war."

Verbon stared at Sid for a moment, sizing him up.

"Very well, I have decided not to kill you. Yet. You might still be useful to us."

"I appreciate that," Sid smiled.

"I want you to listen to my sister."

CHAPTER 16

THE TRAP

My great concern is not whether you have failed,
but whether you are content with failure.
- Abraham Lincoln

"Captain Carlisle, when I have a report I will let you know."

The Air Ops office at Scotland's Lossiemouth air field had just about enough of Janine Carlisle. It was not unusual for minor flight reports to take some time to reach the operations office and her pestering annoyed the clerk.

Captain Carlisle hung up the receiver and began to pace around her small office. Her intelligence unit at Special Operations Executive (SOE) had no contact with their deep cover agent on Belle Isle. She had no way of knowing if Woodard had even made it to the island let alone made contact. And now the possibility he was collateral damage in the air raid weighed on her mind.

Finally, at 1800 hours - fully two days after the Spitfire raid - the phone rang.

"This is Corporal Smythe at Ops. We have the report, Captain. The flight commander reported serious damage with secondary explosions on a U-boat anchored offshore. It has been confirmed as the U-227. The report lists several collateral targets, including some of the small boats loading the U-boat. I am sending pictures."

Just some additional small boats. Even the most routine reports would list strafing of general TOAs, especially attacks on military command targets. To deliberately avoid such a mention could be significant. The U-boat was their target. Perhaps they did not strafe the town itself.

Carlisle sat back and poured herself a scotch.

"Seems like you managed to not get your ass blown off," she sighed out loud. "So, Private Woodard, just where in the hell are you?"

Anisette sat with her brother and Sid over a bottle of wine, courtesy - or so the colonel stated - of the local German commander whose former headquarters they now occupied.

"Brittany was in complete chaos. British and French soldiers and civilians of all kinds flooded south to the Biscay ports. People panicked as the German army swept quickly south. The atrocities they committed in their conquest of France were hideous.

"We took the Madonna from its hiding place here in Redon and were preparing to flee south to Spain. But the collapse of the army was so quick, and the Germans cut us off. The SS came here, to Redon, specifically to find the Madonna. They captured the priest and tortured him. When he refused to talk he was beheaded on the steps of the chapel. The people refused to talk, and many were killed who protected us in our escape, including my mother.

"My brother led a group of us away from where we knew the SS would attack. Another group remained to fight them, and stall so we could escape. They were all killed. We encountered a small patrol and my brother was wounded. I fled through the woods with the Madonna wrapped in its woolen blanket. I came to a road and met a small convoy of British soldiers trying to escape to Saint-Nazaire. I handed one of them the artifact. He promised he would keep it safe."

Anisette began to cry as she told the story.

"That was the last I saw of it. I broke the chain, and failed my people, and God." She looked down, tears dripping onto the floor.

Colonel Verbon placed his arms around his sister and gave her a gentle embrace.

"Anisette was captured and taken to Rennes where she was held at the cathedral. The bishop who now calls himself Monsignor Jacquette tried to persuade her to tell him where the Madonna was hidden, but she refused. After a few days, when they refused to let her eat or drink, she was given to the Prefect of Police in Lorient, Captain Foucault."

Anisette composed herself, and continued.

"I was held in the city's jail for several days. When the local officials returned to their duties, Captain Foucault had made his deal with the German occupiers and became a part of their administration. Eventually I was taken to Belle Isle and held in that miserable cell. I cannot remember much, except for pain and cold. But I refused to tell them anything."

"You were brave to withstand their torture."

"I was not brave, monsieur. I had failed my God. But He came to me in a dream, and gave me his forgiveness. He said the wickedness of the evil in the world visits pain on the righteous, just as He suffered on the cross. He promised me a place by his side in heaven, for my heart was pure. It gave me joy in the face of my torture, and the strength to resist. And He saved me from my tormentors."

With a little help, Sid thought, a little sarcastically.

"So the relic is gone, and there is no way to know what happened to it?"

"God has hidden the Madonna Rosa, monsieur. It is not our place to question His wisdom. Only to take comfort that he has left us a sign, a path to follow."

She removed a small silken handkerchief from her bodice.

"I did not understand at the time, but knew there would be light shining somewhere along my journey. The light to find the Madonna. And now, I pass that light on to you."

"Me? No, mademoiselle. I am just looking for a way back to headquarters. I can't help you find this thing."

"That is not your decision to make. God has made that choice for you."

She handed him the handkerchief. Sid felt something small and round inside, and unfolded it.

"A British dog tag?"

"I hid this in my cell, in a crack in the brick. I barely managed to retrieve it before I was drugged and dragged from the prison. This is the boy I gave the Madonna Rosa to. He promised to keep it safe and gave me one of his tags so I could someday find him. It is the red one - one of two the soldiers wear. Red for the blood of the martyrs who inspired the carving, and the Madonna Rosa He now challenges you to find."

Sid looked at the name on the ID tag.

FITCH, STF, 4978618, C

A squad of American soldiers under the command of Captain Kennedy pulled up to a small restaurant where the main street, Rue de Douves, turned to head to the canal. Kennedy walked in and proceeded to take over several tables.

"I will make this my command center. Lieutenant, you will oversee the deployment of the troops."

Troops? Who do you think you are - General God-Damned Patton? You have a measly squad of twelve.

"Yes, sir."

Kennedy spread a map out across one of the tables as the proprietor reluctantly brought him a bottle of wine.

"We are here - Rue de La Gare. The road turns toward the harbor ... here. Set up to block the bridges at these two locations and seal off the harbor from the North."

"What about the southern routes?"

"The FFI will attack from the South, and they will control the southern escape routes. Either they will succeed in snaring the thieves red-handed, or they will flush them out like rabbits, right into our trap."

"Uh, Captain ... doesn't this go against our orders to remain neutral with the FFI factions?"

"Thieves, Lieutenant. Bootleggers and black marketeers - that's what we're dealing with. No, it is entirely within my authority to arrest these vermin. Or kill them in the process."

Which is why you are hiding out here?

"Yes, Captain."

"D-hour is 14:00. Deploy your men."

What an ass.

Shouting erupted suddenly from outside and the man Sid knew as Marçon burst open the door dragging another man by the collar who Sid recognized as their driver, Derrall. The driver's face was battered and dirty, and blood oozed down his face and splattered over the front of his shirt.

"Marçon, what is this?"

Marçon tossed the driver onto the floor and stood over him, a look of disgust and hatred on his face.

"A traitor, Colonel. I found him listening outside the window, hidden between some boxes. I followed him back to the truck and heard him make a call on the radio. I think he was calling *Le Cercle*."

"*Le Cercle*? Are you sure of this?"

"I heard him give away our position. They are coming, Colonel. They are coming for La Guardienne. This pig has sold us out!"

Verbon stood and walked over to the driver laying prostrate on the floor.

"Derrall, is this true? You have sold out your brothers? You have turned your back on La Guardienne?"

The driver rose to his knees and wiped the blood from his mouth.

"Your foolish superstitions, they will not help you now. Bretagne will burn, and rise from the ashes free and independent. You and your kind are a throwback, the ones who cost us the help of the Germans. Your day is over."

"You are *Parti National*? You would sell us out to the Germans, and now *Le Cercle*? A gang of thieves and murderers? For what, Derrall? An extra loaf of bread, or bottle of wine?"

Verbon was screaming at the top of his lungs, his arms flailing widely. Sid looked at Anisette who sat quietly. She would not interfere.

"Who is coming? Derrall, tell me, and I will spare your miserable life. Who is coming, and when?"

"You cannot run any longer, Verbon. The Americans are on their side, the side of the Church. They have the entire area surrounded by now."

"The Americans?"

"Yes. And they will let the Church do their dirty work. You are going to die, Verbon. You and your superstitious whore of a sister!"

Sid looked back at Anisette just as a loud shot rang out. Anisette jumped at the shock, her eyes widened. Sid turned back in time to see Marçon holding his smoking pistol.

Verbon simply stared at the traitor lying on the floor. He spit on his body.

"We have to get out of here. Come." He moved quickly and took the still shaking Anisette by the arm.

"You! *Américain*. What do you know of this?"

"Nothing. I swear. The Americans would not participate in something like this. Not unless ... ,"

"Unless what?"

It was something he suddenly remembered Captain Kennedy saying that made him stop.

"I know who is responsible. And yes, the Americans are coming, but I think they have been tricked into supporting one of your rival factions."

He stood, removed his coat covering the SS uniform, and walked to the door.

"Colonel, listen to me carefully. The man responsible for this is an American captain - a dirty one. I know what he will do. He will not want the men he commands to be implicated in anything local, so he will just set up a perimeter and let whoever he is working with do the dirty work. They will not have much time before Army command gets suspicious and begins to ask questions. So we use this to our advantage."

"Why should I trust you, and not just shoot you where you stand?"

"Because you need me as a diversion. They will expect you to run, and expose yourself in the streets. You will be arrested as thieves or looters. Or shot - something the captain is itching to do."

"If we stay here, we will be killed."

"Yes. But do not run. There is another way."

Sid grabbed a chunk of firewood and wrapped it in his short jacket. He grabbed a burlap sack laying near the firewood stash, stuffed the jacket inside, and tied the top with a small piece of cord.

"Get in the truck."

"Where are we going?"

"For a swim."

Sid climbed into the cab of the truck and fired the engine. Verbon, Anisette, Marçon, and two guards climbed into the back. Sid backed the truck out of the warehouse and drove a short distance up the quay, then stopped. He opened the sliding window between the cab and the bed.

"Use the truck as cover. Climb down the gang railing and duck under the water, beneath the dock. There will be enough space to get air. Stay there as long as you can. They will not think to look there - they will think you have escaped."

"Where are you going?"

"To surrender. An SS officer will be a prized plum for this arrogant fool."

"They will arrest you."

Sid smiled.

"I have some experience with that. Now go, and stay in the water until everything quiets down."

"What then."

"I will send word, once I finger this dirty captain. Until then, none of us are safe."

The armed men stormed into the warehouse, weapons firing haphazardly, spraying the room with bullets. The room was empty, save for the lifeless body of their informant - the driver known as Derrall.

"Corporal, a truck is approaching."

The guards blocked the road with two Jeeps where Quai Surcouf crossed the canal and readied their weapons as a German truck crossed the canal bridge. It slowed to a stop. To their astonishment, an SS officer stepped from the cab and adjusted his cap as the bolts from the army carbines pulled back at the ready. Light machine gun fire could be heard from down the harbor. The attack at the warehouse had begun.

"Private!"

The corporal relished the thought of capturing a real SS officer in his trap. The private darted forward with three other men, rifles ready. He motioned the officer away from the truck as the others cautiously approached the back.

"*Heraus!* Out! Out!"

When there was no reply, a soldier fired a warning shot into the roof of the truck. Still no response. Slowly, cautiously, one pulled back the tarp and looked inside.

"Empty, corporal," he called out.

A young private, his rifle ready, approached the officer who stood at attention.

"Heil Hitler!" the officer shouted, and snapped to a Nazi salute. The soldier panicked, and accidentally shot a hole in the side of the truck as the other soldiers ducked for cover. This was the first real German he had ever seen face-to-face.

"You speak English?"

He tried to appear composed after firing his weapon. At that, the officer launched into a flood of rapid German that left the young private bewildered. He simply turned and raised his hands in resignation. Another soldier from the corporal's squad frisked the officer, removed his sidearm, and motioned with his rifle for him to walk toward the squad's Jeep.

Corporal Wilson immediately radioed to Kennedy.

"Yes, sir. Right away, sir … ," and he turned to his men. "The captain is saying the FFI scored a blank. The warehouse was empty." Wilson turned to face the officer. "Where are the others?"

The SS officer just looked stoically ahead and repeated, "Heil Hitler."

"Anybody here speak any German?"

The other men just looked at each other.

"So, what now?" The men looked around unsure.

"Captain says to hold until he arrives."

The café was only a kilometer away, so it took but a moment for the captain's Jeep to drive up and screech to a halt at the road block, and turn around. Kennedy did not bother to get out, or even to look at his prisoner.

"Good work, Corporal. Any of the maquis with him?"

"No, Captain."

"And the artifact?"

"No mention of it, Captain."

One of the soldiers who had been ordered to inspect the truck cried out.

"In here, Corporal!"

He pulled out a burlap sack. It was heavy, and he handled it as Kennedy would expect the Madonna would be.

"Hah! I win all around! The Madonna and an officer for a prisoner! There is a promotion in this for me! Bring the prisoner and the artifact to the command center!"

Kennedy's Jeep drove off.

"Command center, Corporal?"

"The café," he admitted, somewhat sarcastically. "Get in, private."

They loaded the sack and the German officer into the Jeep and drove off toward the café.

"Command center?" one of the men laughed.

"That back home is what we call an over-baked ham."

Captain Kennedy looked up from the café table triumphantly as Corporal Wilson escorted his prisoner inside, a pistol held menacingly at his back. Sid noticed he did not look him in the eyes, but instead began one of his irritating scenes.

"Thank you, Corporal. You will remain as a guard. You, you are a prisoner of the United States Army. You are also a thief. Under the articles of war I can have you shot for looting. Do you understand?"

"*Ich spreche kein Englisch.*"

"Yes, yes. Whatever. Corporal, where is the contraband?"

"Private!" the corporal shouted, and the young private brought the burlap sack inside and set it on the table. Kennedy picked it up.

"It is very heavy, and made of wood. I wonder what it could be?"

He smiled, still not having looked his captive square in the eyes yet, and untied the twine holding the sack closed. He pulled out the coat with a heavy object wrapped inside.

"Yes. Just what we expected. Gentlemen, I give you the Madonna Rosa!"

With a flourish he unwrapped the object, then dropped it quickly on the table.

"What? What is the meaning of this?"

"Not exactly what you were expecting, eh, Captain?"

Sid removed his cap, set it on the table, pulled the chair out and took a seat. He grabbed the open bottle of wine and took a swig as the two officers looked in amazement. Suddenly Captain Kennedy realized who he was.

"Woodard! What the god-damned hell are you doing here? And where's my artifact?"

"I'm getting a little tired of bailing you out of jail, Woodard," Major Dawson growled as he motioned to the guard to open the door.

"Not my fault, Major. Captain Dickhead barged into the middle of my investigation just when things were beginning to come together."

"Put it in your report. Guard, I'm taking the prisoner."

The corporal at the desk simply glanced at Major Dawson's orders and shrugged. Woodard, now dressed in a plain jumpsuit, stood and followed him back down the hall. Once outside, Major Dawson began to speak.

"I wanted to get away from prying ears, Woodard. Something has been going on behind the lines. I think your Captain Kennedy ... ,"

"Captain Dickhead ... ,"

"Captain Kennedy ... may be involved. But I need proof. The problem is, I have been ordered to begin training a special squad for a mission deep inside Germany. And I'm putting you on that team."

Sid realized Dawson wanted him out of France, quickly.

"What about Major Codman? I am supposed to report to him on this operation."

"Not any more. The operation has been terminated."

"On whose orders?"

Dawson stopped and turned to give him a nasty look.

"I didn't realize command had to get your approval ... Private."

Sid was not used to being upbraided by his CO, and realized he had overstepped his relationship with the maverick OSS major.

"OK, I get it. What's next?"

"Make your report, and have it sent directly to me. You will board transport to England immediately and report to OSS liaison in Dover."

"What about my notes on this mission?"

"What notes?"

It was not meant as a question. Sid knew something had been stirred up during his absence and he was caught in the middle of it all. That was never a smart place to be. Better to shut up and move on - and get out of France and away from Captain Kennedy.

"Major, I need to radio my SOE liaison before I can wrap this up."

"Yes, I suppose. Keep the Brits happy."

Dawson pulled a small note pad from his shirt pocket and wrote out a brief set of orders granting Pvt. S. Woodard one-time access to the radio shack - contents classified.

"What about the SS uniform? Makes a great souvenir."

Dawson made a note on the orders and gave Woodard a sideways glance.

"That should take care of you, once and for all," he snarled, not so secretly enjoying the notoriety of it all. "And Woodard, go to supply and get a decent uniform. An American one."

Later that night Private Sidney Woodard, dressed in the uniform of a simple American soldier, removed a waterproof pouch he had taped to his thigh. Inside were his notes - and his previous orders, the only proof of his assignment to this operation, the only ace he held if all this blew up.

He started a new page of notes, careful to disguise his literal meaning in his own private encryption code using Scott Fitch's service number as his key.

He folded the papers, placed them inside an envelope with the red identity disc, and posted it to his address of record back home.

"Now, one last thing."

He walked outside and cut across the base to the radio shack.

"I have to make a report. I need access to the radio."

"You? You're just a damn private!"

Sid handed him the orders from Major Dawson and pushed his way into the operator's chair.

"Take a powder, Scooter."

They met at the designated spot on the outskirts of Rennes. Sid drove up in a Jeep.

"Where are you heading?" Colonel Verbon asked, extending his hand.

"Back to England. Flying out of Arromanches."

"Your own Jeep?"

"Not exactly," Sid smiled.

Anisette stepped out of the waiting car and walked to the side of the Jeep. She took Sid's hand.

"I am grateful you saved my life, but it has no meaning, save for my duty to God. Please help us find the Madonna. Find the man from the tag. It does not matter how long it takes. God will grant you success only when He finds us worthy, by His plan, not the intrigues of man."

Sid looked into her eyes, tears flowing once more.

How can I refuse this remarkable woman?

"I will find the Madonna. I promise."

With a soft smile, she turned and followed her brother and his men to the car. Sid watched as they drove off into the Breton countryside.

He gunned the Jeep's engine and roared up the road north toward Arromanches.

CHAPTER 17

THE JADE COAST

Through tattered clothes, small vices do appear.
Robes and furred gowns hide all.
- William Shakespeare

Present Day

I knew I had to decode the cryptic notes to piece these documents together and have any hope of unraveling this mystery. I began with the premise there was a key hidden somewhere in the notes - a phrase that held the pattern of numbers or letters I could use to decode the text. I pulled some note paper out and pencilled in the first forty characters of the notes looking for a pattern. Nothing was apparent.

The only unencrypted phrase was the name "Anisette Durande." Was this the key? I wrote the name out, determined the alphabet number location of each of the letters, and wrote it above each letter. I applied this as a rudimentary key to some of the text, but it revealed nothing.

There are many ways to form an encryption but without knowing Sid's particular bias I could waste a lot of time manually trying to decode this. Instead, I hollered out toward the kitchen.

"Monique, when you get a minute ... ."

I passed the decoding problem off to Monique who jumped at the chance to tackle a new problem. In the meantime, I took stock of what I knew.

Patton's orders juxtaposed with the other documents led me to one explicit conclusion: General George Patton ordered Sid Woodard, OSS, to recover an undisclosed religious object. But the information about Scott Fitch was from 1940 - four years before American forces landed in France. How were these clues connected?

I knew from my last conversation with "Whitey" that he intended to revisit these files and resolve whatever mystery or enigma they posed. He passed away, however, leaving only these subtle clues - a look into the working of his keen intellect, however incomplete. There had to be a context here - Sid would not have left this story hanging in mid-air.

So I was not surprised when the last page of the stapled papers gave me the context I was looking for. In typical Sid fashion, the critical document lay underneath the others - "the foundation upon which truth is built," he would often say. It was a faded photocopy of an article from *The War Illustrated* magazine, August 1940.

> I Was There! - We Swam in Oil When "Lancastria" Sank
>
> None of the sea disasters of the war is likely to surpass in human suffering the wreck of the troopship "Lancastria", which was bombed and sunk in Saint-Nazaire harbour on June 17. Here are some survivors' stories of the tragic and pitiable scenes they witnessed, and of coolness and heroism in the face of catastrophe. (4)

I decided to head for the heart of the story - Saint-Nazaire.

I dropped an email to my benefactor Angus McDonough at the Winnipeg Guardian and promised him an enticing new story about the British evacuation from France, packed up my laptop and a gear bag, and headed south. As I drove through the Brittany countryside - through the homeland of Antoine, Marianne, and Arièle - I reflected on the research I had done on the *Lancastria* disaster.

The *Lancastria* arrived off the port of Saint-Nazaire in mid-July to aide in the evacuation of the British Expeditionary Force from France. As the remnants of the BEF fled south, soldiers and civilians alike gathered in Saint-Nazaire and boarded small coastal craft ferrying evacuees to the *Lancastria* and other ships anchored further offshore in the Loire estuary. Over 8000 people jammed the holds and decks of the converted Cunard liner. Threats of German U-boats offshore persuaded Captain Sharpe to wait for a destroyer escort even as waves of Stuka dive bombers began harassing the evacuation efforts.

At 1548 on 17 June 1940 the *Lancastria* took four direct hits, listed to starboard, then back to port before beginning its death roll. Twenty minutes later it sank. Estimates of the death toll vary - some as high as 5000. Bodies littered the shorelines all along the coast; many were never recovered. Survivors clung to floating debris and waited in the cold, oily water - strafed by German planes, desperate for rescue. Of the entire losses incurred by the BEF in the fall of France, fully one-third died at Saint-Nazaire that fateful afternoon - the single greatest loss of life in British maritime history.

The story of why there was such a loss of life is disturbing and painful. Too many men, women, and children crammed aboard. Too few life jackets or life boats. Too few British fighters overhead to ward off the German attacks. Too few warships to chase away the waiting U-boats. Too little time.

Churchill ordered news of the sinking blacked out. The news of the capitulation of the French government overshadowed the sinking, and the story was lost to the backwater of history, forgotten for decades, reluctant to rise again.

Napoleon was right - history was just the lies we agree upon.

Henri, the manager of my hotel near the Saint-Nazaire waterfront, turned out to be one of my readers, so I autographed his copy of *The Juno Letters*.

"Are you working on another of your books, M. Hewitt?"

"Yes, I hope so. Mostly some research right now."

"Then I am at your service, my friend. Whatever you may need, it would be my pleasure to assist you."

It was always good to make friends in a new city. Henri directed me to the Lancastria Memorial and suggested a café around the corner with a fine view of the waterfront just across the boulevard from the memorial plaza.

Place du Commando consisted of an obelisk honoring a raid on the massive Normandie dry docks built to repair the battleships *Tirpitz* and *Bismarck*. The locks were destroyed in perhaps the greatest commando raid of all time, called Operation Chariot. The Lancastria Memorial erected in 1988 shared this spot, almost an afterthought compared the Operation Chariot memorial, almost lost to history.

As I stood before the memorial I could hear explosions and the screams of the dying. This was a place of death, of pain, but also of heroism.

This was where Private Scott Fitch died. His war record indicated he was "missing in action" - he probably went down with the *Lancastria* and his body was never recovered. That was made clear by Sid's meticulous note taking. Yet his red identity disc - the disc removed from a body for reporting - lay sealed in Sid's file in an old envelope all these years. Where did it come from? How did Sid find it?

I had hoped by coming to Saint-Nazaire I could shed some light on these questions. I checked the church registries in the surrounding communities, the Lancastria Association archives, the records of the Catholic diocese - nothing. There was no record of a Private Scott Fitch boarding *Lancastria*, no burial records, and no records of unidentified bodies from the war in any official sources.

Who recovered his red identity disc and how did they find it?

A block down the beach from the memorial I took a table at Restaurant "Le 16." Le 16 is my favorite kind of French eatery - small, clean, and discrete. It was past mid-day and the café was not busy - good thing, as there were only three small tables outside on the sidewalk looking out on the beach frontage. A slight breeze wafted in off the bay, the sea air comforting.

I ordered a bottle of wine, some bread and cheese, and settled in to begin examining my notes.

"*Monsieur, pardon.*"

I had been lost in thought when the waiter interrupted me.

"*Non, merci.* I have enough wine."

"*Ah, non, monsieur.* You are American?"

"Yes."

"OK. I know plenty English. I am curious - what you are studying. You look so serious."

He pulled up the chair opposite me and sat down, glass in hand, and helped himself to a slurp of the wine.

"Well, if you are interested … ."

"No, not really, but the owner is curious … whether he should ask you to leave. I told him I would check you out."

I had to laugh. The French can be extremely accommodating, or exasperatingly direct. I appreciated both.

"OK. What do you know of the *Lancastria*?"

"The memorial? Not a lot. Just a lot of men died here in the war. That's all."

"Well, that's the gist of it. I am looking for a man who was lost on the *Lancastria*. Officially he is listed as missing in action but we know he died that day. But I believe someone found his body."

"And what is he to you? A relative?"

"No. He is part of a puzzle, part of a job I have to find something, something lost during the war."

"Part of a job? What kind of job is that? Are you a private detective? Do you carry a gun?"

"No, I don't carry a gun," which was not exactly true. "And I am a writer, not a detective, although there is not much difference sometimes."

"A writer. Have I read anything of yours?"

"Maybe. I am published here in France. Part of my first book included the *Campbeltown* raid, where they blew up the locks."

"The Normandie. Yes, right there."

The *Campbeltown* raid, called Operation Chariot, was big tourism business here in Saint-Nazaire, the locks just at the end of the street to the left of the café.

"What is the name of your book?"

"*The Juno Letters.*"

He took a deep drink of the wine, emptying the glass, and left it on the table.

"Never heard of it," and he hurried off back inside.

I went back to studying the transcriptions when I was interrupted again, this time by a heavy-set older man who plopped a dog-eared copy of my book on the table.

"You are M. Hewitt?"

"Yes, I am," and I rose to greet the man. "Larry Hewitt."

"I am Darcell Favro, owner and cook."

"*Mon plaisir*, M. Favro."

"Cut the crap … and call me Darcell."

He sat down with a glass and poured out most of the rest of the wine.

"Justin! Another bottle!"

The waiter returned, dropped a bottle on the table, and headed back inside.

"So, you wrote this crap, eh?"

Crap?

"Yes."

He picked up the book and contemplated it for a moment.

"My wife, she read it. Forced me to. Not my thing, if you follow me."

"I follow you, Darcell. Is there something I can help you with?"

"You are writing another book?"

"Researching, right now."

"About what? Saint-Nazaire?"

His brusque manner amused me … as long as he was buying the wine.

"In part."

"Justin says you are looking for a man. A dead man. I know everything and everybody in Saint-Nazaire. I can help you."

Now I began to be suspicious.

"And what are you looking for? A fee, perhaps?"

He turned and spit on the ground.

"Americans! Why do I waste my time? I starve quite well running this little dump of a café. I am not after a payment."

"What then?"

"My wife … she will want you to sign this little book of yours."

"An autograph? Is that all?"

"*Non.*"

I sat and just waited while he gobbled down most of the rest of my cheese, and killed off the first bottle of wine. He removed a corkscrew from his pocket and opened the second bottle.

"My wife's family … they finance this little café of mine. Why, I don't know. But there it is. If I keep her happy, she keeps me in business. When she finds out I am friends with the famous American writer … ,"

I poured myself another glass, took a long draw, and replied, "I would rather pay a fee."

"Hah! I like you already! We are going to be great partners!"

Partners? What is this guy's angle?

"OK, Mr. Writer, ask me anything you want."

"All right. You know of the *Lancastria*?"

"Of course. The memorial is just across the street. Ask me something more difficult."

"Do you know the name Scott Fitch?"

"Non."

"Have you ever heard of Sid Woodard?"

"Non."

"Do you know anything about the activities of the OSS here during the war?"

"Non." He poured another glass of wine. "Ask me something I know about."

Great. How the hell do I know what you know about?

"OK, let's try something else. I am interested in a church relic, something that may have gone missing during the war, and one the American army may have been looking for. There is an obscure reference in my notes, and I am not really certain what it refers to."

"There were many things stolen during the war. The Germans were quite good at it. The Allies, too."

He smiled at the not so subtle dig.

"Have you heard of something called the 'Madonna?'"

Darcell Favro quickly set his glass on the table, spilling the wine on the table cloth. He looked around the room quickly, then turned back to me and spoke in a low voice.

"M. Larry. You are looking for the Madonna Rosa?"

"I am not sure. Just what is this Madonna Rosa?"

"My friend, do not speak of this openly, I beg of you. Tell no one you seek this."

He looked furtively around again.

"I will explain more to you ... but not here."

Paris

"Bonjour, Professor Dechant. Ça va?"

"Monique! What brings you here, to this god-awful hell-hole? And call me Tristan, please."

Professor Tristan Dechant taught a course called "Technology and the Legal Process" at the university and Monique was one of his favorite students. He managed the university's extensive digital law library. On several occasions the much older professor had asked Monique out for a drink, unsuccessfully.

"I have a problem I was hoping you could help me with."

"Of course. Sit, please, and tell me about it."

She knew Professor Dechant would want at least a drink-date out of this and she had already resigned herself to that. Despite his persistence, he seemed polite and relatively harmless.

"I have a paper written in some sort of code. I was hoping with your computer skills you could help me decode them."

"A code? Whatever for?"

"My friend, the American writer. One of his little mysteries."

"Well, let us see what you have."

Monique opened a file folder with a photocopy of the coded notes.

"Hmm, yes. Definitely encrypted, likely a mnemonic, and not a very sophisticated one by the repetitions. But quite difficult to interpret without the key, nonetheless."

"M. Larry and I thought the name, here ... ," and she pointed to the name Anisette Durande on the second page, "... might be the key."

"Possibly. Not too difficult to test. But I would think not. Anyone going to the trouble to encode this would not put the key so openly on the same page. Certainly a casual observer could not make out the content, but anyone with cryptology experience would have no problem at all. No, I would think it would be something else, something more subtle - and possibly a number."

A number? Monique thought for a moment, then grabbed her cell phone.

"M. Larry. The number on the ID tag. What is it? ... No, not yet, but I am working on it ... yes, I will. Trust me! ... *Merci*!"

She wrote Scott Fitch's military ID number down on a separate piece of paper and handed it to the professor.

"This is significant to the context of the notes?"

"Yes. Quite."

"I will give it a try. It may take a while. May I call you when it is finished?"

He smiled a genuinely warm smile, one Monique knew carried with it a date for drinks after work.

"If you could email me your results?"

"Of course."

She smiled, and wrote her email and phone number on the edge of his desk blotter.

Darcell made a quick phone call. Before I could finish my wine we went hurrying off down the street to a hastily arranged meeting with a Reformist pastor at Centre Evangélique de Saint-Nazaire, Darcell leading the way, keeping a close eye over his shoulder all the way.

"A Reformist church? But wouldn't a madonna relic be Catholic, not Reformist?"

"Yes, my friend, but the Church - a den of snakes and thieves. You will not get a straight answer out of the priests. Too political. But the Reformists - they would like nothing more than to tweak the ass of the giant ... ," he smiled as he hurried up the street.

At a nondescript entrance at 21 Rue Ypres we entered a simple whitewashed building with a modest blue sign that read "Centre Evangélique" in simple white letters. Darcell barged into the pastor's office without knocking.

"Darcell! How good to see you."

"No, I am not coming to services, so don't ask."

Pastor Lorbas simply smiled.

"You think I would even bother to ask? And you must be our American friend?"

"Hewitt, pastor. Larry Hewitt."

"Please, come in and sit down. Darcell is an old friend, and that makes you a friend as well."

"Watch your wallet," the café owner warned.

Pastor Lorbas simply smiled at the good-natured jab and motioned us to sit in the simple chairs. He opened a bottle of red wine and poured three glasses.

"Darcell tells me you are looking for information about a religious object, one perhaps lost during the war. He was somewhat reluctant to discuss it on the telephone, however."

"Yes, it may have gone missing in the British evacuation from Saint-Nazaire."

Darcell began to squirm in his seat.

"Pastor," he interrupted, nervously, "he is talking about the Madonna Rosa."

Pastor Lorbas sat up short and gave a quick look at Darcell. He sat back slowly.

"Darcell said you have a solder's identity disc."

"Yes, from a body that is listed as missing in action. But if the dead soldier was never found, why would I have his identity disc, and why only one of the pair?"

"Which one?"

"The red one."

The pastor looked at me and wrinkled his brow.

"The red one? What does that mean?" Darcel interrupted.

"It usually means someone took the disc to report his body found. What exactly is the connection between the soldier and this artifact?"

"To be honest, I am not sure. I believe there was an investigation of sorts in 1944 as the American army secured the Brittany peninsula. Something brought this to the attention of the American command. That implies it may have been seen after the *Lancastria* tragedy, still here in Brittany. The soldier who conducted the original search for the relic in 1944 was a good friend. He was a member of the OSS and his orders sent him to Brittany, but I can only assume there is a relationship between his assignment and the Madonna. I have no direct proof."

The pastor wrinkled his brow.

"Is there any way to meet with your friend to discuss these matters?"

"He passed away recently, but before he died he gave me a file. It contained notes on his investigation, and an envelope. The red identity disc was sealed in that envelope."

"Hmm," he sat back, stroking his chin. "A small act, it would seem, but one of great significance."

"My thoughts, exactly. Forgive me, Pastor Lorbas, but your reaction to the name - Madonna Rosa. That begs an explanation."

It took a few hours, but Monique's phone buzzed with the anticipated email just as she prepared to leave work. There were three small attachments to the professor's message, each one a translation of one of the paragraphs on the page. She clicked on each and glanced through them quickly. She had been right. The cypher key was Scott Fitch's military ID.

Her phone rang next.

"*Bonjour*, professor ... yes, thank you. I looked them over briefly ... yes, very interesting. I have to ask you to keep this information confidential ... yes, of course ... tomorrow night? Yes, professor. I will meet you for a drink. Seven o'clock. Very well."

She smiled as she forwarded the email to me.

> M. Larry. Read these files carefully. A professor at school helped with the translation. Call me when you have the chance. You owe me for this one - big time!

> Please be careful. M.

Pastor Lorbas rose and slowly paced the floor, choosing his words carefully.

"The Madonna Rosa is a relic from Brittany's Roman past. According to legend it was carved from the cross upon which Saint Blandina was martyred following the Christian persecutions in Lyon."

"And the name 'Rosa?'"

"A spiritual connection to the Virgin Mary. The rose has long been associated with the incarnations of the divine feminine - a critical part of the story of Jesus.

"According to a letter written by an eyewitness, the Christian slave Blandina suffered terribly at the hands of the Roman executioners. She was burned over a roasting pit, her flesh torn by wild beasts in the arena. Hung on a crude pole, she was wrapped in a fisherman's net then gored and trampled by a raging bull. Miraculously, she was still alive when the executioner cut her throat with a dagger.

"Legend says a Christian from a radical sect recovered a piece of the pole some people equate to a cross. A sculptor among them carved a figurine, what was called the Madonna Rosa. The survivors carried that icon before them as they fled Roman persecution to what is now Brittany. The Madonna was hidden for centuries - first from the Romans and later the Catholic Church.

"The church was brutal in its search for the Madonna. A loyal duke of Brittany cornered the sect near the River La Vilaine. They took the Madonna and massacred everyone in the party.

"In 1485 the Madonna was stolen from the church by one of the rebellious dukes vying for independence from the Crown. The rebellion failed, and the Crown and the Church reasserted its hegemony over Bretagne. But the Madonna remained lost."

"Hidden, not lost," Darcell interjected.

Pastor Lorbas smiled.

"The artifact became synonymous with an independent Bretagne and stories of its mysterious power infiltrated every corner of Brittany. Separatism has always been strong here, but there have been so many factions the Church and the Crown were able to keep a tight grip on the people, until the Revolution."

"What changed?"

"Following the beheading of the king nobles from the House of Montfort in Brittany tried to arrange safe passage to England. They were intercepted at a river crossing near Rennes as they fled south - near where the massacre of the Christian sect took place. The entire party - save for a servant girl - was slaughtered. The attackers were just a roving band of opportunists - they found the Madonna hidden among their possessions."

"It is called 'La Rivière' - The River. It is the moment of rebirth for an independent Bretagne."

Darcell's passion when discussing the relic put me on edge.

"I don't understand something. These nobles had the Madonna, but kept it from the Church. I thought the ruling class had succumbed to the control of the Crown. I would presume they would have turned it over to the Church."

Pastor Lorbas sighed and shook his head.

"The history of the Madonna and the separatism that it engenders is very complex, and political. Even among the old nobility there were many factions - those closely allied with the Crown and those merely subservient to it. The church took no official action against the nobles who possessed the Madonna.

"After the attack, however, everything changed. A renegade priest took the Madonna and gave refuge to the little servant girl who survived."

"What do you mean, 'renegade?'"

"Many of the priests in Brittany sided with the separatists against the Church, especially among the rural parishes. As just one of many political intrigues within the Church this was not so unusual. But the taking of the Madonna - this was open warfare against the Church's hegemony.

"The young girl was selected to become the anointed protector of the Madonna. She was named La Guardienne, and her personal seal was a red rose - symbolic of the wild roses at the site of the relic's recovery and the rose as the flower depicting Mary, the Mother of God."

"There is a guardian still today?"

Pastor Lorbas continued without answering my question.

"After the Revolution the church reestablished its influence with the new Republic as the old monarchy and its extant nobility dissolved. The Pope declared the Madonna Rosa a relic of the Church of Rome and issued a decree of excommunication against the renegade priest and all those who protected the artifact. To keep it from the church's hands it once again disappeared."

I found it interesting that the pastor knew very specific details of this legend - especially the dates. I guessed there were details he was withholding from me as well.

"Did the relic surface during the war?"

"That is difficult to say. There are only rumors. We know the Germans sent SS squads into the countryside searching for it."

Darcell began to spit on the floor, but thought better of it.

"Your soldier's disc. It proves the British took it during the evacuation," Darcel interjected.

I was not so sure. If the Madonna left the continent during the evacuation, why would General Patton leading his armor in a rush through the peninsula trouble himself personally with such a matter? Then there was the letter from the French church official denying church complicity in the blackmarket and the refusal of CIA Director Smith to pursue the matter. These things are not in the file by chance. They support the idea that the Madonna was still in Brittany.

I decided to keep these details secret for now.

"Scott Fitch never made it home and his body was not recovered, at least as far as I can tell. If he had the relic, it may have disappeared at the same time. If his body was discovered by someone who mistrusted the authorities, that might explain why it is unaccounted for. They did not report the body, or the recovery of the Madonna."

The pastor wrinkled his brow.

"The first part of your conjecture is, I believe, possible. Many bodies washed ashore after the sinking of the *Lancastria*. The French police, the SS, and the Gestapo were quite thorough in their efforts to secure the bodies. Many of the dead seamen and civilians were buried by people who simply refused to inform the authorities. But there is another side to the story, one not generally discussed openly."

"And what is that?"

"The churches of the major cities and towns were under the control of the authorities, that is true. But many of the rural village chapels remained independent, beyond the reach of the police. Some of these churches were a source of partisan support and many of their separatist followers joined the Reformist movement after the war. If one of them discovered the body ... ,"

"He could be buried anywhere, my friend." Darcell finished off the bottle of wine. "There are too many churches to check them all."

"Darcell, I need to think about this. There is a truth here. Scott Fitch died that day, that I know. Someone found his identity tag, that I also know. And Sid Woodard connected that person through his ID tag to the Madonna Rosa. These facts connect to a logical set of events that did occur - we just don't yet know what they are."

"How will you find out?"

I took a deep breath and sighed.

"I just need to think this through."

As we said our goodbyes, I had one last thought.

"Pastor Lorbas, do you know what happened to the priest - the one who blessed the first Guardienne?"

I could see he was saying a quick prayer.

"He was burned to death, nailed to the altar in his church."

Back at the hotel I checked my laptop and read the email from Monique - especially the last line:

> Please be careful. M.

I opened and read the attachments. I was disappointed, but not surprised, that Sid's notes painted an incomplete picture. The decryption was hampered by Sid's difficult handwriting. Since the letters were not in the form of recognizable words the translation was haphazard at best.

The first paragraph was labeled "FFI" - what I knew to be the "French Forces of the Interior." Certain keywords were evident: fractured, infighting, lack of discipline. One phrase stood out - "civil war." Some names tried to emerge from the cryptanalysis, but again they were difficult to read. Three were clear enough, however: "Cpt Kennedy," someone with the last name of "Verbon," and the first name "Anisette" with the notation, "granddaughter." Anisette Durande was the name written plainly on the bottom of this page.

The professor had written a note here.

> The name written below, Anisette Durande, was added in a different ink. Very recently.

Sid must have added the name to the notes before he gave them to me. This was a critical piece of the puzzle I had not noticed.

The second paragraph appeared to focus on Captain Kennedy. I remembered that name from the story Sid told me of his assignment in Kent when he first met General Patton. He had always suspected Kennedy was dirty, but he could never quite prove it. But here was his own notation that supported those fears. The translation had another note from the professor:

> The word "blackmarket" was written next to the
> name Kennedy and circled. The final sentence of the
> paragraph was translated in its entirety:

> No report to 3rd Army.

The third paragraph was the most complete. I was reading the kind of random dialogue I often found myself stuck in as I thought through difficult problems.

> Four years in hell hole on the island. Finally got her to
> tell me entire story, at least as much as she knew. The
> artifact - rumors only. Body washed ashore? If found
> by G or SS - records. Not found by FFI, or Boucliers.
> Why do they think MR survived? Why still hiding?

> Need to find the body.

I took Sid's advice and decided to focus on finding the body of Scott Fitch. According to the official accounts of the *Lancastria* disaster many of the bodies simply washed up on the beach in the following days. A body floating away from the wreck in the shallow estuary waters would have followed the tidal and wind-driven currents eastward into the hook formed by the island of Noirmoutier. The Jade Coast in 1944 was scarcely populated as coasts go - plenty of small villages and coastal fishing communities. There were no large cities with significant occupying forces east of Saint-Nazaire until the submarine complex at La Pallice. The Gestapo and the SS would be scattered very thin through this part of France - a body on the beach could have been discovered by locals and hidden from the authorities.

I decided to start at the furthest logical spot on my current map where I believed a body could have been found and work backward along the coast toward Saint-Nazaire.

CHAPTER 18

THE FRUIT OF FAILURE

Real knowledge is to know the extent
of one's ignorance.
- Confucius

The tourist and fishing port of La Linier is at the very tip of the peninsula formed by the island of Noirmoutier - a hook that formed a natural barrier to the floating body of Scott Fitch. I hoped to find some evidence of the *Lancastria* sinking - someone still alive that was here during the war, a memorial with names written on it, or a cemetery - anything that could give me a clue to stimulate my search.

"*Je regrette, monsieur.* I cannot help you." The woman at the tourist kiosk was too young to remember even the *Challenger* disaster let alone the war. "Perhaps you could speak to the priest."

The priest was a young man about twenty-five.

"I would be happy to look through the church records and call you, but I know of nothing like you are asking for."

I walked the beaches and spoke to as many people as I could, especially small merchants, business owners - anyone who would talk to me. After an entire day, I accomplished nothing - except to cross Noirmoutier off the list.

Working my way back along the coast I visited a dozen small communes, spoke to the pastors and priests of twenty-three churches, and burned the better part of three days - again, nothing of any significance.

In a café in Prigny I met an old man who latched onto me and in broken English mixed with French made me sit through three hours of stories about the war. My notes started off detailed and organized but ended in swirling doodles as my interest waned. As I drove back to my hotel in La Bernerie-en-Retz, I decided I needed a different strategy.

Over a cup of extra strong coffee and croissants at the café at Le Hotel Rose the following morning I began to have second thoughts about the entire process.

"You look lost with your thoughts, monsieur."

The waitress who also doubled for duty at the front desk wore a name tag that read "Melaine." She politely refilled my coffee and took my plate.

"Yes, I suppose I am trying a little too hard to figure this out."

"The morning is very beautiful, monsieur. Too beautiful to waste it working. Perhaps a nice walk along the beach will help you collect your thoughts."

I looked out the view windows over the beach below. The restaurant has a sunroom - that's the best way I can describe it - that looks more like the bridge of a fishing boat sticking out into the beach area above a public promenade. An artificial sea wall forms a lagoon that keeps a steady water level that warms in the summer - a perfect outdoor swimming area, empty at this early hour. A walk along this quiet beach front seemed a good idea.

"I will take you up on that suggestion, Melaine. Thank you. Can you tell me if there is an official public records office here in La Bernerie?"

She thought for a moment, wondering what to say.

"Only the library, monsieur. But I am not certain what help they can offer you. Will you be staying at the hotel tonight?"

"Yes, another day if it is convenient."

"I will inform the manager, monsieur. *Bonjour.*"

"He has left the café. He asked me if there was a public records office here, so I told him to check with the library. Should I have done that?"

"Yes. Do not try and put any obstacles in his path that cannot be blamed on local officials. That will simply raise his suspicions. Just try and keep an eye on where he goes. Report back to me with even the smallest details."

"I understand."

Melaine looked up to see the hotel manager approaching.

"I have to go."

Perryn de L'Etanche slipped his cell phone back into his pocket and sat on a beachfront bench across the boulevard from Le Café 16, considering his options.

I took my time the following morning getting ready. I had spent the entire previous afternoon combing through public records at the library - burials, deaths, births, lawsuits, land actions - anything that might hold a clue, a key to something I already knew but was simply overlooking. Nothing.

The librarian finally had to ask me to leave - the library had already been closed for over an hour. I knew I had struck out, and overstayed my welcome. So I was in no hurry to start again. I finished my coffee and decided to talk a short walk.

The bay was smooth as glass on this breathless morning. I sat down and stretched in the cool sand and picked up a few loose stones. I tossed them one by one into the quiet water in front of me. The ripples spread away into the distance. Some children ran past, diverting my attention for a moment. When I looked back the ripples had all disappeared.

I picked up another stone and tossed it into the water. The ripples ran away once more. Then again. Something about the stone, the ripples ... what was it?

I looked around but did not see any other stones lying on top of the sand. From where I looked the sand appeared uniform, featureless. Yet I knew that was not the case. I dug around a little, and found a stone small enough not to be noticed on the sandy beach yet big enough to make a ripple in the calm bay easily within reach.

A stone that would create its own unique ripples, but ones that would disappear in a short time.

That gave me an idea.

"Ah, you have returned," the librarian smiled. I was certain she was not really glad to see me back after our exhausting and fruitless session the day before.

"Yes, madame. And I want to thank you for all your hard work yesterday."

She shot me a look that made me realize I had already blown my cover, so I got right to the point.

"I have another request to make. One I hope will be short."

"*D'accord, monsieur*. OK. But I have some cataloging to do this morning and cannot spend a lot of time with you. If this involves more work, I will have to ask that you forgive me until this afternoon."

"With a little luck, I will be out of here shortly. I am planning to leave for Saint-Nazaire later this afternoon."

"Where do you wish to begin?"

"Yesterday I was searching through burial records, perhaps ones that indicated an unknown soldier, or perhaps a mistaken identity. But what if no one wanted the records found? What if the burial itself was covered up somehow?"

"Why, monsieur?"

"There could be a million reasons - none of which are relevant, really. But what might be common to all or at least some of such occurrences?"

"I do not know, monsieur."

"A ripple, madame."

"Ripple?"

"*Une ondulation*. A ripple. Something that caused a reaction, a reaction we can discover if not the action itself - a pointer, if you will."

She looked over the top of her glasses at me like I had been drinking too much wine, and I smiled.

"I want to search the newspapers from 1944 to the present. I have a list of key words ... ," and I handed her a list of words I had carefully tested online to see what kind of results I could expect. The search engines did not have access to the archived newspaper files, but the library did.

"What are you looking for?"

"Someone who is mad. Someone making a stink."

"A stink?"

"American slang, madame, for causing a lot of fuss over something, usually little."

She nodded her head and made "that look" - she knew all too well about people like that.

"It will take time," she remarked as she looked over the list. "There are many words here, but the search is fairly routine. I will give you an access password with a code so you can view the results at your leisure. If you will give me just a few minutes."

I waited in the lobby until she returned and handed me a small slip of paper.

"The results should be ready within the hour. Will there be anything else?"

"No, madame. If this does not work, I promise to leave you in peace."

She smiled, and nodded her head.

"I wish you *bon chance*, monsieur."

I crossed the street to a small café, ordered lunch, then logged onto the library site with my cell phone to monitor its progress. It took about fifty minutes before the results appeared. As promised, I was looking at a list - a long list - of articles that matched with a degree of "fuzzy logic" the search terms I had tested. I clicked on the first few links to get a feel for what I was seeing and how I could manipulate the data.

The files were PDF shots of newspaper articles that had been character scanned for searching. A text version in varying degrees of thoroughness accompanied each article that I could download and manipulate on my laptop.

Everything was, of course, in French. I noticed an icon in the lower corner - an arrow pointing downward, and clicked it. The list of links immediately downloaded to my cell phone as a linked web file I could browse at my leisure. I would need help with the French, however.

"Monique. I wish to speak to Monique."

Her roommate was accustomed to screening her calls from would-be suitors.

"You are American?"

"Yes, tell her it is M. Larry. It is very important."

I could tell she had her hand covering the receiver by the muffled sounds that followed.

"M. Larry! So good to hear from you!"

"Hello, Monique. How did your finals go?"

"Oh, well enough." I knew by her tone she had aced them, otherwise there would have been hell to pay for even asking. "I have absolutely nothing to do except work for Papa, and I am completely bored. Do you have something for me?"

"I have a list of newspaper stories - all in French, of course. I need someone to go through them and look for a needle in a haystack."

"A what?"

"A needle … never mind. I am looking for a clue, a clue to someone making a fuss about something. A ripple, if you will, in an otherwise calm pond."

"I wish you would stop talking in circles. What are you looking for, exactly?"

"I don't know."

"That figures. What do you hope to find?"

"The body of Scott Fitch. But it is unlikely his name will come up anywhere. I think he was buried anonymously, and I am trying to find him. What I am looking for may be buried with him."

"What will give me a clue?"

"Throw a rock into a calm pond and watch the ripples run away."

The phone remained quiet for a moment.

"Just once, a straight answer would be nice. Where is this information?"

"I will email you the downloaded list with my login information. And one more thing. Can you track down a name from the occupation, probably from Brittany? Anisette Durande."

"The name on the note page?"

"Yes. Sid would not have kept it if it weren't important - but that's all I know."

"I will do what I can."

I knew I could count on Monique to do quite a lot more than that.

The librarian ducked inside a small cubicle and hurriedly called a number from her cell phone.

"He has been searching for newspaper stories ... I don't know what! He just spoke some nonsense about ripples ... there are about fifty, all in French. From what I can tell he can't speak French very well ... no, he has not asked for translations ... I already sent him the list ... I couldn't just refuse him! Do you really think he would not report me?"

She listened to a voice on the other end for a short time.

"That is a bad idea. It will simply put him on alert ... do you really think he is that stupid? ... if you insist. I will do it immediately and call you back."

She ended the call without further comment, then looked around carefully to make certain she was not seen. Backtracking to her computer terminal, she logged back onto the "Hewitt" search request, found the list of documents, and pressed "DELETE."

She placed a call from her cell phone but the call simply went to voice mail.

The monsignor is unavailable. Please leave a message.

The waiter cleared my lunch dishes and I sat back intending to browse through the records for a while just to see what I could find. To my surprise the list of matches was gone.

Must be some kind of network glitch. No matter. I can work off the web file I made. I paid my bill and decided to take a leisurely stroll back down the beach on my way to the hotel.

About a kilometer down the beach the late morning was cut by the racking shrill of police sirens. From a distance it sounded as if three cars were converging at a spot back toward my hotel, so I turned around and decided to investigate. Ever since I was a small boy I have had a fascination for sirens - a trait my mother, the ultimate ambulance chaser, imbued me with at an early age.

As I approached my hotel I could easily see the cars, now five strong, encircling the outer edges of the parking area that serves several businesses and the public access to the beach. Officers closed off my access.

"No further, monsieur, for your own safety," the officer demanded.

"What is going on?"

"Reports of a bomb in the parking lot, monsieur. Everyone must stay behind the tape." He turned to holler at another curious onlooker.

I backtracked to where I could cross the access road and skirt around the closed off area, trying to get back to the hotel, but could not get close enough. Another police barricade two blocks from the hotel entrance closed the area off tightly. So I ducked into a nearby café, ordered a glass of wine, and waited out the police.

Lucas Roscheau watched from a discrete distance as the cars first converged on the hotel parking lot, then sealed off the area. He smiled when he heard a muffled "HRRUMPH" echo among the buildings. He placed a call.

"They blew up his car. Pretty funny."

"Have you seen Hewitt yet?"

"No, but I suspect he is nearby."

"He will be detained under house arrest for a while. The LSN have seen to that. We can count on at least two days. That should give us plenty of time."

"*Le Sang Neuf?* The New Blood?"

"The number of players in increasing. Hewitt has obviously hit a nerve although I doubt he is aware of it yet. But it will not take him long to piece this together - especially after the bomb threat."

"Understood. I have someone who can keep an eye on him. They will report to me when he leaves and where he is going."

"Good. In the meantime, we need to try and isolate the girl - at least for now. She's in Paris, but he keeps calling and asking for her help. We can't afford that."

"From what I heard, he has nothing."

"That's what I fear most. He does not take failure well. And sitting around for two days, however unavoidable, will only stir his imagination. But it will give us time for the next step. I need you in Paris by tonight. I will explain when you arrive."

"Understood. I'll catch the next train."

Lucas slipped his cell phone back inside the vest pocket of his waist-length leather jacket, paid his bill, and slipped quietly out the door.

Two hours later the rumor on the street was the bomb was merely a scare, and the area reopened. I walked back to the hotel - just past my checkout time. Melaine was behind the desk.

"Oh, monsieur. I am so sorry about your car. The police have asked that you remain at the hotel while they investigate, I am certain. Sit and have a glass of wine to soothe your nerves."

"What nerves? And what do you mean, sorry about my car?"

"I am afraid the damage done to your car was extensive."

"Damage? Whatever for?"

"The bomb, monsieur. They found nothing, of course, but could not take any chances. It was just a rental, I hope?"

"Yes, it was ... ," I stuttered, unsure off what had just happened. My confusion was soon to be cleared up.

"You are M. Hewitt?"

"Yes, I am," I turned, and stood facing a short thin man dressed in casual summer clothing.

"I am Inspector Mahieu, district police."

"Inspector," and I offered my hand. He did not take it. "Can you explain to me what is going on?"

"I was hoping you could do the same for me, monsieur. Perhaps we should sit and have a talk."

The police captain promised to explain his decision to incinerate my car to the rental company.

"We have already determined the bomb threat was a hoax. Nonetheless, the information we had about the alleged bomb was very detailed. Our forensics team has concluded whoever planned this little diversion had an extensive knowledge of explosives and technology. A prank threat would never have been so specific. So you see, monsieur, we really had no choice."

The mindset of the French bureaucrat is one of the few constants in the universe. I sat staring at this little man trying to understand what he was saying, the justifications behind this ridiculous situation, but I was completely at a loss. Through the window of the café I watched as a tow truck hauled away the remains of my Peugeot.

"You will, of course, remain here as a guest of the prefect until the investigation has concluded."

A guest of the local police? House arrest was more like it.

"But Captain, you said there was nothing connecting me to the bomb threat, that my car was randomly selected - at least according to the threat."

"You are correct. However, we must be very thorough in our investigation. I am certain you can appreciate my situation."

Situation? The captain left his calling card on the table, stood and snapped to attention, and dismissed himself. The scene looked more like a bad period movie - I half expected Humphrey Bogart to step in and invite me for a drink.

Instead, I was confronted by the hotel manager.

"So, you will be staying with us a little longer I am told. I hope we have no further disruptions, monsieur."

"This was not my fault!"

"So you say. Nonetheless, we are not used to such things here in La Bernerie-en-Retz. This is not the big city."

"Used to such things? Neither am I!"

He stood and looked somewhat indignant.

"I am not the one whose car was blown up in my parking lot, monsieur. I will be keeping my eye on you!" and he stomped away indignantly.

The five men of the council met in emergency session. The voices in the room rang out in a chaotic sharpness, concern in every one.

"A bomb threat? Les Boucliers have never stooped to such things."

"Portier Verbon, what do you know of this?"

"What? You accuse me of this thing? Every man here knows I disagreed with the council's position. Why would I act alone, knowing the shadow of blame would fall upon me?"

"Do you stand before us and deny responsibility?"

"I fear the American - what he may do. I fear he is in league with the Church - yes, that I admit. But that is all I claim. My hands are clean."

The council dismissed him, but remained behind closed doors for another half hour. When they emerged, they refused to look at him.

Portier Verbon knew they did not trust him.

I left the table and walked across the public square to the swimming beach. I meandered along the water's edge, just thinking, reflecting.

This a warning. Someone is trying to push me off of my investigation. Pastor Lorbas warned me about the factions that might try to interfere, but this was a little over the top. I have nothing. I am no closer to finding out the location of Scott Fitch's body or resolving the mystery of the identity disc.

Or am I? Why the bomb threat - here and now? Was I closer than I realized? Did I have some critical piece of information I simply did not recognize?

I was missing something. Pastor Lorbas said the Madonna was at the heart of violent passions between collaborators and the faithful. The church letter hinted at collaboration and the black market.

I sat where a stairway led from the beach up to the promenade and took off my shoes and socks, rubbing my feet in the warm sand. An inscription on the bulwark in both French and English caught my attention.

> HMT Lancastria - Sunk 17 July 1940
> This promenade is in remembrance of those who in
> death washed ashore into the caring arms of the
> people of La Bernerie-en-Retz.
> Dedicated 17 July 1952

The slightest breeze wafted sweetly along the promenade, filled with tourists. I watched a young couple stop and admire an old ship's wheel outside of a small antique shop across the walkway from the steps.

Was this really about the *Lancastria*? Or something else entirely?

The police captain stopped by the hotel in the morning and interrupted my coffee.

"We have determined you were not complicit in this unfortunate incident, monsieur. You are free to leave as you wish. I have personally interceded with the rental company on your behalf. They will be delivering another car to you within the hour."

And with that he was off. I hoped to not see him again.

While my rental car drama was playing out I received a series of emails from Monique, each with an article or two attached and comments. So far nothing too relevant appeared, but I knew she was scouring these archives with her usual tenacity.

Nothing yet about the woman Anisette, but she suggested I call the father at the Catholic Church in Prefailles, just up the coast. She had found something about a small collection of period artifacts and an attempted break-in. Nothing specific, but tantalizing nonetheless.

As promised, a driver from the rental agency arrived with my car - not the elegant Peugeot they had destroyed, but some small off-brand model that was so small I barely fit. Someone's idea of a joke - a little retribution, perhaps. But it was transport, so I headed towards Prefailles and an appointment with the priest.

As I drove away from the hotel loading zone the manager dialed a number on his cell phone.

"He has left the hotel."

CHAPTER 19

THE TIN BOX

Regard your soldiers as your children,
and they will follow you into the deepest valleys.
- Sun Tzu

"M. Hewitt. Welcome. Thank you for calling ahead."

"Thank you, Father. I appreciate you taking the time to see me."

"You have undertaken quite a task, monsieur. I hope God has blessed you in your quest."

"He walks with me, but sometimes I think He is as much a trickster," I smiled.

"Ah, the trickster. An interesting comment. That ideology plays a major role in formative religions, and even forms the basis of the early stories of Heaven and Hell, and the Devil."

"Do you believe in the literal interpretation of the Devil, Father, or of God's active intervention in our daily lives?"

He reflected for a moment, then smiled.

"This is a very complex and difficult world. God places people along their paths and guides them - not for what they actually accomplish, but as a test of their faith. A man or woman who trusts in God and follows a righteous path will do work on behalf of others, regardless of the measures of achievement society values."

"And what of prayer? Would you say a prayer for me to find my missing soldier?"

"Of course I would, but prayer does not itself guarantee success. I do not believe God answers our prayers through intervention but rather through the resolve prayer solidifies in our own thoughts to do God's work. The result is the same in the grander scheme of things."

He offered me a glass of wine.

"Now, you said you are interested in a particular soldier."

"I have an identity disc from a soldier named Scott Fitch. I believe he was killed when the *Lancastria* was sunk in 1940. His body was never recovered and he disappeared from the public record after that. I believe his body washed ashore along the coast. Nothing in the German records indicate they recovered the body, although there were hundreds of soldiers who could not be identified. There is no record of him in the British files either."

"I know of no unidentified graves here in Prefailles, but perhaps there are other things that may be of help to you. Please, let's take a walk."

We left the foyer and walked outside to the cemetery and toward a small stone building off to the side.

"The priest here during the war was named Father Joseph. He provided comfort to many of those fleeing the Germans, and those that suffered under the occupation. One of the more unusual things he did was to collect artifacts from the British evacuation - things that washed up on the beaches, mostly. Over the years much of this had to be discarded, but the documents and letters became a passion of his, especially after he retired. He lived in this cottage, and after he passed the church turned it into a small museum of sorts."

He unlocked the door and we stepped inside. I was amazed by what I saw. There was a single room with library shelves along one of the side walls. What had been the water closet had been gutted of the rude latrine and was now used to house the extensive card catalogue index. A small table sat in the center with two chairs. A row of old wooden file cabinets ran along the far wall and several glass display cases took a prominent place by the window that overlooked the cemetery. The private library looked completely out of place in this tiny village.

"I can see you are surprised."

"This is very impressive."

"Since Father Joseph's passing the library has grown substantially thanks to a partnership with one of the schools in Saint-Nazaire. The library is accumulating one of the more unique collections of period artifacts under the supervision of the school. The church has donated use of the building but the school manages the collection and contributes the funds for maintenance. It is not open to the public, but I asked for permission to let you examine its collection. The school was most accommodating."

"Are you familiar with the collection?"

"No, I am afraid not. I was only recently appointed to this church - I am from Nord-du-Calais originally. But if you wish to spend some time here, you are quite welcome to look through whatever you wish. Nothing inside the library is digital I am afraid. The school is preparing a project to convert the entire collection, but for now you will have to do your research the old-fashioned way."

He gave me a teasing smile. I was glad I still remembered how to use the library card system and the "stacks" we suffered through in college.

"Of course, nothing can leave the cottage, but you may copy or photograph anything you wish. You can arrange with my secretary to return the keys. If you need to take several days, simply coordinate your entry with her. I wish I could be more helpful."

"Thank you, Father. This is an amazing opportunity, even if I don't find what I am seeking."

"Good luck, monsieur. Please call on me if you need anything."

"One more thing, if I may. There was a small news story, about a burglary here recently."

"Oh, nothing too important. Our groundskeeper found a man late at night on the property. He was surprised trying to enter the cottage - probably someone looking for a warm place to stay the night. It made the incident list in the local paper - nothing more."

"Nothing was stolen?"

"No, monsieur. I hardly believe the artifacts were at risk in any event. They are not valuable, just to the curious. Good morning, monsieur."

"Thank you, Father."

He left me to examine the storehouse of small treasures by myself, and I settled into a small desk and pulled out a note pad. Luckily I still had cellular service or I would have missed the email from Monique.

> M. Larry
> Here are a few interesting stories. You will like the
> one I labeled "Ripple" - it might be worth exploring.
> M

I looked at the three other stories first - interesting, but I didn't think they appeared relevant. When I got back to my hotel I would go through these in greater detail. But Monique was correct - the "Ripple" story caught my attention.

> M. Larry - I have paraphrased the story and
> eliminated what I thought was irrelevant. I can send
> you the full text if you wish. M

> 6 Apr 1952
> The small coastal commune of Pornic was treated to
> quite a spectacle when a man walking through the
> town center carried a large sign saying "Rumors of
> my death are greatly exaggerated!"

> The man, Vincent Dupris, returned home to Pornic
> from Spain only to find his own grave in the
> commune cemetery marked by a common pauper's
> stone.

> "I left France when the Germans invaded Poland and
> returned to find my headstone in the cemetery. The
> church has refused to listen to me. One more time - I
> am not dead."

> The expression derives from the popular form of a
> statement by the American writer, Mark Twain, which
> appeared in the New York Journal of 2 June 1897:
> 'The report of my death was an exaggeration'. (5)

The local magistrate of Pornic has promised to look
into the matter. Meanwhile, M. Vincent cannot work
or receive assistance as he is legally dead.

I checked my map and found Pornic about nine kilometers further down the beach. After I was finished with this library, Pornic would be my next stop.

I emailed Monique.

Keep looking, but I liked your "Ripple."

I was mostly interested in the document archives. The assortment of letters, orders, and memos had been collected from people all along the coast of Brittany following the war. It was remarkable how many people kept these most personal of belongings that washed up on the shore or were found on the remains of the dead. An inscription above the document archive - a quote from a woman who brought a letter to the church for safekeeping in 1946 - said it best.

I have read the letter a thousand times. I was holding
the heartstrings of a family in my hands. This man is
now my brother.

The documents had been carefully preserved and protected with plastic covers in binders. I could easily leaf through the collection and read these most precious and private moments of men who would never make it home to family from the shores of France.

The letters themselves were not particularly remarkable. I remember once reading a critique of the document restoration process where the archivist explained her duty was to record and protect the mundane. It was the context of the documents that imparted to them value and significance. After five hours of reading I began to appreciate the validity of that observation. I decided to take a break.

Father Victor saw me walking around the cemetery grounds and decided to join me.

"How is your search going?"

"There is a lot of material, Father. Most of it is what I expected - plain and unrelated. I am mostly looking for clues. But in the larger context, it shows just how focused our lives are on family and little things compared to world war."

"Confession is like that. The things people are concerned with most are very small things. I cannot recall the last time someone wanted to talk about world peace." He smiled a knowing smile as we walked along. "What kind of clues are you seeking?"

"Perhaps a name, a location. Usually something that appears out of context. It's what I like to call a 'ripple' - something just a little out of place."

We walked along in silence for a moment when the Father stopped and turned toward me.

"Perhaps I know of something you may want to look at. Come, let me show you."

We went back into the library. On a shelf behind a glass door were several personal objects that had been discovered on the beach - a tiny doll I could see going home as a gift for a small child; an ornate wooden letter opener; a pipe.

"This is what I wanted you to see."

He removed a small tin box from the shelf and placed it on the table. On the underside of the box was a coded reference number, and he went to one of the file cabinets and removed a small folder with the same number on it.

"This box was recovered near here along the beach. There is a description of the circumstances of this file, as well as a collection of letters that have not been on display - we have only so much room to display restored material. I don't know if this is relevant, but you may find the story interesting. I have some work to tend to, so I will leave you to your own discovery, let us pray."

He smiled, and left the library.

Inside the folder I found a handwritten account of the recovery of the tin box.

ITEM #21287

After the liberation local authorities began to investigate the disappearance of French citizens in what has been called "Nacht und Nebel" - the Night and Fog. A baker in the village of Prefailles disappeared in July 1940 without a trace. When his wife tried to make inquiries into his disappearance, and confronted the local police prefect, she too disappeared.

The bakery lay abandoned until after the liberation when family members cleared out the remaining personal effects and sold the property. Inside was this tin box filled with letters addressed to a British serviceman none of the family knew. An attempt to locate family of the serviceman was unsuccessful.

The letters were still in their original condition - yellowed and brittle, but still legible. I cautiously spread them out on the table, careful to handle them only by the edges. There were eight in all, and no envelopes. An envelope would have given me a return address and perhaps the location of the soldier when he received them - or at least an indicator of his unit. But it was not to be.

As I read the first letter I struggled to hold back my emotions. Tears filled my eyes and my breathing became labored and shallow. The letter was addressed to "My dear Scotty."

4 Oct 1939

My dear Scotty,

We were all so excited to read your first letter home. It sounds like sitting around waiting for your ship to sail is terribly boring, but Mother says you seem in good spirits. Father is so proud you joined his regiment.

Cousin Mary joined us for dinner last night. She has enlisted in the ATS and was on her way to her assignment when she stopped by. She looks very smart in her uniform. When I am older, I want to join, too.

Mother says you are to look out for George when you leave. You know how he gets ... she regards him just like her own son.

Please write often. I do miss you so.

Your loving sister,
Martha

There were five others from Martha - the younger sister. The last of these was dated May 12, just two days after the invasion of the Netherlands that ended with the evacuations at Dunkirk and the disaster at Saint-Nazaire.

The seventh letter was quite different. As I read it, my hands began to shake and I felt a cold chill run through my body.

17 June 1940

We finally made it to port after a crazy drive south.
Boarded a ship - Lancastria. Next stop - home!
George thinks its great fun. I am scared. German planes are still overhead.

I met a remarkable woman. She was beautiful, but terribly frightened. She helped us find Saint-Nazaire.

Her name was Anisette.

Anisette! The name written on the note in Sid's file.

I thought back immediately to Antoine Bouchard and the Juno Letters - letters penned but never sent, hidden in a tin box, and not discovered for nearly seventy years. Here was a letter written by Scotty after he boarded the ill-fated *Lancastria*, hours before its sinking. Hours before thousands perished in the explosions, the burning oil, and the heartless sea.

The letter had never been mailed.

"M. Larry. I have some news for you."

I was halfway to Pornic when my cell phone rang. I had emailed Monique with a transcription of the letter hoping it might assist her search in some way.

"I tracked down some additional information about your Scott Fitch at the War Records Service. The letter talks about his father and how he joined the same regiment. Robert Scott Fitch was a soldier in the Sherwood Foresters regiment in World War I. I double checked with public records in Nottingham and he had a son, Scott Thomas Fitch. So this appears to be the correct Scott Fitch."

"That's good news."

"There is more. The letter had a brief reference to what I presume is a friend named George. So I checked the regiment list and found several Georges in the outfit. One in particular stood out. A 'George Sherrat' joined the regiment at the same time as Scott. I am sending you a group photograph taken in September 1939 just before they deployed to France. Let me know what you think."

"One last thing. There is a Commonwealth cemetery in Pornic. I checked their online registry, but found nothing even close to Scott Fitch.

"Gotta go - got a date!"

She hung up.

Monique hurried up the street and covered the short distance to Café Brasserie. She smiled at the handsome man sitting at one of the small tables on the sidewalk along Rue Saint Marc, the man she had met at one of the business dinners hosted by the landlord of her father's café, M. Soullant.

"Bonjour!" she called cheerfully.

The man, wearing a waist length leather jacket and sporting a jet black pony tail, rose and smiled back.

"Bonjour, Monique. Please, sit and enjoy a bottle of wine with me before dinner."

She tossed back her long hair, pulled out the opposite chair, and sat down.

This one is very handsome, she smiled to herself.

She couldn't help but notice the tattoo on his right wrist.

"Your tattoo. I have seen it before - on my American friend's wrist."

Lucas Roscheau smiled at her.

"It is a popular style. Nothing more."

You are a liar. What is going on?

When I pulled into Pornic I stopped at a small café, ordered lunch, and checked my email. There, attached to the details from Monique's searching through the military records was the photograph. The caption listed all the soldiers' names. Standing at the far right was S. Fitch (Pte). Next to him, with his arm over Scotty's shoulder, was G. Sherrat (Pte).

Even with the slightly grainy and faded picture I could see Scotty was a handsome young man, slightly built. George was the taller of the two, and while Scotty held a stoic expression you could see in George's face the soul of an adventurer. Scotty wore gloves - the only one in the photograph.

I couldn't stop staring at his face. Once again I felt the questions grinding against each other, almost like trying to force the pieces of a jigsaw puzzle together where they did not fit. I looked again at George, then Scotty - what was wrong? What doesn't fit?

The Pornic War Cemetery was less than a kilometer from the café so I decided to walk, enjoying the late afternoon sun. Located next to the main Pornic commune cemetery, the War Cemetery was a simple resting place - neat rows of bleached white headstones I had seen in so many places throughout Europe. The number of dead men and women wasted in these wars numbs the senses.

The cemetery was one of the Commonwealth War Graves Commission sites where approximately 1.7 million war dead are buried in over 23,000 locations worldwide. Monique had already checked their online database and quickly ruled out an obvious answer. I knew I would not find Scotty, but I looked for "George Sherrat" just on a hunch. No luck.

Most of the soldiers buried here were victims of the *Lancastria* sinking, washed ashore along the beach in the following days and weeks. I was moved by a lone headstone standing apart from the carefully laid out sections - a single Indian soldier, forever resting with, but separated from, his comrades. I logged back on to the War Graves registry to find out his name, but there was no record.

I found nothing in the cemetery that helped. The site listed 160 unknown graves - many not within the confines of the cemetery itself, and memorialized with the phrase "Buried Near Here."

I called Monique.

"Neither the database nor the registry are any help. There are 247 graves in the cemetery, but 395 WWII-related deaths in the database. Over one hundred sixty of the records are marked 'Unidentified.'"

"That is too bad, M. Larry. We could spend a lot of wasted time chasing shadows there."

The solution to the Madonna Rosa mystery was not here in Pornic War Cemetery.

I drove the six kilometers back to my hotel and over dinner at Le Café Rose began to chew through my notes along with the local shrimp. I guessed the story of the wrongful burial played a key role in this mystery, and blocked the day tomorrow to investigate the common cemetery in Pornic. Even though I struck out at the War Commission cemetery, something about it still buzzed around my head. Was I reading more into this than the evidence suggested? Was I letting my frustration get the better of me and seeing connections where there were none?

As I worked, a man brushed by my table, catching the edge of my shoulder with his waist, pushing me slightly aside. He dropped a newspaper on the table as he passed. I watched him leave the café then looked where he had come from. The only place he could have been was the bathroom.

I looked around the room - no one was paying any attention. The man had disappeared to the right once he hit the street, and I could not see him through the window. I turned my attention to the newspaper left on the table, annoyed with his rudeness. The marks on the front page arrested my annoyance.

A series of words had been circled from the front page stories, in order from left to right, top to bottom. I wrote them down in sequence, then opened my translator app and typed them in. I received the message loud and clear.

Leave La Bernerie and stop meddling in these affairs

I looked back at the photograph, then at the warning screaming at me from my computer translator.

The photograph had hit a nerve. Someone was watching me and was upset. The warning told me the answer was here. I scribbled on my notepad:

I am close, maybe too close.

⸙

CHAPTER 20

A PAUPER'S GRAVE

What the eyes see and the ears hear,
the mind believes.
- Harry Houdini

The following morning I drove the short distance back to Pornic. A lone grounds tender was working in the commune cemetery, edging the grass that slowly tried to reclaim the ground markers of the dead who could not afford to raise a proper headstone. As I slowly walked through the neat rows of graves, the worker left his tools and walked off to the maintenance shed. A few minutes later a priest approached me through the rows of markers.

"Bonjour, monsieur. I am Father Bioche"

"Bonjour, Father."

"Ah, by your accent I presume you are American?"

"Yes, Father. My French gives me away?"

He smiled and stepped forward to shake my hand.

"My gardener tells me you appear to be looking for something in particular. Perhaps I may assist you."

"Thank you, Father. Yes, I am looking for something, although I am not certain exactly what it is."

He cocked his head slightly, and smiled.

"Perhaps it is the journey you seek, not a destination."

A journey. Each of the mysteries that have consumed me in my travels throughout Europe these past months have been journeys. As each appeared to conclude the path opened even wider, and every time folded back upon itself. I remembered wandering the German cemetery in Normandy looking for the common grave of Antoine Bouchard. That seemed such a long time ago, yet the smell of the sea air mixed with wildflowers still haunted my memory, the same smell that inundated my senses in this tiny village resting place.

"You may be right, Father," I smiled back, and we began to slowly walk back along the rows of headstones and common markers laid in the ground. "The markers, Father. There is an equal mix of elaborate and very plain grave markers."

He looked down at the ground as we talked, weighing every word, measuring the tapestry I began to weave to explain my visit. I could sense he was anticipating more than a casual tourist conversation.

"Marking our ancestors' final resting place is a serious affair for Bretons and, indeed, all Frenchmen. Our lineage is ancient, and our families are very proud."

"Yet there are many plain ones."

"The destitute and wanderers who find their final home here."

"And unmarked graves? Are there many here in the village?"

He hesitated.

"Some." His avoidance caught my curiosity. "You ask for a purpose?"

"I am a writer. I am researching a story, and in my reading I discovered there was a man who returned from Spain where he fled as the war broke out only to find someone buried in a grave with his name. The man was named ... ,"

"Vincent Dupris." He stopped for a moment, then began to walk a different direction. "He is here. He passed away in ... 1989, if my memory serves. For a short while his story brought many of the curious. He rests peacefully now."

At the far side of the cemetery we found the marker for Vincent Dupris. It was a rather plain upright stone. Father Bioche knelt and removed a single weed growing at its base.

"When was the mistaken burial?"

"I do not know, exactly. I would have to check the church records."

"And the grave for the man who had been wrongfully buried? Is it still here?"

Father Brioche stood up and sighed.

"Some things are best only for God to know."

I turned and stood to face him.

"I have travelled a long way to find this man, Father. Please."

Father Bioche stood quietly for a moment, and sighed.

"If you must. Over here."

He led me to the far corner of the cemetery where about a dozen graves sat in small neat rows. Each grave was marked by a small square stone inscribed with a date and the words, "*Connue que de Dieu*"- Known Only to God. A pauper's stone.

"Which one is it?"

"Here, from 1952 when M. Dupris returned." The priest pointed to the fifth stone from the end. "I am afraid we know nothing about the man resting here, except he has been embraced by God. After all, what else does one really need to know?"

That last comment was directed at me intentionally. I knew it was time to do a little detective work - without the help of the priest.

"If you don't mind, Father, I'd like to remain and do some writing. I like to write in places that inspire me. It's a beautiful day, and I'd just like to sit here and work awhile."

"As you wish. The cemetery is open to all who seek to contemplate eternity, my friend. We ask you leave when it gets dark, but otherwise you are welcome to remain as long as you wish."

"Thank you, Father. I appreciate your help."

As he walked away, he turned.

"Be careful, monsieur. Sometimes finding what you seek brings more than one anticipates."

I sat on the overgrown grass and began to make some notes, assembling the pieces of this latest puzzle and pulling from them questions I needed to answer. I let my mind wander, to float among the inconsistencies, seeking that perfect moment of clarity that rarely rises from the void.

It would not be today.

Instead, I wrote down a number of practical suggestions, including the one I circled:

Who is buried here? Scotty?

On a second page, I began to jot down what I knew.

When was the body buried? - Germany invades
France.

Was that right? If so, the date on the original stone would have been sometime between May to June 1940. Germany invaded the Netherlands May 10, which ended the so-called "Phony War," and followed by invading France later in the month. The British evacuated Dunkirk, and later Saint-Nazaire aboard the ill-fated *Lancastria*, June 17.

I placed a big question mark on the note. Something simply did not fit. I took my phone from my jacket pocket and double-checked my email for Monique's message. I scrolled down to the news story.

I fled to Spain when Germany attacked Poland ... .

September 1939. Almost a year before the sinking of the *Lancastria*. But something else caught my attention. A casual reference in the story gave me a clue to what was bothering me.

... his own grave in the commune cemetery marked by a common pauper's stone.

A pauper's stone. I moved close to the stone in the ground and examined it carefully. The inscription on it was clearly marked on a clean face in 1952. But the words "a pauper's stone" still stuck in my head. If they had used a pauper's stone in the first place, it means there were no funds from relatives for the burial. A relative would have known the body was not Vincent Dupris, a stranger would not. Why Vincent Dupris? And the stone itself?

I looked up to make certain I was not watched, then dug with my hands down into the dirt and turned the stone over. Distinctive gouges had been chiseled out of the stone where the name and date had once been, but the words "Connue que de Dieu" had clearly never been cut into the back side of the stone. Was this the same stone that marked the original Dupris grave?

Had they simply reused the stone and turned it over to save money, and time, in marking the unknown body? A pauper's stone, a pauper's grave. But the original date - could it still be read?

I brushed away the dirt clinging to the gouges and tried to make out any marks more distinctive. Out of the corner of my eye I saw movement, and looked up to see the groundskeeper back in the rows, occasionally casting a glance in my direction. I didn't want to be seen violating the stone's resting place, so took a closeup photo of the stone's face with my cell phone and put it back. I gathered up my things and headed toward my car, taking a moment to acknowledge the worker with a nod of my head.

Back at the hotel café in La Bernerie I pulled out my computer and uploaded the photograph. I enlarged the gouged out area and began to play around with many of the image-editing filters to see if I could coax out any telltale markings - possibly a name or a date.

Wherever I found what appeared to be more carefully inscribed marks, I copied the section and pasted it into a separate file in layers. After about an hour, and twenty-two layers later, I started to work on the composite photo. By showing and hiding successive layers, eventually enough parts of the original inscription emerged to reveal one inescapable fact.

The stone was once marked with the date '22 June 1940' and the last name, "Dupris."

Why June 22? The real Vincent Dupris left France in September 1939. A relative should have known he had left France, and most certainly would have known this was not his body. Yet the unknown man in the grave was buried shortly after the sinking of the *Lancastria*.

I emailed Monique.

> Graves registration, Pornic, France. Who authorized
> the burying of Vincent Dupris, 22 June 1940?

Monique returned my email before I finished my lunch wine.

> Give me something worth my time. This was too
> simple. Authorized by M. G. Varnadoe, listed as a
> cousin and the owner of the plot. Authorization form
> dated 22 June 1940, but the recording date officially
> was 18 July. Give me something challenging! M

A burial authorization backdated to the date of burial? Someone was in a hurry to bury this body. Dupris' cousin was involved, and he had to know this was not his cousin, but gave up his plot - possibly knowing he had left France. Why?

Occam's Razor states all things equal, the simplest answer is the correct one. However improbable, the simple solution was the cousin needed to hide this man's body, a body brought to the church following the sinking of the *Lancastria* when the German and French authorities scoured the beaches looking for bodies of soldiers washed ashore. This one they missed. And at least one person, perhaps several, conspired to hide it from the authorities.

As I finished my glass of wine I noticed one of the men sitting at a side table watching me ... a little too closely. As I looked in his direction, he folded a newspaper and rose. For a brief moment I noticed a mark on his right hand, between the thumb and forefinger. It all happened too quickly to make out the symbol, but as he walked away quickly I looked down at my own tattoo - the comet on my right wrist. His mark - a tattoo - was on his right hand. That was not a coincidence.

I emailed Monique back.

> Significance of a tattoo on the right hand, between thumb and forefinger on the loose skin. Couldn't see it clearly from a distance ... Perhaps a cross? Something else, significant to Brittany? Not much to go on.

I decide to stay another night.

The telephone rang in Rolland Soullant's office in Paris late that afternoon. The voice on the other end was subdued but concerned.

"Sang Neuf knows about the writer. They are going to intercept him."

Roland hung up the phone without responding. He reached for his cell phone and typed out a quick message:

> Leave La Bernerie immediately.
> Expect my call. R.

He placed a local call.

"We have a problem. Get back to Saint-Nazaire as quickly as you can. Wait for my call."

He sat back in his chair and began to tap his pen on the edge of his desk.

You have stirred up a hornet's nest, my brother. Perhaps it is time for more drastic action.

The text message screamed at me from my cell phone as I waited for the hotel clerk to complete my request to keep my room for the night.

> Leave La Bernerie immediately.
> Expect my call. R.

I hadn't heard anything from Roland Soullant since the close of the "Three Angels" convention several weeks back. And that was only a fleeting comment, one that opened my eyes to the undercurrents my Angels stories had stirred. I wasn't sure just what he was concerned about, but knew to trust his motives.

"Okay, that is one additional night. Will there be anything else?"

"Sorry. I have decided to check out."

Melaine look at me like I was crazy.

I checked out of the hotel, casually stepped outside, crossed to my rented car, and quickly drove out of town heading north back to Saint-Nazaire.

CHAPTER 21

THE RED DISC

For every promise, there is price to pay.
- Jim Rohn

"What the hell are you doing here?"

Darcell Favro threw up his hands in disbelief as I walked into Le 16.

"I'm not sure. I've eaten your cooking."

"Ha, very funny. Didn't you get the message to leave La Bernerie?"

"Yes, I did." How did he know about that? "I left."

He hurried to the door, looked around the sidewalk and across to the beach, then scurried back, grabbing my arm.

"They are here, in Saint-Nazaire."

"Who?"

"We thought you would have better sense than to come here! Roland said you were smart! Didn't you talk to him on the phone?"

"No. Just a text. You know Roland Soullant?"

He didn't hear me.

"We have to get you out of here, right now. Stay put while I make a call."

He jumped up from the table and ran back to the kitchen. When he returned he had his cell phone to his ear, turned slightly away from me. His behavior made me nervous, and I looked around for a convenient way out of the café. I was watching him speak furiously in French that I could not follow when his eyes shifted to the door and he stopped. I saw him hang up the call.

"He tried to call you, but lost the signal. Lousy cell service," he spat. "We have to get out of here!"

Two men stepped into the café and blocked the entrance. One looked menacingly at Darcell, the other directly at me. As I stood the man staring at me shook his head slowly.

"*S'asseoir* - sit."

I glanced over at Darcell who slowly backed toward a table and also sat down. He glanced furtively at me with a look of resignation.

"Not my fault."

No one spoke. The men in the doorway did not carry weapons - at least none I could see. There was nothing extraordinary about their appearance. The afternoon was warm and they both wore short sleeved shirts, rather plain next to the tourists strolling the nearby public walkway. Clean shaven, neatly kempt. Not what you would expect from organized crime thugs, which is what I suspected they were. I quickly convinced myself Darcell was mixed up with something dirty - otherwise, why the connection with Roland Soullant? If these men openly opposed Roland, and were willing to show themselves in public, I could be in some real trouble.

So I just sat and waited, and contemplated a quick exit out the back. They appeared to be waiting as well, patiently.

The next twenty seconds dragged on when a third man stepped thorough the doorway. He didn't bother to look at either me or

Darcell, but quickly inspected the kitchen, refrigerator room, and wash area before exiting out the back door. I guessed he was standing guard just outside - it wouldn't be wise to try and escape in that direction. I had missed my opportunity.

My hands began to sweat, but I deliberately breathed slowly to control my anxiety and tried to appear calm. Darcell was clearly on edge, tapping his foot annoyingly on the floor.

She entered with a quiet grace that contrasted oddly with the tension in the room. Both men at the door bowed their heads slightly, deferring to her as if to royalty, but did not relax their posture as guards.

"Bonjour, M. Favro." She stopped briefly and smiled in Darcel's direction. "A glass of wine for the American and myself, if you please."

"Oui, madame." He practically jumped out of his seat. As he returned his hands trembled slightly, nearly spilling the wine. When he finished, she smiled again at him.

"Merci. You may leave, monsieur. Please do not stray far."

Darcell nodded his head and carefully slipped between the two men at the door. I wondered why she let him leave, wondering where he would go, who he would try to reach.

"Do not be alarmed for your friend, monsieur. I have given explicit instructions he is not to be harmed. I trust he understands the situation enough to exercise proper judgement."

The situation?

"And now, I must ask your forgiveness for this somewhat dramatic entrance. It was necessary to ensure everyone's safety."

The calmness of her voice and the degree she seemed to control the behavior of the men standing guard helped me relax, if only a little. She took a sip of the wine while I studied her face.

She was perhaps in her late 80s or early 90s, but her movements were strong and fluid. Her eyes shined with a clear brightness that belied her years. Something about her elicited calmness - I guessed it was her voice. She returned the glass to the table and smiled at me, looking into my eyes. I felt captivated ... perhaps captive was a better word.

"You do not like the wine, monsieur?" Her teasing tone both surprised me and relieved me of much of my anxiety.

"I am sorry, madame. I am just a little on edge."

I reached for the wine glass and could not hide my slight trembling.

"Please, monsieur. You are not in danger. The men have a difficult duty to attend to, and they sometimes appear a little intimidating. Please, let us become acquainted, and perhaps friends. I am Madame Laconier."

"*Enchante, madame.* Larry Hewitt."

She smiled, her warmth flooding over me.

"*Enchante.*"

Who are you? And what do you want?

Darcell hurried down the street and ducked into a small café. He placed a quick phone call.

"She has him, at my café. What should I do?"

He listened for a short while, and interrupted a few times with "... I didn't tell him to come ... ," and " ... not my fault ... ," but generally spent more time listening.

"*D'accord.* I agree. I will keep an eye on him. What do you think they will do?"

He listened for a short while, a deep frown on his face.

"You know what this will stir up, do you not?"

Again, he listened.

"He needs to know. Otherwise, he will stumble from one crisis to another, with me stuck in the middle. I will take him back to Pastor Lorbas. Hewitt needs the truth if he is to keep his wits about him."

He hung up just as another man with jet-black hair pulled back into a ponytail and wearing a short leather jacket despite the warm weather entered the café and motioned him outside. He put away his cell phone and quickly followed.

"You have me at a disadvantage, madame."

With another sip of the wine, she lowered her silken shawl.

"You have been asking about a man, a soldier who disappeared following the terrible tragedy in the harbor in 1940."

"Yes, the sinking of the *Lancastria*. How do you know I am looking for him?"

She carefully avoided answering me.

"We, too, have been searching for him. Since the end of the war."

This was the link ... between Scotty's identity disc and the notes in Sid's files - however sparse they were. I looked again at Mme Laconier. She would be the correct age ... .

"Tell me, monsieur. How do you come to search for this man?"

This was a curious question. I had assumed by the posture the guards took, and the sureness of the woman's manner, that they knew who I was and why I was looking. Somehow I had triggered their interest - perhaps the priest or the gardener in Pornic, or maybe they were listening to certain key phrases traveling the Internet. Who knows? And I doubted they were ready to say. But it was clear they did not know as much as they pretended.

Be careful what you reveal.

"I am completing a request from a friend who recently passed away. He asked me to try and locate the soldier named Scott Fitch."

"For what purpose?"

"Personal reasons. I believe he knew of him during the war."

"So you do not know the nature of their association?"

"My friend left me a few files - parts of his life that needed closure. I agreed to help tie up some loose ends for him."

"And you are planning to write about these 'loose ends?'"

How does she know I am a writer?

"Again, you have me at a disadvantage."

"I am aware of who you are, monsieur, and your work. I did not know your Antoine or Marianne. As Bretons, your stories of them are well known to us, however. You did their memories a great service, and as a French woman who also lived through those sad times, I thank you."

Why would she think I should expect them to know Antoine or Marianne? Was she from Pont-Aven, or the surrounding countryside?

Or connected somehow with the conspiracy network that Antoine stumbled into, the one that ordered Marianne's arrest?

"I do not have much to write about, madame. At least right now. But I hope to find something worthwhile to put into words. That is what I do. But dead ends, they are more common. So far I am not having much luck."

I was hoping to flesh out more information from her. Why else would she be here unless I was close to finding something they also wanted?

She sipped a little wine, and calmly, soothingly, called my bluff.

"You are being less than candid with me, monsieur. But I understand your caution."

She left the issue simply laying there on the table. No threats, no accusations.

"What is your interest in this man, madame? Perhaps knowing that would put me a little more at ease."

She smiled that irrepressible smile of hers again, and sat back.

"We are dancing, monsieur, in a cautious paux-de-deux. As a gesture of good faith, I will break our little impasse."

She took a last sip of the wine, closed her eyes momentarily, and began to speak, clearly, with focus.

"The man you are seeking ... I met him on the road to Saint-Nazaire during the British evacuation in 1940. I was fleeing an SS death squad sent to retrieve a religious object entrusted to me. He was a soldier traveling with a small convoy. They stopped to examine their maps, and I pointed the direction to Saint-Nazaire in exchange for a promise - to take an icon and keep it safe from the Germans."

The icon? Did she mean the Madonna Rosa?

"After the war I could not find him. I waited for word he would return, but the years passed without any contact. We began to search for him, and to watch and listen for word that might alert us the icon had surfaced.

"Eventually we learned he was listed as missing from the sinking of the *Lancastria*. But there were whispers the icon was still in Brittany. We could never be certain, and no proof ever surfaced. But in my heart I know the icon is not lost. And this man, Scott Fitch, holds the key to its existence."

"This icon. Exactly what is it?"

"A madonna and child, carved from the cross that bore the death agony of Saint Blandina."

When she mentioned the name of the Christian saint, the men at the door crossed themselves. She stopped for a moment and let the words sink in.

"Madame, are you Anisette?"

She looked up at me, startled.

"Anisette Durande was my maiden name."

I reached for my computer case and removed the faded envelope from the side pocket. I pulled the red identity disc out and laid it on the table.

"*Mon dieu!*" she gasped. A tear immediately rolled down her cheek. "Where did you get this?" she barely whispered.

Mme Laconier took a deep, slow breath as she finished her story.

"That was the last time I spoke to your friend Sid. We discretely inquired as to his whereabouts, to see if he had discovered anything new, but the American army was too preoccupied to assist us. After the liberation there was so much work to rebuild our lives in Brittany. So many people had been killed, so many disappeared. I came to realize this catastrophe - not the war itself - was the darkness we had always feared. I did not know why the Madonna remained lost after the liberation, but it was not my place to question God's plan. So we waited and watched all these years."

"Waited for what?"

"I did not know. I guess for something to change ... a ripple in a pond, if you will."

A familiar metaphor.

"How did you know I was looking for this man Scotty?"

"Like you we searched the local churches and records. I always believed the cemetery in Pornic was important. When the news of the man returning from Spain was in the newspapers people thought it humorous. But I felt it was one of the clues to the fate of the Madonna. So we moved quietly into the areas where we believed we would see some sign, to wait and watch."

"The groundskeeper at Pornic?"

"Yes. One of many."

"Why didn't you simply contact me? I would have been willing to help you."

"There are others, my friend, who would kill for the Madonna. They are also watching you, and waiting. It is a sad truth we Bretons fought more against each other than we did the Germans. The warring factions committed atrocities during the occupation - the separatists, the communists, the reformists. Few were ever brought to justice. Some have grown strong within the independence movement, hiding just beneath the surface. We could not be certain if you were allied with any of them."

Multiple factions? That would explain Roland's frantic text message. Even he did not have control over this chaotic predicament.

"And what of Roland Soullant?"

At the mention of his name Anisette dropped her eyes, her voice barely heard above the noise from the street.

"M. Soullant is a friend. That is why we came to believe you were not a part of the factions."

Anisette Laconier was deliberately evasive. This was something I wanted to know more about ... some other time.

"Madame, I wish to help you. Sid gave me the disc because he wanted to bring this story to an end. Life simply caught up with him - too many commitments, too few years. He gave me his notes, including one with your name written on it, as a charge to complete for him."

"And why would he pass this challenge to you?"

"I was his friend - one of only a few who knew his real story. I owe him nothing of value, nothing tangible. Yet I owe him a debt that can never be repaid for the stories he told and the trust he showed me in revealing his deepest secrets. We shared a bond I cannot explain, but feel so deeply ... a debt of honor I would give my life for."

She raised her eyes to mine.

"You may yet be asked to make that sacrifice, my friend."

<hr />

CHAPTER 22

TURNING THE TIDE

*We swallow greedily any lie that flatters us,
but we sip only little by little at a
truth we find bitter.*
- Denis Diderot

Darcell and the man with the pony tail hurried up the street toward the Centre Évangélique de Saint-Nazaire where Pastor Lorbas waited for them.

"Please, sit down, gentlemen. We have to move quickly."

"Father, this is Lucas Roscheau. He works for Roland Soullant."

"Monsieur, if Roland has sent you I expect you are fully briefed."

"Yes, Pastor Lorbas."

"Good. How many men do they have?"

"Three. Two at the front door, just inside. One at the back."

"Weapons?"

"I could not tell. Perhaps handguns."

"That is not their style. I suggest that means they arrived unarmed. Darcell, how did you escape?"

"I was caught by surprise when Hewitt showed up. I had no time to get him out. Mme Laconier dismissed me."

"Dismissed you? And the men at the door, they did nothing?"

"No, Father. And no one followed me. Mme Laconier told me to not venture far."

"And yet you are here. I wonder how smart that was."

"I think it was more a warning than a command," Lucas suggested. "If not, they would have followed him. I was very careful to watch them. He was not followed."

"Then stay away, for now. We need to get word to M. Hewitt where to go and how to react to the meeting. You cannot go back, it is simply too dangerous."

"Is Hewitt in danger?"

"I don't think so. Mme Laconier is after what he knows and she cannot be certain he does not already have the Madonna. She has waited too long to be careless now."

"But her men. They have acted in haste before."

"Yes. That is why it is best he remain in close contact with Mme Laconier until we can warn him. Did you recognize either of the men at the door?"

"No. But the man at the back entrance - it is Portier Verbon."

Pastor Lorbas sat back in his chair and sighed as he looked away.

"I was afraid of that."

The three men sat in silence for a moment.

"How do we contact Hewitt?"

Lucas pulled out his cell phone.

"I have an idea."

"Bonjour, Monique. Ça va?"

"Bien, M. Grimaud. Et toi?"

"I am well. A beautiful day today. How is your father?"

"Grumpy as ever. Luckily, he thinks I am still in school today so I do not have to work!"

Monique strode happily down Rue Vivienne enjoying the banter with the other business people on the street, stopping to talk with friends. The afternoon was warm and the sweet smell of flowers filled the streets of Paris, now busy with tourists. The narrow street was jammed with cars going nowhere fast - a perfect day for a stroll through the City of Light.

A man suddenly grabbed her arm.

"What are you doing? You are hurting me!"

He steered her quickly into a seat in the next sidewalk café.

"Give me your cell phone. Hurry."

His mannerism caught her by surprise as he looked around furtively. He did not want to be noticed even in this public place. She did as she was told, and looked around quickly for a way to escape.

The man dialed a phone number and spoke firmly to her as he waited for the connection.

"I am a friend of Lucas Roscheau. You are calling your writer friend, M. Hewitt. Be happy and cheerful, but tell him only what I have written down for you to say. His safety depends upon you at this moment."

M. Larry? What is this about?

He hastily spread a paper with a script preprinted on it for her to read as a familiar voice answered the phone.

My cellphone rang. One of the men at the door grunted *"Non!"* and moved quickly to take it from me. He showed the name on the caller ID to Mme Laconier, who nodded her head.

He handed me the phone after putting it on speaker.

"Hello."

"Bonjour, M. Larry. I have some additional information for you."

It was Monique. She sounded guarded, concerned - not her usual cheerful self.

"I performed some additional searches through the war records. There are some inconsistencies among the list of missing soldiers I sent you. The information is worth examining. Where can I meet you?"

"I am at a café. Where are you?"

"At the Library Etienne Garnier at the Océanis campus. I am afraid the documents are all on microfilm. I think you need to come see me."

What was she talking about? What soldiers' list? The War Records data is online, and searchable by a standard browser. I pay a nice premium for complete access to their records. And what the hell was she doing in Saint-Nazaire?

"I am a little busy right now. Can this wait?" I was looking for confirmation in her voice. She took the hint.

"At breakfast you told me this was important. And I think it is. I may have found your missing soldier."

When she heard this, Mme Laconier raised her eyes to mine, and nodded her head. For my part, I realized this was a ploy to get me out of here - just how she knew I was in trouble I did not know, but I did not have breakfast with her as she claimed. She wanted me away.

"OK. I will be there shortly," I replied, watching Mme Laconier all the while. She indicated by her expression she had agreed to let me go.

"Very good. I am on floor 4, room 416."

"Room 416 ... OK, I am on the way."

When the call ended, Mme Laconier raised the shawl back over her head and rose.

"Continue your research, monsieur. I do not believe either of us has the answer to this puzzle yet. I do hope you will be willing to work with us to resolve this mystery ... despite the anxiety of your friends."

She smiled, and walked gracefully to the front door and turned. I rose and stepped toward her to take her hand.

"We will speak again - less dramatically, I assure you. Perhaps you will have more information you can share. And please, tell your young lady the university library has only three floors. Perhaps you should call her back and arrange to meet elsewhere."

She handed me a small sealed envelope, smiled again, and disappeared out the door.

Monique lowered her cell phone.

"I am sorry I frightened you. There was no time to explain. Lucas will call you."

As he folded his paper and put it into his shirt pocket, Monique saw a familiar tattoo on his right wrist - a comet. He rose and disappeared into the crowded street.

The university was near the waterfront but about five kilometers away. I had ditched the tiny rental car on my return to Saint-Nazaire the night before so I hailed a cab. I wondered why Monique was in Saint-Nazaire until I entered the main entrance of the library.

"You were not followed?"

Darcell Favro waited just inside the door.

"No. Mme Laconier left with her men. Why are you here? And where is Monique?"

"Your young lady friend is in Paris. We enlisted her to give you an opportunity to get clear of Les Boucliers."

"What the hell is going on? And who are Les Boucliers."

"Come, my friend. I have a car."

We drove north to the nearby commune of Trignac. As we drove I discretely opened the envelope Anisette had given me. Inside was a business card with a solitary phone number printed on the face. A handwritten note on the back read simply:

If you need to contact me.

I stuffed it into my shirt pocket as the car stopped across from a small public square in the center of town - very open, and yet secluded.

"Why are we here?"

"We are meeting Lorbas and another person - who you already know. It is time you understand just what you are mixed up with. Good - they are already here." He exited the car and called, "Follow me."

We crossed the street and took a seat on a concrete bench inside the grass- and tree-lined plaza.

"We will wait until they decide it is safe to show themselves."

The cloak-and-dagger intrigued me. I figured I had already survived the meeting with the Saint-Nazaire mafia, or whoever they were, so this should be a piece of cake.

I was surprised to see the "familiar face" walk up beside Richard Lorbas. I stood, tense and on alert.

"It has been some time, monsieur." Lucas Roscheau extended me his hand.

"M. Roscheau. Last time I saw you I believe you were trying to kill me."

He smiled.

"The last time I saw you I saved your puny neck, so we are even."

I cocked my head, unsure what that last comment meant. He smiled slyly, enjoying my discomfort. "For another time ... ."

Pastor Lorbas began.

"Gentlemen, it is time to lay out for M. Hewitt what he has uncovered, for his safety as well as our own," and he turned to face me. "You met Les Boucliers today - The Shield, the society sworn to protect the Madonna."

"And the woman?"

"She is La Guardienne. She is the most powerful woman in Brittany, and for that reason wields tremendous influence. She is somewhat of an enigma. She goes by the name Laconier, but no one knows who she really is."

"I do. Her real name - at least her maiden name - was Durande. Anisette Durande."

"Durande? Are you certain of this?"

"Yes. And I addressed her as such."

The men all looked at each other, unsure what to do next.

"That puts you in a position to do her severe harm, monsieur. I am without words to explain why she let you simply walk away."

"I know why. But perhaps you need to fill in the gaps for me first."

"Of course. Les Guardiennes have been the keepers of the holy relic since the time of the Revolution."

"The Madonna Rosa."

"Yes. The Madonna surfaced briefly during the war as the SS scoured the countryside searching for it. It then disappeared, and has been sought by competing groups ever since. Factions that do not play nice, if you get my message."

"Yes, I do. Clearly." I decided to keep the story Anisette told me secret for now.

"The women descendants of the original Guardian have been responsible for protecting the hiding place of the Madonna, and the responsibility is passed from mother to daughter. It remains with her until she bears a woman child and she comes of age. The men of the lineage form the backbone of Les Boucliers. The boy children are taken away and raised by the family to be warriors, and assume a different name. No one outside of Les Boucliers knows the identities of La Guardienne's blood relations."

"The chain. She spoke of a chain."

"Yes. *Le Chaîne*. It remained unbroken until the German invasion. Since then, La Guardienne's daughter and granddaughter have both come of age, but the chain cannot be whole without the Madonna. Mme Laconier is an old woman. If she dies before Le Chaîne is passed, it spells the end of the relics's power over the hearts of Bretons."

"Explain that to me."

"Brittany has always been of two minds - both French and Breton. Nationalism is very strong, and many groups - socialists, communists, anarchists among them - have tried to organize politically to break Brittany from French hegemony. But the political parties have no power, and the social groups fight among themselves. During the war it was the Parti National Breton, but they allied with the Germans who, in turn, turned their backs on them when the Vichy government formed to run France. The Breton Parti was systematically hunted down and its people disappeared.

"But the Madonna transcends the petty politics. It represents the independent spirit of Bretons as no political party can. For that reason, it is a threat - to the Church and to the government. And why controlling it would give any faction significant prestige and power."

"And these people - Les Boucliers?"

"They are a private army. They have always provided protection for La Guardienne and the Madonna, but were nearly exterminated by the SS - that is why the relic was hidden, even after the Germans were routed. Since then their numbers have steadily grown. They exist as shadows scattered throughout Brittany, watching, listening for rumors - signs of the appearance of the relic. As Mme Laconier ages, they have become increasingly dangerous.

"One of the men who detained you today was Portier Verbon. He threatens to lead Les Boucliers into even more violent directions. Only Mme Laconier's influence keeps the Shield intact. Once she passes without restoring the relic, Les Boucliers will disintegrate into even more competing factions - as does the powerful economic control they exert over what one might call a secret underground economy. They control much of the commerce in Lorient and Saint-Nazaire. They infiltrate the unions and political organizations. Some say they are behind the bickering that unsettles every political party, every general strike, every disruptive movement. Anything that shifts the power away from themselves."

"I don't get it. What power does the Madonna have."

"It is carved ... ,"

"I know, from the cross of Saint Blandina."

"Yes. Because of that it has symbolic power over the faithful. The Church realizes La Guardienne and her network operate outside of their control, and they cannot tolerate that. The government fears their influence. If either of them can find the Madonna, that power evaporates. And there are others searching as well - those seeking to wrest the power away from La Guardienne for their own purposes."

Lucas Roscheau interrupted.

"OK. Enough of the history and social studies. Why did she contact you? What do you know?"

"Just how is Roland involved in this?"

Lucas did not like the question.

"Ask him yourself. You are a member of the Comet. Now answer my question."

Lucas looked agitated. I knew the only reason I was not in danger from him was Roland's influence. But I knew to watch my back.

"I have been looking for a dead man, a soldier who disappeared in Saint-Nazaire harbor during the British evacuation. I believe those inquiries alerted Mme Laconier and Les Boucliers to my search."

"And why do you know of this man."

"That is my secret. At least for now."

That answer sat badly with Lucas. He snarled at me and was about to explode when the pastor cut in.

"We all have our secrets, gentlemen. At some point it will help to share them all. But that must be based on trust - a trust that must be earned. For now, let us remember we share common goals."

"And what might those be?"

"For one, keeping your sorry ass alive," Lucas snapped.

When I finally was alone, I sat back and tried to reconcile what I had just learned. I took out a sheet of paper and began to map out the factions wrestling for control of the Madonna Rosa.

> Anisette - La Guardienne
> Les Boucliers - private army - carrying the artifact before it?
> Portier Verbon - potential personal threat, hot head

The Circle - any still remaining?
Communists
Separatists
The Church
Reformists within the Church
Reformists not aligned

I reviewed the list with growing concern. I immediately texted Monique.

> Mixed up with something. Complicated. Please stay clear. Stop any more research for now. Wait for me to contact you.

"Papa, M. Larry sent me a disturbing text message. I think he is in some sort of trouble."

"Hah! Another café owner he owes a bill to, I bet!"

"Oh, Papa, stop. I am serious."

Marcel could see by the look on her face she was concerned.

"Very well, I can see you are upset. What is going on?"

"A man stopped me on the street just now. He had me call M. Larry and read a message for him to go to the university in Saint-Nazaire to meet me. Then he disappeared. Then I got this text from M. Larry."

She turned her phone around and showed him the text message.

"What do you know of this man? What is his name?"

"I do not know, but he said he was a friend of Lucas Roscheau, a man I met for lunch the other day. Lucas at first seemed pleasant enough at lunch, but after a while he began to ask me questions about M. Larry. Little things at first, like 'I saw that writer in your café. Do you know him?' ... things like that."

"So? He has written about our café in his books, in the newspapers. Perhaps he is just curious."

"I thought so, too. But when I began to be a little suspicious, he dropped the subject completely. Like he was afraid I might find something out. And now this. I am afraid ... for M. Larry."

"He can take care of himself. And if not, what is one less American in Paris? But you, I am more concerned for you."

"Papa, the man today ... he had a comet tattoo, just like M. Larry ... and Lucas!"

Marcel looked up, his cocky voice becoming serious.

"That settles it! You will stay here until this is cleared up. With mama and me."

Before he even finished his sentence she was gone. Mama Carré walked out from the kitchen just as the door closed behind Monique.

"And this is why I wanted sons!" Marcel barked, and stomped off to the kitchen in disgust.

"What are you fussing about?"

The clock in the church struck one in the afternoon as Monique turned the corner to the door of her flat. On a hunch she ducked into a side doorway where she could watch the entrance to her building. She waited for barely a minute when a man she did not recognize appeared from the other direction, stopped in front of the doorway to look up and down the street, then stepped into the alcove.

"Too bad for you," she whispered, and turned back down the cross street. At the next corner she hailed a taxi.

"The university."

"We are closing soon, madame."

"I will be just a few more minutes. Merci."

Monique rubbed her reddened eyes and jotted down the last few notes before placing her laptop in her bag. She turned back to the first page of notes, made a minor correction, and stared at the word circled at the top of her notes - RIPPLE.

"M. Larry. I hope for your sake I am right."

Her cab waited in front of the library as the lights of Paris slowly pierced the enveloping dusk. Exhausted, she slipped into the back seat.

"Le Café Reuban Vert."

Tonight she would sleep at her parent's apartment above the café.

"I am sorry, monsieur. I cannot issue you a ticket without a passport or a valid national identity card. Perhaps you can arrange to take the next train."

In disgust, he simply had to watch as the train pulled out of Gare du Nord and headed for the coast at Calais. He dialed a number on his cell phone.

"She boarded the Eurostar."

"You lost her?"

"I followed her as she left the café - she spent the night there. I didn't expect her to go to London! I couldn't just board the damn thing. You really think I would carry identification on me?"

"She obviously planned this. I think she knows someone is following her. See if you can find someone to catch her in London. In the meantime, keep monitoring her communications. She is not as careful as the American. She will make a mistake."

"Have you anything to declare, miss?"

"No. I have only a day bag with me."

"And your reason for visiting the United Kingdom today?"

"My sister goes to school here. We are planning to party during the break."

She flashed a demure and flirtatious smile at the customs agent who tipped his hat and smiled in turn.

"Have a pleasant stay, miss."

He couldn't help but watch the slender brunette in the pink blouse, stylish miniskirt, and high heels saunter down the passenger walkway and disappear into the washroom at the far end as other passengers slipped by, avoiding the random customs check.

He did not notice the red-head, wearing jeans and sneakers, and a blue vest over a red blouse, exit the wash room and casually stroll out to catch a cab. A man stood waiting nearby - waiting for the return of the brunette. He would have a long wait.

CHAPTER 23

HER NAME WAS ANISETTE

Pleasure is the flower that passes;
remembrance, the lasting perfume.
- Jean de Boufflers

"Good afternoon, Miss Carré. Mrs. Gunderson will be with you shortly. Please come in."

The administrator in the private nursing home met Monique in the foyer and bade her wait in the library. She was here to see Mrs. Lorraine Gunderson, retired Director of Nursing of the prestigious Imperial College School of Medicine, now a resident. A nurse brought her in a wheelchair, but she stood and with a little assistance took her place in the leather chair next to the fireplace.

"Some tea, if you don't mind."

"Yes, ma'm."

Monique stood and made her formal introduction.

"Good afternoon, Mrs. Gunderson. I am grateful you agreed to meet with me."

"Think nothing of it, Miss Carré. What with the wheelchair and all, it is a little hard to maintain formal pleasantries. Please, sit while Marie brings us tea."

The afternoon sun streamed through large windows that looked out on a beautifully tended garden. Two residents sat at a small table enjoying the warm afternoon. The nurse entered with tea and cakes.

"I hope my visit is not tiring you."

"Oh, not at all. I appreciate the opportunity for company. I am actually quite well, save for the fall I took recently. With just a little help I am still fairly mobile, but I know better than to push my limits before I am fully healed."

Know better, indeed. Monique's research revealed Nurse Gunderson was known throughout England as a relentless advocate for patient care. One account began with the simple words, "She is a force to be reckoned with."

"Now, how may I help you?"

"You were a nurse during the war. I read an article that you attended to many of the survivors of the sinking of the *Lancastria*."

"Oh, my, yes. That was so long ago. I was just a young nurse back then, and very intimidated by the whole affair. There where so many, and their wounds so horrible. Many were burned, and others had ingested oil into their lungs. The doctors really had no idea how to treat such an influx of patients at one time. It was horrible."

"Yet out of that experience, you developed quite a reputation I have read."

She smiled.

"I am afraid I got into a touch of trouble over it."

"And you were released."

"Yes," she laughed. "Oh, it was quite traumatic. My parents were horrified, and I was certain my father would die of a stroke any moment he became so upset. But I stood my ground. I had exposed the weaknesses of the medical treatment process, you see, and that was something no one in the hospital wanted to make a fuss over."

"Yet you prevailed. How?"

"A young reporter who was writing a story on the hospital was told by a patient how his nurse had been fired for showing up a doctor, and he tracked me down. Oh, it made quite a fuss. But one day I received a summons to appear before a minister at one of the government buildings. I was certain I was in a lot of trouble what with the wartime censorship and all. While I was waiting in the lobby, the prime minister Mr. Churchill walked through, stopped, and shook my hand."

"Winston Churchill?"

"Yes. I was somewhat amazed. He said he had only a brief moment to talk, but asked what all the fuss was about. Well, I told him a thing or two. I made his aide quite nervous, I am afraid, but Mr. Churchill simply took my hand and told me to go and 'give them a good bashing.' The next thing I knew I was back at hospital in charge of a ward of extremely sick soldiers with my own nursing staff.

"By the time the wounded began to stream in following the Normandy invasion, we had developed what we now call triage, procedures for handling the most serious of injuries, and increased the survivor rate tremendously. After the war I took a position with Hillingdon Hospital, which later became a part of the Imperial College School of Medicine where I served until I retired."

"With quite a distinction, from what I read."

She blushed, and took a sip of tea.

"Why an interest in the *Lancastria*?"

"I am looking for a soldier who was listed as missing on the *Lancastria* manifest, but his body was never found. He was only twenty or so, and after a rather complex search I have come to believe he may have survived, at least to where he made it aboard a medical transport. He probably arrived with no identification."

Mrs. Gunderson drifted off for a moment, forcing Monique to stop short in her discussion.

"Yes, there were many. I cannot recall how many died on the voyage home, but it was all too common. And so many were burned beyond recognition, and their identity discs missing."

"What would have happened to a soldier who survived, but was unaccounted for?"

She paused for a moment, then spoke in almost a whisper.

"Yes, there were some. We tried so many ways to reach them, those with such traumatic injuries that they could not tell us their names. For some, it was simply hopeless."

"The man I am looking for was named Scott Fitch. Does that name sound familiar to you?"

"No, dear. I am afraid not. So many remained unidentified - some even that could speak, but suffered selective memory loss. One in particular had an effect on me. I had been attending rounds with a doctor, and we had been trying to care for the poor boy - he was barely alive, his lungs terribly injured by oil. The doctor had decided to just send the poor lad off to die in the psychiatric ward. It was shameful. He struggled so just to breathe. He suffered complications of anoxia, and the lack of oxygen resulted in considerable brain damage.

"In my spare time, I nursed him in the psychiatric ward, trying different things to help him clear his lungs. He eventually recovered sufficiently to return to a convalescent hospital, but I knew he would struggle the rest of his life.

"Just before he was moved, I tried to get any name from him at all, of a relative or sweetheart. Maybe focusing on someone he loved would help him remember. He did manage to give me a name, and I searched for her for quite a long time, but without success."

"Do you remember her name?"

"Let me think - her first name, Ann ... something ... French sounding ... ,"

Monique nearly gasped out loud.

"Anisette?"

"Why, yes. Anisette. How did you know?"

"Anisette Durande?"

"He only said, 'Her name was Anisette.' I never knew her last name."

"I believe I know who the boy was."

"Not was, dear."

Monique looked at Mrs. Gunderson in disbelief.

"He is still alive?"

"Yes. I have called on him several times each year afterwards, and he is still alive. He is a resident at Brighton Hills. Do you really think this is the man you are looking for?"

"I am going to find out," she stated emphatically.

"How may I help you, dear?"

The doctor was not impressed.

"The patient is very fragile, Miss Carré. He trembles, often uncontrollably, and has difficulty sleeping. I fear disrupting his current condition would be harmful."

"The patient has a name, doctor. It is Scott Fitch."

Monique stood her ground emphatically.

"So you believe, but without proof, it is just speculation. And, miss, you are not family. You have no standing to speak to him."

"I believe I can confirm who he is. Are you telling me this not important?"

"Miss, I appreciate your concern, but you are not a psychiatrist, and without a bonafide interest in the patient, I am afraid there is nothing I can do."

"I want to ask Scotty a few questions."

"Miss, let us assume he is this Scott Fitch as you say. You still have no standing. Only a relative could make a request to visit him."

"Mrs. Shannon Latham, please."

"Yes, this is Mrs. Latham."

Monique hoped this phone call would unlock the impasse and get her into Brighton Hills to see the man she believed was Scotty.

"Good afternoon, ma'm. My name is Monique Carré. I work for a writer from America working on a story about missing servicemen from World War II. I believe you may be the niece of a man named Scott Fitch who served with the Sherwood Foresters."

"Why, yes, I do believe my great uncle served in that unit, although the family moved from Sherwood after the war."

"Ma'm, we have possession of one of his identity discs from that period - one of two the soldiers wore. I am trying to find out just how his ID disc came into the possession of the man who put us on this search."

"Oh, dear, I'm afraid I cannot tell you much. No one in the family knows much about him during the war. All I know is he was missing."

"I believe he was aboard the converted ocean liner *Lancastria* when it was sunk in Saint-Nazaire harbor following the defeat of France."

"Oh, my. I am afraid I cannot be of much help. You say you have an identity disc?"

"Yes. I was hoping to find out how it came into our possession, and, of course, return it to your family."

"Oh, if it were really his that would be delightful. We have so few things of him in the family archives. My mother was a great one for collecting family memorabilia."

"Is your mother still alive?"

"Yes, but I'm afraid she is not all too well these days. I don't think she would be up to an interview."

"Yes, of course. But as a relative, perhaps I could ask you to accompany me to talk to him?"

"Uncle Scotty? But he died in the war."

"Actually, I don't think so. I have evidence - very strong evidence - that he is the man I have found at Brighton Hills. But since I am not a relative, I cannot see him. I have tried, but the doctors have refused. However, if you claimed to be his relative."

"But how could I know if he is Uncle Scotty?"

"May I come and visit with you? I would like to tell you what I know."

"Why, yes. If there is a chance, yes. Perhaps you could join me for tea."

"Miss, I have to insist you stop wasting my time."

"Doctor Mattingly, this is Mrs. Shannon Latham. She is a relative of Scott Fitch, and wants to speak to him."

"Miss Carré, you have no proof of his identity. This fishing expedition of yours is over!"

The doctor was interrupted by his office assistant who opened the door to speak to him.

"I am sorry, Doctor, but there is an urgent phone call for you."

"I am afraid our conversation is finished, ladies. If you will excuse me."

Monique and Mrs. Latham were ushered outside as the assistant closed the door to his office. Monique took Mrs. Latham by the arm and whispered.

"Wait here. I do not think this is over yet."

It took only a few minutes before Doctor Mattingly, his face flushed, opened the door to his office and stepped out.

"So, why am I not surprised you are still here? I must state for the record I am opposed to this, but ... come with me."

As they followed the doctor down the hall, Mrs. Latham looked quizzically at Monique.

"What was that about?"

Monique just smiled.

"A little help, from a very important friend."

"I have to insist the nurse remain with you at all times. If you say or do anything to upset him, the interview is over. Have I made myself clear?"

"Perfectly, doctor. Thank you," and Monique dismissed him just as quickly. She pulled a chair up close to the bed and sat down.

"Hello, Scotty."

Her voice was soft, reassuring. The man in the bed did not respond. His hands shook, his face a dark gray pallor.

"He shakes all the time, miss. And sleeps very poorly. We have to medicate him to get him to rest at all."

"I don't think he is at peace, and that is why his hands tremble, why he has such a difficult time sleeping. He has retreated from the world to hide from his fear and shame."

"Shame? Shame for what?" Mrs. Latham stepped close to the bedside.

"I believe he thinks he failed in his duty … to fulfill a promise he made."

"To who?"

"To a beautiful young woman he met during the evacuation from France. The woman gave him a precious artifact to protect. I think he lost it when the *Lancastria* was sunk, and he lives with that shame."

She sat for a moment, tears filling her eyes.

"I need to ask him some very pointed questions," Monique spoke, almost in a whisper.

"Will it hurt him?" Mrs. Latham could barely speak.

"I don't know."

"Scotty, can you hear me? I talked to George."

His eyes widened, although he kept his head still, his gaze focused on the ceiling.

"Georgie? Is he all right?"

The nurse took a sharp breath, surprised he spoke - directly, purposefully.

"Yes, Scotty. He is at peace."

"He died, you know. That day, on the boat."

"Yes, Scotty. I know."

Scotty just laid there, quietly.

"She made me promise."

"To protect the Madonna."

"Tell her I tried. Tell them both I tried."

"You tried, Scotty. That was all she could ask."

Scotty turned his head and looked at Monique, his eyes glistening.

"They tried to get in the boat. But there was no room. They grabbed the pack to toss it ... but I held on. I held on tight."

His eyes began to cloud once more, the brief moment of perfect reality dissolving into the safety of his private oblivion. Monique took his hands, still trembling.

"Anisette says she forgives you."

At the mention of her name a single tear rolled down his cheek. His hands stopped trembling and he closed his eyes and slipped off to sleep on his own for the first time in many years.

Monique travelled all night by train and arrived in Saint-Nazaire in time to slip into my café table at breakfast.

"Where did you come from?"

"London."

"What? How did you find me?"

"The man at your hotel told me you hang out here - it's what I would have expected. You are perhaps a little too predictable, M. Larry," she smiled. "*Un café, s'il vous plaît*," she called to the waiter.

"I hope for the sake of my expense account you have something interesting for me."

Monique simply smiled. She nodded to the handsome waiter when he brought her the coffee, took a sip, and placed the cup on the table with a mischievous grin.

"Scotty is not the man who was buried in Pornic. I think it was his friend George."

"Why do you think that?"

She looked at me and smiled.

"Because I found Scotty."

I stared at her in disbelief.

"Still alive?"

"The artifact was in his backpack when he and George were separated in the attack. He called him Georgie."

My head began swimming as the truth began to dissolve out of the fog.

"The letters. The tin box - and the Madonna - were in Scotty's backpack."

"He was in a lifeboat. He told of men trying to toss it overboard. But he held on, until something happened. That must have been when he was hurt."

"And separated from the backpack. That means it would have floated along the same path the body would have. That is how the tin box was found ... and that means the Madonna was also found. On the beach - near Prefailles."

"M. Larry, Scotty remembers very little of that terrible time. In fact, he is barely cognizant of anything. But he did remember Anisette. He has lived with the pain of knowing he failed her, and has suffered terribly ever since. But I think he is a peace now."

"Why do you say that?"

She stopped for a moment, collected herself, then tried to speak. The confident law student, researcher, and woman of new Paris could barely speak the words, blinking back her tears.

"I told him Anisette forgives him. He cried, and fell asleep. The nurse said he has never slept without medication."

CHAPTER 24

A BIG FISH

*There is frequently more to be learned from
the unexpected questions of a child
than the discourses of men.*
- John Locke

Monique told me she could stay for a few days to help me.

"To keep you out of trouble, M. Larry. Another set of eyes will help."

I brought her up-to-date on the recent developments with Les Boucliers and the meeting with La Guardienne. She told me of the man watching her apartment and slipping what she guessed was a tail at the train station. Her eyes lit up with the intrigues.

"I could really enjoy this!"

I couldn't help but admire her self-confidence. If she only knew how deep the passions, how complex the relationships, and how dangerous the waters could become.

"How can we find out who is the unknown soldier buried in Pornic? My guess ... we do not want to simply go and ask."

"No, Monique. It's probably George Sherrat, and his body being heavier and floating lower in the water was carried further up the coast than the knapsack by the currents. But taking a direct approach could alert our competition we are closing in on the truth. That is something I want to avoid, at least for now."

"So what do we do?"

"We play a little tag team."

"Again, with the American slang. What on earth do you mean?"

I looked at her and sat up formally.

"Why certainly, madame, I would be pleased to help you locate your missing great-uncle's resting place. In Pornic, you say?"

She cocked her head and took a sip of the coffee.

"You Americans are a strange people."

I took it as a compliment.

We sat and concocted a good backstory to use as a starting point for Monique's investigation.

"Things began to heat up as soon as I asked about Scotty. That tells me this is sensitive ground - and whoever is watching feels emboldened by our secrecy. Pretending George Sherrat is your relative gives you a reason to drill down for answers. This will put a lot of pressure on whoever is watching us. And stepping out into the open may push the watchers back a notch or two - long enough for us to make a move."

"A move to do what?"

"To dig up the body buried in the pauper's grave."

"What! Are you crazy?"

"Well, you and I are not going to dig it up. But if we can get the church to do it, all the better."

"You think the relic is buried with George's body?"

I considered her question carefully.

"It's a good sell, but I'm not sure."

"Again with the slang - a 'good sell?'"

"It seems a likely spot - and that bothers me. If it were that simple, someone would have figured it out by now. Someone knew the body was not Vincent Dupris. If the artifact was buried in the same grave someone would have known. Why have they remained silent all these years? What would be the reason for the figurine remaining buried there when everyone wants it?"

Monique took a sip of wine and considered this last statement.

"You are making an assumption, M. Larry, that everyone who covets the Madonna Rosa actually wants it found."

I hadn't considered that. I'd been so absorbed with tracking down the details I missed a compelling point.

"Monique, for over two hundred years Les Boucliers kept the Madonna hidden. Yet I have been assuming they want it found - and revealed. You are suggesting this may not be the case."

I could see that legal steel-trap of a mind churning.

"The Catholics want the artifact - and have been seeking it for centuries. Your story about Sid and Anisette confirms this. The collaborators - the Circle? They kidnapped and imprisoned Anisette Durande, and tortured her to reveal it to them - but she did not know where it was. You said a rift developed in the Church - and the Reformists became involved. That is at least four different factions seeking to recover the icon."

"And there are others. Someone may betray a confidence thinking it is safe, or in a panic. But what I hope is local officials do not make a connection between you and me. The tourist season is in full swing, and it is likely such inquiries might be commonplace. I am hoping we may catch someone a little off guard."

I pulled a list printed on plain white paper with the names of several of the unaccounted-for men who actually perished that sad day - the list I was using to try and weed out potential grave sites. I crumpled it, mussed it up with some dirt from the café floor and dribbled some coffee on it, and handed it to Monique.

"I think this looks realistic enough. You will see it shows names crossed off as found, and the cemeteries they were discovered in. There are only two left on your list. Harry Penderton and George Sherrat."

"This is fantastic! How did you think of it?"

"I spill a lot of coffee."

She laughed, then a serious look came over her.

"M. Larry. In legal research the sources are well known. The documents are mostly public, but you have had little luck with such things. Where do I begin?"

"I have looked in all the obvious places. This is why I have attracted attention, and why they blew up my car. It's time to change the focus, and start looking where no one else has. Places no one has thought of before."

"But they are watching you."

"That is why we have to work separately. Let's meet every day - but no emails and no cell phones. It's hard to say who is watching what."

"Where do we meet?"

"I'll pick a spot, and leave a message at my hotel. A different time each day, just to be safe. You can call the hotel and ask for a reservation - the owner is named Henri. Just identify yourself as 'Monique' - I will tell him what to do."

"*D'accord*. What's first?"

"A visit to Pornic for you. Use your backstory to poke around and see what you can discover. Look for the unusual, something no one else may have noticed. I'm afraid I cannot tell you more."

"And you, M. Larry?"

"I am going fishing."

"Fishing?"

"For a very big fish."

The boys sat on the end of the dock, their fishing poles lazily hanging over the side. A lively card game was in progress - it was clear the fish were not biting this morning.

"No fish today?"

One boy looked up from the hand he was holding.

"No, monsieur. Not today."

He threw a pair of cards down on the dock as the other boys groaned.

"You couldn't tell he was holding? Who taught you how to play cards?" I laughed.

"I suppose you can do better?" the boy who collected the pot teased.

"Let a foreigner into the game?"

"Ten euro to buy in."

I smiled at the taunt.

"*D'accord*. I'm in."

I set down my backpack, dropped two five-euro notes into the pot, and took back change enough to play the next several hands.

"Watch him, monsieur. He cheats," one of the boys snarled.

Twenty euros later I had to call it quits.

"Too rich for me, boys. You must've seen me coming!"

They all looked a little quizzically at each other at my use of slang, and one of the boys just shrugged his shoulders.

"Can I ask you a question?"

"You have paid for the privilege," the boy with the hot hand shot back.

"I'm a writer. Children's books, mainly. A little too young for you guys ... but I was hoping you could tell me about any local legends I could embellish for one of my books. You know, sea monsters, zombies, pirates - that sort of thing."

They all just looked at each other and shrugged.

"You mean to tell me five boys growing up on the seashore have never heard any fantastic stories?"

"How much?"

"Ten euro?"

"Too cheap. Thirty."

"Thirty? You already took twenty from me. Fifteen. Nothing more. And only if the story is good."

"Twenty-five, and I'll take you to the old man who saw the thing."

"Twenty."

"Done."

The fish would have to wait another day.

"He is just *vieillard fou* - a crazy old man. He walks the beaches taking anything that washes ashore. Sometimes he sells the junk to the stupid tourists, like you."

I liked this boy. Blunt, irreverent, but plugged in to the soft underbelly of the Jade Coast. Just what I would expect from a twelve-year old.

"Hey! Old man!"

We rounded the corner where a rock wall jutted out into the upper reaches of the beach and saw an old man sitting on the edge of the sand, a walking stick in hand.

"*Ah, bonjour, Martin! Comment va tu?*"

"A little richer today, thanks to this American. He wants to talk to you."

"An American? Well, bring him closer ... you know, my eyes."

He had a sly grin on his face as I approached and offered my hand in introduction.

"I am Leone Langille, monsieur. How may I help you?"

"He is looking for stories, old man. Like the stories you tell to frighten the little kids."

"And what are these to you, my American friend? Sit, and let us talk."

"You are on your own ... that is, unless you have more euros to spend."

"No, Martin. You've made enough off me today. Thanks."

"As you wish. I am off."

M. Langille chuckled as the boy disappeared back around the rock wall and up the beach.

"He is the ring leader, as American novels like to call them. But he is a good boy. Now, how can I help you, my friend."

"Martin says you walk the beach, collecting things."

"Yes. I am too old to fish any more. The mind is willing, but my back ... so I keep busy doing a lot of things. I help in the museum, and each afternoon I take a walk to keep in good condition. And sometimes I find things. I've been living on this beach all my life."

"I asked the boy about stories - sea monsters, things like that. I was actually looking for something else."

"And what might that be."

"Stories of ... well, bodies, to put it bluntly."

"Bodies?"

He looked at me suspiciously.

"I am a writer, and I am looking for information about the men who died here in 1940. About the sinking ... ,"

"The *Lancastria*."

His response caught me by surprise.

"Yes, the *Lancastria*."

"July 17, 1940. A terrible day."

This man was no itinerant wanderer.

"What can you tell me?"

He sat back and took a deep breath.

"Walk with me."

His cottage on the upper reaches of the beach did not fit the picture I had of him living in some rude hovel. The home was small, but elegant. It looked centuries old.

"I have lived here all my life, as did my father, and his father before. It has been in our family for over two hundred years. I am sure Martin left you with quite a different impression."

I laughed.

"According to him, you are a wandering scavenger."

He laughed with a deep robustness that belied his older years.

"I have always scoured the beaches, ever since I was a little boy. Always some special treasure to be had." And he smiled remembering. "I was a just boy during the war. We managed to survive the German occupation with little interference - this is such a small commune. The French authorities had little to steal from us. My father was a fisherman, and the boats kept fishing even during the difficult years. Life was not so bad here."

He ushered me to a small sitting area with a view of the bay.

"The days following the sinking were terrible, however. The Germans scoured the beach looking for survivors. And bodies, of course. They collected much of the debris, scouring for anything of value, any intelligence."

He went to a cupboard and removed a half-full bottle of local red wine and poured two glasses.

"My father told me to stay off the beach after the authorities grounded the fleet following the sinking. But I went with him to work on a small skiff. I saw something in the water and went to investigate. I was quite terrified at first."

"A body?"

"British, from his uniform. I could tell. Papa sent me to get the priest. Men from the village came and took the poor soldier to the church. Everyone wanted to keep it such a secret - afraid the authorities would come."

"What about identification?"

"There was a small identity disc like all the soldiers wear ... they had two of them you know."

Yes, I knew.

"The name. Any chance you remember the name on the disc."

"No, it's been such a long time."

My heart sank. I hoped this was the break I needed to complete the circle. He stood and walked back to the cabinet - I figured to get another bottle of wine - just what I needed to soothe my spirits after this disappointment. Instead, he pulled out a small book.

"I have kept it here."

He thumbed through the pages then presented the open book to me. There, pressed between the pages, was a green British soldier identity disc. The name was faded, but visible.

SHERRAT, GFS, 4978735, C

It was George Sherrat - the friend from the photograph!

"Do you know what happened to the body?"

My heart raced, adrenaline flooding my senses. I desperately tried to maintain my sense of control.

"The priest buried him in the church cemetery even though he was not Catholic."

"In the grave meant for Vincent Dupris?"

He smiled mischievously.

"Who is the girl?"

"A waitress from Paris. We don't know much about her."

"Why is she here? His mistress?"

"Not that we know of. These Americans ... not as sensible as the French."

"Find out. Monitor their communications. I don't want any surprises."

Portier Verbon hung up the phone and looked out the window over a perfect blue sea, flat calm in the warm summer afternoon.

"Calm, yes. But a storm is about the break in Brittany unless we can keep him from finding the Madonna."

CHAPTER 25

LE SANG NEUF

No one is so brave that he is not disturbed
by something unexpected.
- Julius Caesar

My phone rang early the next morning. It was late after work in Winnipeg and I could tell Angus McDonough was a few pints into blowing off some steam at his favorite pub.

"I figured somebody dumped your body into the Bay of Biscay, which was why we have not heard anything from you. Thought about it a few times myself."

"Sorry, Angus, but things have been a little crazy here."

"Yes, and you owe me some copy."

"It's coming together."

"Coming together? What the hell does that mean? If you were on staff ... ."

"I know, you'd have given me the boot by now. That's why I am not on staff."

"You freelancers are a pain in the ass. What have you got?"

"I was confronted by a secret society - guardians of an ancient religious relic lost since the war. That story is a killer in and of itself ... the soldier Fitch was entrusted with the artifact during the evacuation. He lost it when the *Lancastria* was sunk, but its gets better. Items from his backpack were recovered - and it appears the artifact may have been among them. We decided his body washed ashore and was buried secretly to keep it from the Germans.

"It turns out Scott Fitch is still alive - a resident in a nursing home in England. His story alone is worth all this trouble. He has carried the memory of his failure to protect the relic with him all these years - it was the trigger that brought him out of his stupor, if only temporarily.

"The body that washed ashore was his friend George Sherrat. I talked to the man who found him when he was a boy and he still had his identity disc. He confirmed George was buried in Pornic as Vincent Dupris, and later exhumed when the real Vincent Dupris returned. I believe he was reburied in what is now an unmarked grave in the Pornic cemetery. I think the Madonna Rosa is buried with him."

Angus McDonough listened to my explanation quietly.

"You seem pretty convinced about this, but you still have only circumstantial evidence."

"There are groups searching for the relic - factions that have been at war with each other for years. They are all watching, waiting for us to find it."

"If you find it. These factions - are they real or just the imagination of a few right-wing zealots?"

"That's hard to say. The Parti National was very real, but their numbers were decimated by the Nazis and French police after the armistice. Germany saw the cooperation of Vichy as far more valuable, at least in the early stages. Most of the leaders ended up in Natzweiler."

Once again, the specter of the French concentration camp where Marianne died and Gela kept the accounts for the Money Train reared its ugly head.

"And the bomb threat - that was real. Then the visit from Les Boucliers - the society guarding the Madonna Rosa, and two other threats. People are watching me. I am getting close."

"So what are you planning?"

"I want to dig up the pauper's grave."

"What? An exhumation? Are you crazy ... ?"

Why do people keep asking me that?

I put the phone down and let him rant for a few moments before rejoining the conversation.

"... can only guess what legal will have to say. But you're on your own with that. In the meantime, I need a story! A lead article? I'm not financing this little jaunt of yours just for kicks!"

I promised to throw him a bone by morning.

"Angus, I have someone helping me here. A law student, the daughter of a friend. I need Ellen to OK some additional expenses ... "

He cut me off.

"Of course you do! I wish I had never given you that damn credit card."

"Have another pint, Angus. You'll have your story in the morning."

I put Monique up in a hotel down the street and dashed off an email saying "Angus gave me the go-ahead" to Ellen Richardson, Angus' personal assistant. Monique insisted on being my partner in this investigation, and I appreciated a fresh set of ideas to help sort this out ... and keep an eye out for trouble.

The next morning Monique and I met for coffee at a spot arranged by my friend Henri.

"I tossed and turned all night thinking this through. These factions - they are converging on us, I can feel it. It means we are too close for comfort, but I am still not exactly sure if we are on the right track."

"You are having second thoughts about George Sherrat being the one buried in the cemetery?"

"No. But the Madonna - we are assuming it is buried with him. The more I think this through, the more I think that's not the case."

Monique took a sip of coffee and frowned.

"I have been to every place in Pornic and Prefailles I could think of, and have nothing. The more I pushed about the Dupris burial the more I got stoned ... ,"

"Stonewalled," I corrected, chuckling.

"Stone-walled? I will never get your slang correct. Anyway, these people - if they think the body and the Madonna are buried together that means they did not know where the body was. I mean, how hard would it have been to dig up the grave? An hour or so, two men with shovels, on a dark ... ,"

"... and stormy night ... yeah, I thought of that. I agree they didn't know - maybe didn't know about a body at all. In the confusion following the sinking, then following the liberation, it would have been easy for information to get muddied. But someone knew.

Someone buried the body, and that someone likely hid the Madonna. The question is, who?"

Monique began to doodle on a napkin.

"Do I think they are watching us? Yes. Do they have any information we do not? No, I do not believe so. Perhaps they see us focusing the search in a smaller and smaller area, and are simply sitting back waiting for the right moment."

"The question is," and I savored a long slurp of coffee before continuing, "the moment to do what?"

"I feel like a mouse about to be pounced on," Monique reflected.

I had the same feeling.

"I think you're right. They are simply waiting for us to make a discovery before they move in. The problem is, there are too many of them to manage effectively. Too easy for one to slip through and hit us - perhaps even violently."

"So what do you suggest."

"Publicity. Lots of it. All focused on the grave in Pornic."

"You said the other day you wanted to go about quietly. Why the change?"

"To disrupt their thinking, perhaps make them a little desperate. Desperate men make mistakes. I'm going to claim we have located the Madonna Rosa, and we have evidence it is buried in the pauper's grave. Give these factions something to really focus on."

Monique nodded her head, thinking through the potential complications.

"Let me go after the publicity - the innocent young girl, looking for her long, lost great-uncle. Blah, blah, blah ... ," She smiled. "Maybe find a cute reporter or two in the process."

"Do you ever stop?"

Monique just grinned.

"OK, you take care of the press. I am going to demand an exhumation. Better yet, get the church to request one from the local authorities - that'll really stir things up."

"How will you do that?"

"By calling a friend. If the artifact is there, at least it will be uncovered in public - and whether Les Boucliers or the Church gets it will be decided by the courts. In the meantime, between you and me, I don't think the relic is there at all. That's too easy. We need to keep searching."

"So how do we find it?"

I smiled at her.

"I have no idea."

Monique sat at a café with Millard Gayman, editor of a news service on the Jade Coast, Le Communiqué, and wrapped the handsome newsman around her little finger.

"My great-uncle was a British soldier in the war. He disappeared following the sinking of the *Lancastria* in 1940. My mother moved here as a college student after the war and tried to find him. Instead she met my father and eventually settled in Paris."

M. Gayman had been a young ambitious reporter, fed up with the slow pace in his hometown of Brest, and decided to start his own service using both the Internet and the tourist pages of local newspapers scattered throughout Brittany. He was aggressive, intelligent, and totally transfixed by the beautiful Monique. He kept meticulous notes while trying not to stare into her beguiling eyes.

"OK, and why are you looking now?"

"My mother is in poor health, and I made her a promise to find her uncle's grave before she passes. I am afraid I am about out of ideas."

"And his name?"

"George Sherrat; Sherwood Foresters. The majority of his unit evacuated at Dunkirk. A small group had to flee south and boarded the *Lancastria*."

"And why do you think he died in the sinking."

"He was listed among the soldiers who boarded, according to the manifest," she lied, "but there is no record of him returning to England."

"And why Pornic?"

"Someone sent me a story about a man who returned to Pornic from Spain to find someone buried with his headstone. I have tried to find out more information about this, but without success."

"The wrong grave? That's a nice hook. That I can sell."

I would sell anything to impress you.

"What do you hope to gain by this publicity? What is our goal?"

Monique took a sip of wine and sat back, crossing her slim legs specifically to catch his attention. This was the moment of truth, and she knew instinctively how to close this deal.

"I am getting desperate, Millard. I have searched through the official records, been to the churches, tried everything I could think of. The local officials have been no help. So I thought about going public ... but I am concerned for my privacy and that of my family. I need someone to help me, to act as an intermediary. Someone I can trust."

Millard Gayman blushed momentarily, squirmed in his seat, and took a too-hot gulp of coffee.

"I think I can help you, Monique. We can keep your identity private, and I can create a separate email account at the paper and direct replies there. We can meet regularly to go over them ... if you think this will help."

Gotcha, as my American friend would say.

She smiled, a twinkle sparking in her beautiful eyes.

"Yes, I think that would be very nice."

Le Communiqué featured the story the following day and it hit the hundreds of small newspapers and web sites that promote Brittany tourism throughout the following week. Monique read the headline and smiled.

Pornic, Brittany

The Rumors of My Death

Imagine coming home from an extended stay and finding out you are officially dead. Vincent Dupris of Pornic returned home in 1952 to discover his own grave in the local cemetery. Local officials wrongly buried another man in his grave. The body was exhumed, and the late M. Dupris laid peacefully to rest after his passing in 1986. Now that mistake is once again big news in this little commune on the Brittany coast.

The story went on to say how a student from Paris believes her great-uncle George Sherrat was the man wrongfully buried in the Dupris case, and she is seeking information about the whereabouts of the body to attempt to confirm his identity.

"It's the same girl? This is a load of crap! I don't believe any of this. Too convenient. Too timely. Keep a close eye on her."

"Portier, with this publicity, we have to be careful. We cannot afford to be exposed."

Portier Verbon stopped, and considered that last statement carefully.

"That's just what this is about. They are close. And they are using this story to push us, to shield themselves from us. Something is about to happen. No, M. Author-Man, we will not back off. Just the opposite. We are going to move in close - close enough to hear you sweat."

"We need to meet with La Guardienne to discuss this. And get the approval of the council."

Portier began to pace wildly.

"The council is weak. They will do what she wants. They have no spine. La Guardienne lost her control when she lost the Madonna. This is my decision. My responsibility."

The men in the room looked nervously at each other.

"And that writer ... he is also mine."

Angus McDonough's news service picked up the story with a little careful prodding and it spread to the major French newspapers and news web sites the following Monday.

> Pornic, Brittany
> Priceless Religious Icon Buried in Pornic?
> An ancient carving of the Madonna and Child lost
> during the German invasion of France is buried in an
> unmarked pauper's grave in the small coastal
> commune of Pornic, according to the American
> author, L.W. Hewitt of the popular Juno Letters
> series.
>
> The Madonna Rosa, the ancient symbol of Breton
> independence, disappeared following the German
> invasion of France and was hidden in the nearby
> commune of Pornic. A local official with ties to the
> reformist church allegedly placed the artifact in the
> grave of an unidentified soldier when it was
> discovered he had been inadvertently buried in
> someone else's grave.
>
> Following an anonymous tip, Hewitt followed a series
> of clues and located what he believes is the hiding
> spot. A request for an exhumation of the grave was
> denied by local officials for lack of proper standing.
> An official of the Luçon diocese refused comment
> when asked today if the Catholic Church would lay

claim to the religious object, once thought to have resided at the Abbey of Saint-Sauveur-le-Vicomte in Lower Normandy.

Portier Verbon read the article and threw the paper across the room.

"I told you he would sell out to the Church! I told all of you! I demand a council gathering ... tonight! We have been stabbed in the back by that writer. If they do not back me, we will act by ourselves."

Roland could barely suppress his laughter when he read the headline in the Paris newspaper. Gilbert was less impressed.

"What is he doing now? Why is he going public? What does he hope to accomplish, besides alerting the factions to his progress?"

"A good question. But I think he is masking his motive."

"And what is that?"

"By exposing his target, he also exposes those who seek to wrest it from him. It will force everyone back a step to two - perhaps just enough to give him a little more breathing space. It is a clever move."

"One that could get him killed."

Roland laughed.

"No, Gilbert. I don't think so - not now. Just the opposite. But Hewitt has a knack of tripping over the very thing he is seeking - a sort of Chaplinesque foolishness, if you will. His instincts are very sharp, but they tend to move ahead of the evidence, and his judgement. That is why he is so good at turning up the undiscoverable, and stirring up trouble at the same time."

Gilbert simply looked at Roland with a blank stare.

"I don't get it."

No, nephew, which is why you work for me, and why I turn my good friend loose in the world to stir up the status quo. Each to his strengths.

"It is time now to make a move. I need an appointment with the Archbishop in Rennes."

"Rennes? Do we have connections there?"

"Tell them M. Soullant wishes an audience, at his earliest convenience. Then book a suite on the train. It will make a nice vacation."

The three priests met in the bishop's office in the cathedral at Rennes.

"His Excellency will be meeting with M. Soullant tomorrow afternoon. What is your recommendation?"

"You have read the reports?"

"Yes. The priest in Prefailles was careless in granting him access to the archives. He is new and not fully aware of the significance of the situation."

"Time erodes even the strongest of walls, Father. It was inevitable someone would discover the truth behind the Madonna Rosa."

"The question becomes, how do we ensure the Church can manage this unfortunate turn of events."

"He has met with Mme Laconier. That will place Les Boucliers on alert. The father in Pornic has sent word trespassers in the cemetery have been run off by the local police three times since. This news is creating passions we cannot deny."

"Then we must act decisively. I will advise His Excellency it is in the best interest of the Church to uncover the grave, to protect the relic from theft or harm. We will have to create a reasonable story to cover the truth."

"The American writer affords us that opportunity. We shift the publicity toward his 'untiring detective work' that resolved this long-standing mystery."

"We must have protection for the artifact. We should anticipate a strong, possibly violent reaction."

"Les Boucliers would never attack the Church openly, Monsignor."

The monsignor stood and walked slowly to the draped window looking out over the courtyard.

"Les Boucliers are not my only concern."

"How did you get the church to intervene?"

Monique arranged to meet with me privately after the Paris news service picked up the next story from its connections in the French church.

> The French Catholic Council today expressed its
> concern the Madonna Rosa allegedly buried in an
> unmarked grave in the coastal commune of Pornic
> could be subject to theft or desecration if left
> undisturbed. Sources confirm a formal writ for a
> church exhumation of the grave has been requested.

"I didn't. Frankly, this smacks more of Roland Soullant - although for the life of me I don't know what connection he would have, especially with the Church."

"Roland Soullant? The industrialist?"

"A friend. And a fellow member of the Comet."

I turned up my right wrist and showed her the tattoo.

"I have seen this before. I have been meaning to ask you about it."

"Where?"

"On the man I met when all this started - Lucas Roscheau. And then another - the one who made me make that phone call."

"Lucas? You know Lucas Roscheau?"

"I met him at a dinner M. Soullant hosted, and he asked me out. He seemed a little too interested in my relationship with you, M. Larry. And when I asked him about his tattoo his answer was vague. I didn't trust him."

"You are right to not trust him. I would stay clear of that one."

She smiled.

"I would not worry. He has a lot of competition. Now, what is this Comet all about?"

"A consortium of sorts, almost like a family. People who can call on Roland for resources and assistance from time to time, and render it back when asked. He has been extremely helpful in the past ... and is connected somehow to La Guardienne, although I have not had the time to ask him about this."

"You think he is behind the exhumation request."

"I would bet my life on it."

Portier Verbon stood before the council of Les Boucliers seething with anger.

"He has sought the aide of the Catholic Church! I should have killed the bastard when I had the chance."

Anisette Laconier put down the newspaper and sat back.

"No, Portier. You are wrong. M. Hewitt would not have so openly betrayed his promise to me - or to his friend, Mr. Woodard."

"The dead man? An easy trust to betray!"

"No, Portier. A harder one, especially among men of character. Something else is happening, I am certain of it. We must remain patient."

"Patient! Next we will see the Church lay claim to the Madonna. They can dig up that grave and we will never see the relic again!"

Mme Laconier simply smiled at the headline in the newspaper.

"I do not believe so."

The council nodded in agreement. Portier Verbon stormed out of the meeting.

Portier Verbon drove along the back roads toward Saint-Nazaire, his rage building.

She is leading them into oblivion. They will dig up the grave, and the Church will steal the Madonna. That will be the end of it.

"Not if I can help it."

"Portier Verbon. What brings you to Saint-Nazaire?"

Perryn de L'Etanche was a small, wiry man who grew up among the docks of Saint-Nazaire. Picked on as a boy, he learned to fight - viciously if necessary - to protect his small "enterprise" as he liked to call it - stealing small items and selling them on the streets. When he was a young man he joined "Le Sang Neuf" - the New Blood, a communist faction that controlled the movement of drugs through the harbor. Now aged fifty-two, he presided over the loose Le Sang Neuf empire, enforcing his directives with an iron fist.

He was a man to fear. A man who did not compromise.

"We are close to finding the Madonna."

"So I hear. We have been watching this writer friend of La Guardienne."

Portier spit on the floor. De L'Etanche looked up quickly.

"You are having a spat with Mme Laconier?" he openly mocked him.

Perryn de L'Etanche maintained guarded relations with Mme Laconier, despite his rancor with the other separatist organizations in Brittany - including his own communist party.

"She has become weak in her old age. She trusts this American."

"And you do not?"

"I would kill him rather than spit on his shadow."

Really. A break in Les Boucliers? Such a thing is unheard of.

"I take it you are not here for a social visit?"

This Portier Verbon dances like a chicken on a hot plate. What is he up to? Can he be trusted?

"No. I need your help."

"To do what?"

"To keep the Madonna Rosa out of the hands of the Church."

"And into your possession?" Verbon looked at de L'Etanche and scowled. "Now, my friend, relax. We have been watching this little drama play out. And had a little fun with some minor disruptions … ."

"The bomb threat?"

"Yes, I must say that was a bit of brilliance. Just enough detail to force the authorities to blow up his car. No risk. Nothing to trace back to Le Sang Neuf."

"That was you! And what was the point in that? Some fun, at my expense?" Verbon was furious. "The council blamed me for acting outside of their control."

Perryn de L'Etanche lowered his voice.

"We had our reasons. And I do not need to explain them to you."

His defiant voice forced Verbon to back down. He knew this was not a man to excite.

"But, Portier, we are all friends here." He resumed a more congenial tone, having put the excitable Verbon in his place. "What is it you wish from me?"

"The council will not act. La Guardienne chooses to wait and trust the American. I need soldiers … to take back the relic before it can become lost in the bowels of the corrupt church."

"Another 'La Riviere?' How fitting. What's in it for me?"

CHAPTER 26

BEST LAID PLANS

The best laid schemes of Mice and Men
oft go awry,
And leave us nothing but grief and pain,
For promised joy!
- Robert Burns

Monsignor Lacrosse smiled as he read the letter in front of him.

"Father, the Archbishop has approved the exhumation and has taken affirmative steps to lay claim to the Madonna with the district court. He has requested an order assigning custody of the relic to the Church."

Father Bioche was uneasy.

"Your Excellency, I have been besieged by reporters requesting access to the exhumation. I fear we will have a difficult situation to control once the digging begins. I am afraid we are not prepared to provide much in the way of security."

"The archdiocese will assume that responsibility, Father. Fear not. We have already contracted with a private security company to transport the relic to Rennes. They will provide ample security at the grave site and besides, the publicity alone will ensure the activity is carefully scrutinized. I appreciate your concern, Father, but this will be carefully orchestrated."

As Father Bioche drove back to Pornic he could not help but worry.

"... and of course we would be pleased to have you witness the exhumation. Your assistance in this matter has been greatly appreciated."

I listened closely to the invitation by the aide to Monsignor Lacrosse of the Rennes diocese trying to read between the lines. The exhumation was moving forward rather quickly and the Church wanted to make certain I was within a discrete but visible distance from the activity.

"I will be there, most certainly. And please express my appreciation to Monsignor Lacrosse."

I hung up the phone and sat for a while thinking. What if the Madonna really is in the pauper's grave? More importantly, what if it is not?

Perryn de L'Etanche spread the map of the district out on the long table in the back of the warehouse that served as Le Sang Neuf's temporary headquarters.

"The arrangements are complete, and we know all the details. Here is the plan. The security van will leave Pornic Cemetery and travel west along the frontage road ... here, along the D213, Route Blueu. As soon as the relic is loaded aboard, Team A will block the 213 here ... ," and he pointed to the highway bridge over the river, " ... and here, at the highway overpass. This will stop all traffic in between.

"Team B will block the security van from the front and behind while Richard and Romain in Team C cross the highway from the opposite frontage road."

One of the men interrupted.

"The security guards will be armed, Perryn."

"We have infiltrated the security company. One of our men will ride in the passenger seat. He will disable the driver, and remove the threat of his weapon."

The other men looked nervously at each other - they understood what "disable" meant.

"Team C will take the artifact, cross back over the highway, and leave up Rue de Chauvé using the back roads as cover. They will rendezvous with me here ... ," and he pointed to a small side road that broke off of the D97 highway, where La Hourserie met Les Platennes Le Clion.

"Team C will reenter the highway and will drive north before turning back to Pornic - they will expect us to be driving away not toward the commune. The car will be abandoned just below the de Gaul bridge, leaving nothing but empty vehicles for the authorities to stop and check. By the time they complete investigating the stalled vehicles, the artifact will be safely away by boat from the Pornic fishery dock."

"And where is the boat headed?"

"Back to Belle Isle."

Back to the traditional home ground of the collaborators, and the Citadel.

Romain Varnadoe studied the plan carefully while appearing to remain slightly disinterested.

"Romain, you will join Team A. Blocking the highway and abandoning these vehicles in place is the critical piece of the plan. The chaos will freeze the authority's response and give us time to remove the artifact."

A good plan, Romain nodded.

"And what of Portier Verbon? Where does he fit in?"

Perryn de L'Etanche just smiled.

"He does not 'fit in,' as you say. He has insisted on accompanying the relic, so he will join Team B as they cross the highway to retrieve the artifact from the van."

"And how do we ensure he does not interfere - try to take it himself?"

"Because he will be shot with the driver's pistol and left on the road ... and Les Boucliers will be blamed for the theft and both bodies."

The men in the room laughed, and nodded in agreement.

All except Romain Varnadoe.

The sun sank into a blood red sky over the Bay of Biscay as a lone bicyclist stopped beside the storage warehouse on the far side of the port and leaned his bicycle against the wall. He entered through a side door.

Ten minutes passed. As the twilight deepened, two small trucks approached the warehouse from different directions. Five men exited the trucks and moved quickly to the doors, stopping to examine the entrance before disappearing inside. The drivers remained at the wheel, their engines running.

After five minutes, one man emerged from the warehouse door and gave a signal to the driver who reached for his cell phone.

"All clear."

He remained at the wheel and waited. It took only a few minutes for the car to arrive.

Inside the warehouse the men waited, anxiously. Romain Varnadoe sat at a small wooden table with only one additional chair. One man stood guard at each of the doors while two stood near the table. One held a small foreign machine pistol conspicuously at the ready. No one moved when the door opened and Mme Laconier stepped into the warehouse flanked by two men carrying pistols.

"Watch what you say, blood man. Your life is mine," one of the men whispered hoarsely.

Mme Laconier sat across from the trembling Sang Neuf and folded her hands on the table.

"You have something important to tell me, I understand."

The softness in her voice filled Romain Varnadoe with more fear than the man with the pistol.

"Oui, Guardienne."

Romain stared down at the table, unable to look Mme Laconier in her eyes.

"Speak freely. If you tell me the truth, you have nothing to fear from these men."

You will certainly kill me when I tell you.

"Le Sang Neuf plans to steal the Madonna when it is uncovered."

"I am not surprised by this. Certainly you would not risk meeting with me for such news?"

"No, Guardienne. There is more. One of Les Boucliers has joined them, and has betrayed his brothers."

Mme Laconier sharpened her stare.

"And who would this be?"

Romain Varnadoe began to shake, unable to control the trembling in his hands.

"Speak, snake!" one of the guards demanded.

Varnadoe folded his hands in prayer.

"Please, Guardienne, do not kill me, I beg of you. I speak the truth."

Mme Laconier sat back for a moment, assessing the fear spewing from this man.

"You must tell me his name. Please, do not be afraid."

He looked up for the first time, tears streaming down his face.

"Verbon, Guardienne. Portier Verbon."

"Liar!" screamed the guard, and pulled his pistol from his waistband.

"Stop!"

Mme Laconier looked fiercely at the guard who took a sharp breath and returned the pistol to his waistband.

"There is more, Guardienne."

"Go on, monsieur," she spoke softly again.

"They will block the security van from entering the highway along the frontage road leading from the cemetery. They will kill the driver, and make it look like Verbon was the killer. Then they will kill him with the guard's weapon."

"And what of the Madonna?"

Mme Laconier remained stoically calm despite the revelation Portier Verbon had betrayed their sacred trust.

"They will pass it to another vehicle across the highway, to another transfer point, then to a boat in the harbor. From there, to Belle Isle."

"The Citadel," Mme Laconier spoke quietly. "Yes, and the circle is complete. You have heard these plans in person?"

"Yes, Guardienne."

"You are a part of the operation?"

"Yes, Guardienne."

"How will they breach the security van?"

"They have a man infiltrated into the security company, Guardienne. And the cemetery - the man who operates the backhoe."

"I see. And why does Portier join with Le Sang Neuf?"

"He says you are weak, and you will let the writer give the Madonna to the Church. He says you have betrayed your vow to God."

"Why would he try to work with Le Sang Neuf if they plan to kill him?"

"He told Perryn de L'Etanche he needed men to pull this off, and he would share the spoils."

"Spoils? What do you mean?"

"He promised de L'Etanche a free hand in Lorient and Saint-Nazaire with the aide of Les Boucliers and the Madonna. He says Bretagne will flow red with the blood of the French oppressors."

"A civil war. Yes, we have feared this."

"And de L'Etanche. Why does he want to kill Portier instead?"

"He said he has no need for such an idealistic fool."

"And his plans for the relic, monsieur?"

"To strengthen the grip Le Sang Neuf has over the ports, Guardienne. He says carrying the Madonna before him will make him the most powerful man in Bretagne."

"Yes, I see. Any why do you risk your life to tell me this?"

It was the question he feared the most.

"My soul. Guardienne. I fear for my soul. In my confession I was told to seek forgiveness by denouncing my sins. If Le Sang Neuf succeeds in stealing the Madonna, I will be forever bound by the excommunication. I will burn in Hell for eternity, Guardienne. As will my children."

The excommunication. Is this man telling the truth? Is his fear of eternal damnation so great? And the confession - will the priest break his vow and speak of this to the monsignor?

"Let me kill this dog now, Guardienne. He lies to implicate Portier, to set us up in a trap."

Mme Laconier closed her eyes for a moment, then reached forward and took Romaine's hands in hers.

"God has touched your heart, Romaine Varnadoe. I believe you are telling the truth. You must leave this place while there is still time, with your family. My men will not harm you, but I cannot protect you from Le Sang Neuf if you remain."

"Yes, Guardienne."

"Go into the mountains. Tell no one, not even a priest. I will pray for you, to receive God's forgiveness. Go, and live your life in God's grace."

One of the guards at the door stepped forward and motioned Varnadoe to stand.

"Take him home. Gather his family and a few possessions and see he is taken to safety."

"Where to, Guardienne?"

"Le Chambon. Take him to the presbytery. Tell them La Guardienne seeks their sanctuary one more time."

I parked the car and waited on the street corner for Monique, anxious for the morning to play out.

"Bonjour, M.Larry! An exciting day!"

"Yes, let us hope."

We walked together the few blocks to the cemetery where a crowd had begun to gather - mostly reporters and a few tourists. In the back corner sat a large backhoe, its giant claw waiting like a prehistoric scorpion to scour the earth.

"Ah, M. Hewitt. A fine morning," Father Bioche smiled. "I am so happy to finally see an end to our mystery. There certainly is a lot of interest."

"Yes, Father. I want to thank the Church for their assistance in expediting this unusual request."

"We all seek the truth, monsieur."

The Church had filed for an official decree of ownership over the artifact, stating in its brief that since it had resided on church property for well over fifty years there could be no challenge to its ownership. In an unusual move, the court instead appointed an arbitrator to take possession of "any artifacts buried with or near the remains approved for exhumation." The Archbishop at Rennes privately flew into a tirade against the French court, but in the end was forced to issue a press release far more conciliatory.

I smelled Roland Soullant's influence wafting over this new development.

A private security company van was parked a few meters from the grave, and the arbitrator overseeing the exhumation stood in a small group that included the mayor of Pornic, Inspector Mahieu, and the district coroner.

"Like so many vultures … ," Monique whispered as we approached the grave.

At precisely nine o'clock the backhoe roared to life as several policemen stepped in to move the curious reporters and onlookers back a safe distance.

"You look quite composed M. Larry. I figured you would be bristling with excitement at this moment."

"Something doesn't feel right, Monique. I can't quite put my finger on it."

Portier Verbon turned onto Route Bleue about five kilometers from the rendezvous point. As his car accelerated to speed he heard a small "pop" and felt the steering wheel begin to shudder uncontrollably.

"Damn! Flat tire," and he pulled over to the side of the road. He exited the driver's side and walked around to the shoulder to examine the tire. Before he could walk back to the trunk to retrieve a spare, another car pulled up alongside.

"Just a flat," he called out, and gestured for the driver to continue on. Instead, two men exited from the back seat. One pointed a pistol directly at him as he quickly stepped forward.

"You will come with us. Now!"

"Where is Verbon? He is not here!"

Le Sang Neuf used short-range walkie-talkies instead of cell phones to ensure privacy.

"Neither is Varnadoe!"

"What about the dig?"

"The backhoe has started ... ," The voice became lost in background noise of the giant machine.

"Is the van in place?"

Nothing but static.

A man monitoring the radio traffic placed a call from a public phone in the commune's central square.

"Two men are missing - Verbon and Varnadoe ... yes, the digging has started."

Perryn de L'Etanche slammed down the telephone receiver and spit on the table in disgust.

"Verbon has set us up. Warn the driver. Order him to drive directly to the boat. And that Varnadoe. Kill him. And his family. No one betrays Le Sang Neuf."

"What about Verbon?"

"I will deal with Portier Verbon myself."

The shutters on over a dozen news service cameras clicked furiously as the backhoe clawed the hard ground. A television crew from Saint-Nazaire tried to keep people from interfering with their news reporter who kept a running commentary. As we slipped around behind the tractor to get a better view, Monique saw Millard Gayman of Le Communiqué.

"Bonjour, Millard," she smiled and slipped her arm in his.

"Bonjour, Monique. An exciting day today, *n'est il pas?*"

"Yes, it is. I must say, I was caught completely by surprise by all this talk of the church relic."

"Yes, it seems your great-uncle was an unwitting player in a much bigger drama. This will make a great story."

"Yes, so it seems."

So I hope.

I left Monique to her reporter friend and walked back to Father Bioche who nervously watched from the edge of the safety tape.

"We will soon have an answer to all your hard work."

"I hope so, Father. I would like to be there when the casket is raised."

"Yes, of course. As soon as the excavator finishes I will take you to the grave."

As we stood waiting, I noticed two men in uniform approaching the safety tape.

"Who are those men, Father?"

"They are from the security company the church has hired to safeguard the artifact, monsieur. They will join us at the grave site, and transport the relic to the office of the arbitrator at Rennes."

I studied the men carefully. Perfectly pressed and starched uniforms. Not the norm for such a low-paying job. One of the men held a clipboard with what appeared to be a work order attached. As he shifted his stance, talking briefly to his partner, I saw the telltale symbol tattooed on the skin between his thumb and forefinger. I had seen this before - a small red rose.

The small fishing boat sat tied on the inside of the commercial dock just below the General de Gaul Bridge, its engine running. The captain and its mate sat below decks. It would be at least a half-hour before their special cargo arrived - plenty of time for a cup of coffee.

Through the small cabin windows they could see the superstructure of a large barge slowly pass on the outside of the dock. To their surprise it slowed and stopped, pushed by a large tug.

The captain left the cabin and stepped on deck to see the barge blocking the entrance to the channel.

"Hey, you cannot tie up there! I have a cargo to move. You there! Make an opening!"

The pilot of the tug flipped the captain an obscene gesture and disappeared below decks, leaving the barge blocking the fishing boat from entering the waterway.

The backhoe pulled away from the trench to let a worker with a shovel clean up the edges of the trench and check the depth. After a few minutes digging he stood up and shrugged his shoulders.

"Father, what is going on?"

"I am not certain. They should have reached the coffin by now."

The worker exited the grave and the backhoe carefully scraped out the tailings left behind and took another bite of the dark earth. Then another. And another.

The worker excitedly climbed up onto the backhoe and talked to the operator, then jumped back into the trench. He dug a hole straight down into the center of the trench. About a half-meter later he again climbed out, and gave a signal to the operator.

Once again the giant monster clawed at the earth, deeper now, grabbing the last two meters of earth before pulling back and shutting down. Excitement buzzed through the crowd of reporters as the worker beckoned Father Bioche to step into the taped off area.

"Monsieur, please come with me." His voice echoed with concern.

The worker quietly spoke to the father in tones no one else could hear. I watched, knowing now what he was saying despite being unable to hear their conversation. Father Bioche turned and looked at me, his face twisted with exasperation.

"The grave is empty, monsieur."

"Empty? Perhaps just not deep enough?"

"No. They can tell from the soil. This ground has never been dug before. There is no casket. There is no body."

I looked up to find Monique, standing on the other side of the tape with Millard Gayman, and slowly shook my head. She immediately grasped my meaning and turned, dragging the newsman with her as frantic cries from the reporters began ringing out.

I just stood, oblivious to the reporters' questions, and stared at the empty hole.

The radio crackled with frantic voices and static.

"The grave - it is empty! Repeat - the grave is empty! What do we do?"

"This is Team A - we are surrounded by police!"

"Team B - it's a trap ... ," then some noise in the background, " ... no, don't shoot ... ." Nothing but static.

Perryn de L'Etanche spit on the floor when he heard the news and screamed at his radio operator.

"Tell the van to get the hell out of there, fast. It is a trap! Move!"

He grabbed his pistol and stuck it quickly in his waistband, grabbed any incriminating papers from the table, and moved quickly to the back entrance of the warehouse. His men beat him through the door when a voice cried out over a loudspeaker.

"Stay where you are. Drop your weapons and stay where you are."

Shots rang out as frantic voices cried in alarm. One of the men fell in a volley of gunfire, the other threw himself on the ground. The gunfire continued.

Perryn de L'Etanche slammed the door behind him and ran quickly to the side door. He opened it slowly and quickly looked outside. The parking lot was a barricade of police cars, lights flashing. Special weapons police in defensive positions trained their heavy automatic weapons on the door waiting for a command.

He slammed the door shut, backed up inside the warehouse, and tried to decide what to do.

"Perryn de L'Etanche. We have the building surrounded. You cannot escape. Exit the building with your hands up. You have exactly thirty-seconds to comply."

The voice on the bull horn went oddly quiet.

"Shit," was all Perryn de L'Etanche could mutter. He felt for the gun in his waistband.

If I get off a shot, in the confusion I may be able to get to cover.

"*D'accord.* OK, OK. I am coming out! Do not shoot. I am not armed."

He opened the door slowly and looked around.

"Your hands in the air, de L'Etanche. Now!"

He walked, feigning confusion, slightly to the left in the direction of a group of metal shipping containers.

If I can reach the backside of these containers, I might slip away. Just a few more meters.

He faced the police cars, hands halfway extended, ready to grab his pistol when the moment was right. A lone policeman stepped toward him, pistol at the ready.

"Do not move. You are under arrest."

Something about the policeman was not right. De L'Etanche looked at his face, then at the hand holding the pistol. He could see a small tattoo.

"You are not the police!" He frantically grabbed for the pistol hidden in his waistband.

Three shots rang out, and Perryn de L'Etanche staggered back against the containers. In disbelief he stared, confused and in shock, as the policeman stepped to within an arms length, placed his pistol to de L'Etanche's forehead, and fired.

The tug fired its engines and the giant barge slowly eased back down the causeway.

"It's about damn time," the captain shouted. He looked at his watch. His special cargo was due any minute. "Prepare to make way," he called out, and entered the wheelhouse.

The mate began to clear the dock lines. He watched as the opening to the channel slowly cleared. He could make out the superstructure of a boat on the outboard side of the barge waiting to enter the harbor - probably why they are moving that damn barge - and looked down to secure the aft mooring line in the dry well. As he looked back up, the barge cleared the opening, and he stared at the police boat as it powered full steam into the harbor.

"Fishing boat *Chérie*. Remain fast and prepare to be boarded."

The voice echoed from the loudspeaker through the warehouses on shore as the captain emerged back on deck. Police stormed the docks from the shore.

"Shit."

CHAPTER 27

THE MADONNA ROSA

The Rose is without an explanation;
She blooms, because She blooms.
- Angelus Silesius

The chaos at the cemetery following the backhoe debacle gave me the chance to quietly slip away without having to face the ire of the reporters. I cut through a small opening in the hedgerow fence and walked quickly to the far side toward the gate to the Pornic War Cemetery. It was the quietest place I could think of, and I wanted to be as far away from the commotion I had caused as possible.

I closed the gate behind me and walked slowly among the graves, thinking, wondering.

"George, where are you?"

How could everything have gone so wrong? The body wrongfully buried in the same time frame, the exhumation and reburial, the attempts to scare me away - they all pointed to the pauper's grave. But an empty grave? I had felt something was wrong, but I at least expected to find something there - if not the Madonna, at least George Sherrat.

There was no way to know if he was buried here in the War Cemetery. So I just sat in the freshening light of the late morning, the cooling breeze off the Jade Coast swirling gently through the trees and hedges surrounding this peaceful place. In many cemeteries I had visited in Europe I could feel the soldiers calling to me. But not here.

I so desperately wanted to believe George Sherrat was here, peacefully sleeping in one of the many unidentified graves. I closed my eyes and let my senses reach out to the soldiers around me - one last try to reach into the perfect void. Despite the pain, the horror, and the agony forever transfixed in the essence of the Jade Coast, here all was quiet. The souls rested peacefully.

The Madonna Rosa was not hidden on this sacred ground. And neither was George Sherrat.

"You've given up?"

Angus couldn't believe what he was hearing. After the cemetery fiasco Monique and I agreed to meet back at Le Café Rose in La Bernerie. It was far enough way from Pornic to avoid the reporters, but familiar, comforting. Roland told me my "nesting habit" would one day come back to haunt me, but today I didn't care. Besides, this was where Monique had to catch her train back to Paris.

"Angus, I know in my heart George is here somewhere, but short of digging up the entire Commonwealth War Cemetery I'm not going to find him. And to be truthful, I don't think he is in the cemetery at all."

The phone was quiet for a few moments.

"What about the relic."

"It's not in the cemetery. I know it's not, but I can't really say why. I can feel it. I can almost taste it, but when I walk into the cemetery, that feeling goes away. It's not there."

"Not exactly your usual dispassionate analysis, my friend."

"No, you're right. I can't tell you why I know. I just know."

"I want a story anyway - maybe you can do a comedy piece on the exhumation you did ... something." His sarcasm oozed from my cell phone.

"I understand. I'll pull something together."

I hung up the phone as Monique walked through the front door of the café and threw her purse down on the table.

"I took care of Millard. I need a glass of wine before I head back, but first ... ."

She looked around, I presumed for the bathroom, then walked over to the kitchen window.

"*Le salle de bain?*"

"Through the kitchen door, in the back, madame."

"Merci," and she disappeared through the kitchen entrance.

That's not right. The man with the newspaper - he came out the door behind me. That was the bathroom. Maybe the woman's room was separate. I dropped the thought just as fast.

Monique asked for a glass of wine when she returned.

"That was disgusting. One shared bathroom. You men should learn to sit when you pee. You certainly know how to pick the finer cafés, M. Larry."

"One bathroom? Are you certain?"

"Yes - a sign with both MEN and WOMEN on it. Should have included a warning from the health department. I am surprised you picked this - you are usually more ... discerning."

She passed me a teasing smile, recalling the arguments I have had with her father at Le Café Reuban Vert over just about everything, including his bathrooms. But something about it bothered me. I rose and walked to the back.

"Where are you going?"

"Just checking."

I pulled on the door knob. The door was unlocked.

"This door. Is this a bathroom?"

The waitress bringing Monique the glass of wine looked up and smiled.

"No, monsieur. The bathroom is in the back, through the kitchen. That is a door to the back alley, and, of course, the prayer room."

She turned and headed back to the kitchen. I pulled the door - it opened to a short hallway. Midway down the hallway was a door with a sign that read *Salle de Prière* - Prayer Room in English. The hall extended a few meters further. When I opened it I was standing in the alley that looked out on the promenade.

"What was that all about?"

"Monique, the man with the newspaper ... he came out that door. I just figured it was the bathroom, but it's not. It is a back entrance that opens onto the promenade. There is a prayer room of some sort off of the hallway."

"Ah, oui. A prayer room - Reformists, mostly. Such things are common, especially in the city."

That nagging knot in my stomach returned. I looked at Monique who was busy arranging her taxi to the train station.

"Le Café Rose ... oui," she answered, and hung up.

"You're taking a taxi? We could walk there faster than waiting for a taxi."

"You could walk there. I am going to enjoy my wine."

She smiled at my kidding. I was going to miss her, but she had to get back for the start of classes. We had reached a dead end anyway, and I knew I could only stretch the expense account so far without a compelling story. We enjoyed a few minutes of quiet, the aroma of the wine soothing.

"Oh, there's my taxi. Please let me know how things go. I had so much fun!"

I couldn't help a slight laugh. I had a feeling she was going to be a good investigative partner. I walked with her outside and after a quick hug, she was off. I was left alone standing on the sidewalk. With a sigh of resignation, I turned and looked back at the café.

Why had I stopped at this little café in the first place, the one with the dirty shared bathroom? This was not the only café in the center of the commune.

Le Café Rose. The man with the newspaper - he came out of the door that leads to the promenade. He left the message written in the newspaper to try and frighten me away. What had I written in my notes that day? ... "I am close, maybe too close."

I couldn't stop staring at the name on the side on the building with the shared bathroom.

Le Café Rose

Could it be that simple?

I dashed back to my table and frantically scrolled down my list of emails. How many days ago? No - too far ... Scroll back up. Yes.

I was looking for Monique's email that carried the news story about Vincent Dupris.

The date. What was the date?

"Here it is. April 6, 1952."

I sat back and stared at my computer screen, not really focusing on anything. Three months. Three months difference.

There had to be a record. I'd been looking in the wrong place!

I left the café and walked briskly through the street to the center of the commune and police headquarters.

"Oui, monsieur."

"I would like to speak to the coroner."

"Coroner?" The clerk looked at me, unsure of what I was asking.

"Uh ... *les causes d'un décès*," I tried to explain in very poor French.

"*Un moment, monsieur.*"

She disappeared through a door in the back and when she returned my good friend Inspector Mahieu was close upon her heels.

"Oh, it is you again. You haven't caused enough trouble here for one day? What have you done now?"

"Inspector, I am sorry for the confusion. My French is not very good."

"So I have noticed."

"I want to speak to the coroner, Inspector."

"The coroner? For what purpose?"

"A simple request, Inspector. I am looking for a record."

"Of what, monsieur?"

"A body."

He looked at me over his glasses.

"Maybe the one you lost in the cemetery this morning? I swear, monsieur, someone sent you here just to antagonize me. First the car bomb ... ,"

"Uh, you blew up my car, Inspector."

He ignored me.

"Then all this talk of an exhumation. The empty grave. Now this? Why do you hate our small commune so much, monsieur?"

"The coroner's office?"

He sighed, and resigned himself to my insistence.

"Follow me, if you must."

We walked through the back and down a short hallway. Through a rippled-glass door without a sign we entered a small work area with two large chest-type refrigerator doors. A young clerk was working at the computer.

"Is Monsieur DeLange back from Pornic?"

"No, Inspector, not at the moment."

"I see. This is M. Hewitt. He wishes to ask you about a record in your files. Please see to his request."

With that, Inspector Mahieu abruptly turned and left through the door with the rippled-glass.

"Oui, monsieur. How can I assist you?"

"Madame, I am seeking a record from 1952. Do your records go back that far?"

"Oui, monsieur. Do you have a name of the deceased?"

"Sherrat. George Sherrat. But I doubt the body would have been recorded under his name. It would be unidentified."

"Without a name ... perhaps a date of death?"

"The body would have arrived here sometime around the first week of April 1952. If my hunch is correct, it would have remained here for a while - as long as three months, perhaps."

"That would have been unusual, monsieur. Let me see ... ," and she began to type into the computer records.

"Ah, oui. This may be what you are looking for. An unidentified body was received from St. Giles church in Pornic on April 25, following an exhumation at the public cemetery, according to the records."

"And does it say what happened to the body?"

"Let me see ... it was released to ... the Commune of La Bernerie, monsieur, by court order."

"And the date?"

"17 June 1952, monsieur."

I retraced my steps back to the café and around behind to the promenade. I stood at the top of the steps and gazed again at the memorial on the seawall.

Dedicated 17 June 1952

Weeks of fruitless searching, disappointments, and frustration evaporated. The gentle lapping of the waves on the beach lulled me into that quiet, that perfect understanding.

Two children chasing each other across the beach dashed up the stairs and nearly ran into me as I stared, contemplating the sea, the memorial, and the understanding that filled me with awe.

In the four corners of the memorial plaque, cast in bronze, were tiny reliefs. Roses.

I was standing in front of George Sherrat's grave, the memorial to the dead of the *Lancastria*. In a quiet ceremony few today would have been around to witness, the tiny commune of La Bernerie set the exhumed body of George Sherrat forever in a place of honor and respect.

I blinked back tears as I spoke, barely whispering.

"Hey, George. It's been quite a journey. We found Scotty, you know. I am sure he will be joining you soon."

I turned to leave and stopped in my tracks. I hadn't noticed before, but now it all made perfect sense.

The sign above the door to the back of the café - another entrance to the prayer room - was decorated with small painted red roses.

Standing on the sea walk I telephoned the number on the small card Anisette gave to me.

"I wish to speak to Mme Laconier."

"I am not familiar with that name, monsieur."

"Please tell her Larry Hewitt wishes to speak to her."

I left my cell phone number, although I guessed Les Boucliers already had it.

I met Anisette back at Le 16. Darcell agreed to host our private meeting at the café and, despite his objections, he left us alone. I had to promise him I would pay for the wine when he returned.

"Thank you for all you have tried to do, M. Hewitt. I was so hoping this would finally put the disappearance of the Madonna to an end. You appeared so certain it was buried in the pauper's grave."

"That's what I believed, although I must admit I began to have my doubts. And to be frank it might have been."

I emptied the glass of cognac and set it back on the table.

"We all act in predictable ways, madame, despite our best efforts to disguise our actions. This is a truth I always seem to fall back upon when I get lost.

"You see, disposing of a body is no small feat - even in time of war. It kept buzzing around in my head - why didn't anyone know where this artifact was buried? It's the little things that matter in an investigation, like when I found Leone Langille, who as a boy discovered George's body. One of the boys playing cards, the boy who introduced me to Leone, was what we call a 'shark.' He cheats, as one of his friends warned me. When I remembered that everything became very clear.

"Someone wanted the Madonna Rosa hidden, and used the very public controversy of Vincent Dupris' wrongful burying as a diversion. People were watching this little drama play out while in the meantime George's body and the Madonna were conveniently slipped away and reinterred.

"The problem was, there were no records of a reburial. That's because we simply were looking in the wrong place. We should have been looking up someone's sleeve for the ace of spades."

Anisette looked at me with an uncertain look.

"Do all you Americans talk in such circles?"

I laughed.

"That's what Monique asks me all the time. It's a card game feint - I make you look one way while I play the ace from my sleeve. In this case, George was reburied - quite openly and legally, so as not to draw attention, but just not in a cemetery."

"Where then? Did you find him?"

"Yes. In a monument to the unknown soldiers who died along the Brittany coastline. No name, no records. A crypt above ground, all official and legal. It would have been so simple to just place the figurine in the crypt at the critical time - a place no one would ever expect."

Anisette cocked her head, as if anticipating something.

"But that is not what happened."

Anisette looked at me, a slight exasperation finally showing through her usual calm and composed expression.

I lifted Sid's old battered briefcase from the floor and placed it on the table.

"They hid it in the prayer room - behind a plaster wall. Everyone who participated in the hiding has either passed or moved away. It was the perfect hiding place - one that no one remembered."

She slowly reached out, almost afraid to touch the briefcase.

"Is it really here?"

Her voice choked with emotion, her words forced through the pain of her life, the disappointments, the patience of waiting all these years.

"It is beautiful."

I only had to smile for her tears to begin flowing.

"I am ashamed to admit I had lost hope many times along this journey. I prayed for strength - begged for it at times. If not for the return of the Madonna, then at least a sign. My own lack of faith, my own weakness, was a test by God. At my own moment of crisis, facing my own death at the hands of my jailers, I resolved to believe in my fate. I resolved to wait in God's shadow until He chose to send a messenger."

As she caught her breath I swallowed, and gave an embarrassed laugh.

"I can assure you, madame, I am not God's messenger. Just a determined writer. One that could see the plaster had been redone in one small spot on the wall. I had to beg the café owner's forgiveness for busting it open."

Anisette laughed, that twinkle returning in her eyes that so captivated Scotty and Sid, that kept the forces of chaos at bay for so many years.

"What now, Anisette? What of Les Boucliers and the defection of this man Portier?"

"How can I fault him for losing faith? He is young, impatient. Things could have turned out much worse. We must rebuild his trust, but spring flows eternal after a cold winter. I am thankful we have an opportunity to help my grandson restore his faith."

"Your grandson?"

I simply shook my head as she smiled, almost shyly. What other secrets of the Madonna Rosa story lay hidden away, never to be known?

Anisette finally reached out and touched the clasp on the briefcase, the strength of her years of trial returning.

"The Madonna will be in protection again, waiting for God's plan to continue to unfold. We are just links in a chain of faith, forged to connect the past and the future when the purpose of the Madonna is revealed."

"And that purpose will be?"

"It will be decided by God, my dear friend. Not by man. It will lead no armies to victory, as so many have wished. It will give no man power over his brothers. That is the biggest secret of the Madonna. But it will surface one day. The destiny of the rose is to bloom in the sun."

To bloom in the sun, after so many years. I smiled.

"And what now, for you?"

"My time as La Guardienne is coming to a close. The mantle passes to my granddaughter very soon, and I can join God with a joyful heart ... at a much later date, of course."

She smiled and rose from the table, the briefcase in her grasp at last. She stopped for a moment at the doorway and smiled, then disappeared into the streets of Saint-Nazaire.

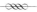

A SINGLE RED ROSE

*Mystery glows in the rose bed and the
secret is hidden in the rose.
- Farid ud-din Attar*

I opened the Sunday Guardian and read the first of a series of features entitled "The Madonna Rosa." The series spread like wildfire throughout the French newspapers and online in the weeks that followed. I recreated the history of the relic, the trials of the faithful, and wove an intriguing story of the woman known now to the world as Anisette Durande.

As for the artifact, I wrote that it remained lost. Perhaps it was still in Pornic, perhaps in the War Cemetery. Perhaps it was lost to the sea. It would be for someone else at some future time to discover.

The blogs and conspiracy theorists insisted it was all a giant scam to sell newspapers. There was no relic. There was no body. Just a lot of lies.

Once more my email was filled with wild claims. I was the instrument of Satan, defying and slandering the Church. I was in league with the Church to suppress the truth - that I had secretly found the Madonna, and it was hidden away in the abbey at Rennes. Still yet, I had found the relic and sold it on eBay. For a while I became the hated villain from America, and had to carefully watch who I talked with and where I took my morning coffee.

My book sales exploded. And Angus McDonough was once again my best friend.

"I need more, anything more. You said you had the rest of Sid's files? Keep working on them, my friend. And pumping out the copy. This is a goldmine!"

Monique sent me an email. She was contacted by her friend in London, Mrs. Latham. A beautiful older woman had visited Scotty at his convalescent hospital. She told Monique the two of them held hands and cried together. When she left, she gave Scotty a kiss.

Scotty passed away peacefully in his sleep shortly thereafter. At the mystery woman's request, the family agreed to have a single red rose tattooed on his right hand, between the thumb and forefinger, just before he was laid to rest.

I had one last task before I could continue working on Sid's papers. Angus warned me I had to face the "snarling wolves" as he like to call them and pay my dues.

"Tell us, Mr. Hewitt. You have made a claim this Madonna was an ancient symbol of Breton independence. There is nothing on the Internet, except news of your fiasco in Pornic. When we asked in Redon no one could tell us anything about it."

As I looked up and tried to craft a plausible reply I caught sight of a beautiful young woman, her tawny hair long and held in a single braid, walking quietly through the crowd of reporters. I caught her out of the corner of my eye as she appeared briefly, hidden by the crowd, then reappeared again, if only momentarily.

A pushy reporter in the front interrupted my distraction.

"You claimed you had evidence the artifact was buried in the unmarked grave. Yet it was not. What evidence did you have and when will you make that evidence available to the press to inspect?"

Before I could answer, the vision of the young woman appeared again, to my right, for the briefest of moments.

"I'm sorry. Your question again ... ?"

"The evidence! When will you make the evidence available? And what about this secret society?"

I looked down for a moment at my notes, trying to decide what to say. When I looked up again, the woman was standing quietly at the podium. She smiled, a softness in her eyes I had seen before, a gentleness in her movements that belied a subtle strength. She held in her hand a small glass vase with a single red rose. She placed it on the podium, turned, and slipped back through the crowd of reporters.

I tried to follow her with my eyes, the din from the anxious questions rising louder, clouding my thoughts. The insistent reporters asked again and again, but I could not hear them through the void. At the back door she stopped, turned, and smiled again. With a slight nod of her head, she passed through the door and was gone.

With the chaos rising around me, I picked up the rose, breathed in its mystery, and closed my eyes ... .

"No, ladies and gentlemen. There is no evidence. I simply misread what I had gathered, and misunderstood. I allowed myself to be seduced by the mystery surrounding the Madonna Rosa - as have so many in the past."

One reporter in the front angrily confronted me.

"How can you, as a historian, justify the claims you made? What does this do to your credibility?"

I refocused my thoughts and stood my ground.

"I am not a historian. I write features and fiction. I never claimed to have evidence, only questions. The Madonna Rosa was lost in 1940 during the British evacuation from Brittany - that I know. The body of George Sherrat was intentionally buried in Vincent Dupris' grave to hide him from the SS - this I also know. The people of La Bernerie took his unclaimed body and reinterred him in a memorial as a show of honor and respect for all those who died aboard the *Lancastria* that terrible day, and like many 'Unknown Soldier' memorials chose to keep his identity a secret.

"But we did not find the Madonna Rosa. Neither did we find this secret organization so many of you have written about - without evidence, I might add."

Someone from the crowd shouted, "Do you think it is lost for good?"

The crowded room quieted for a brief moment.

"Someone told me once the Madonna Rosa was not missing, only lost to the eyes of men. God knows where it lies. That has to be good enough."

The crowd groaned, and I heard a voice off to the side caustically exclaim, "What a croc!"

I turned and began to leave the podium and the cameras behind. A young woman reporter up front called out one last question.

"Will it ever surface again?"

I stepped over to her, took her hands, and remembered the words Anisette told me as she said goodbye.

"The destiny of the rose is to bloom in the sun."

A SPECIAL THANK YOU ,

A young boy from the East African country of Eritrea joined our large multi-cultural family in September, 2014. Almost immediately he was diagnosed with a rare form of bone cancer. A few days before Thanksgiving he and I moved to Seattle leaving the big house, the dogs, our four other foster boys, and my beautiful bride behind.

We lived for the next seven and a half months at Ronald McDonald House (RMC) next to Seattle Children's Hospital (SCH). That is where *The Madonna Rosa* was conceived, written, and published - all from the kitchen table at RMC and the cafeteria at Children's - in between clinic visits, chemotherapy sessions, major surgery, the hospital school, sleepless nights, pain, and stress - and ultimately a triumph over the cancer.

We had the best doctors, surgeons, nurses, and aides that we could have hoped for at Children's Hospital. Their tireless devotion to their patients' care, their humor and compassion, did as much to help this child survive as did the cancer treatments.

I want to thank the friends I made at RMC and SCH among the parents, children, and staff. I have struggled trying to write the essence of that experience - perhaps one day I will be able to sort it all out.

We lived in an odd bubble isolated from those around us, unable to freely embrace family and friends, but knowing all along what we were doing was necessary and vital for this child's survival.

I published *The Madonna Rosa* the day we moved home to "Mom's house."

Life is sweet. Thank you everyone.

L.W. Hewitt

NOTES AND EXPLANATIONS

The Persecutions of Lyon

The backstory of *The Madonna Rosa* is based on the accounts of the persecution of Christians at Lyon in 177 A.D. The events as described in the text are taken from generally available history and should not be considered suitable for citation. The story of the Reformist sect of Christians that carried the Madonna into Brittany and the subsequent events are fiction.

The rose has long symbolized the Virgin Mary and her relationship with Jesus in Christian writings. As with many religious beliefs, there are numerous variations that make the Madonna Rosa plausible.

The Madonna Rosa

The Madonna Rosa as a religious artifact is fiction. I have tried to reconcile the differences in capitalization rules for the term "Madonna" by using "Madonna Rosa" as a proper noun; "Madonna" when substituting a single word for the proper noun; and "madonna' when using it as a single entity reference, as in "A madonna. A very valuable one." In some cases I deliberately used lower case to indicate the character was unaware of the significance of the relic.

Conflicts were inevitable. In such cases I generally opted for capitalization out of respect for religious tradition and keeping with the Chicago Manual of Style where a word is substituted for a proper name.

The Church

Capitalization of the word "church" follows generally accepted guidelines. When referring to the universal Church, the word is capitalized. The name "Catholic Church" is a single term and always capitalized. This also can make some interesting inferences while reading the story. The opinions expressed by characters in the story are simply that. The role of any religious organizations and individuals in the story are purely fictional.

The Citadel

The Citadel on Belle Island was built beginning in 1549 as a naval base to provide protection for ships from pirates. It served as a POW camp during WWI for German soldiers, and a site for artillery and radar in WWII when occupied by the Germans. The story of the prison compound is fiction.

Military Officer Ranks

In narration I generally follow the National Geographic Style Manual for displaying military ranks - with one exception. When introducing a character I generally use a slightly different form to ensure the name and rank are explicitly clear. This differs from the style manual and standard military usage but is adopted for reader clarity purposes. Use of ranks in dialogue are less formalized.

Ranks in the German officer corps and the SS often were conflicting and overlapping. For clarity, I use the Wehrmacht forms of Oberst for Colonel and Hauptmann for Captain, although these were generally not used for SS officers. You will see the phrases "Herr General, Herr Oberst, and Herr Hauptmann" used repeatedly in the dialogue. These were acceptable norms for addressing army officers without using their surnames. However, this less-formal form was forbidden by Himmler in the SS. The acceptable address was Kamerad. However, some readers may confuse this with the Hollywood portrayal of the Russian Army's version, so I use the German army designation in the book.

Use of Dialect

The speech patterns of the working class in various countries use a more standardized form of dialect to represent certain people in the story, and use it sparingly at that. Dialogue that would normally be in a different language is written in more formal English.

REFERENCES

1) Gignac, J. (1907). Anathema. In The Catholic Encyclopedia. New York: Robert Appleton Company. Retrieved May 7, 2015 from New Advent: http://www.newadvent.org/cathen/01455e.htm

2) Forces War Records. (2015). Name Search. Retrieved from https://www.forces-war-records.co.uk

3) Chmelda-Bericht, p. 18, NID-14615; "Der Druck auf die französische Währung," Bank-Archiv, 1942, pp. 484-85; Rass, "Menschenmaterial," p. 240.

4) Eisenhower, Dwight D. (1948). Crusade in Europe. New York: Doubleday. p. 179

5) I Was There! - We Swam in Oil When 'Lancastria' Sank. (August, 1940). The War Illustrated, Volume 3, No. 49, Page 136. Retrieved from http://www.thewarillustrated.info/49/i-was-there-we-swam-in-oil-when-lancastria-sank.asp

6) The Reports of My Death are Greatly Exaggerated. (n.d.). The American Heritage® New Dictionary of Cultural Literacy, Third Edition. Retrieved May 08, 2015, from Dictionary.com website: http://dictionary.reference.com/browse/the reports of my death are greatly exaggerated

7) WW2 Remembrance 1939-1945. (n.d.). Sherwood Foresters. Retrieved from http://ww2remembrance.blogspot.com/2010/07/5112680-pte-victor-dunne-15th-bn.html

THE JUNO LETTERS SERIES

L.W. HEWITT

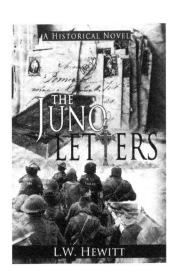

The Juno Letters reveals a web of intrigue, love, tragedy, and heroism that reminds us how the two devastating world wars that defined the Twentieth Century changed the lives of its children, and their children's children, forever.

For a complete listing of the books in the series, and links to purchase ebook, print, and audio editions, please visit oaktreemanor.us

Feel free to contact me at hewitt2961@icloud.com

About the Author

I have coffee most every morning at my "office" - a small table in a 1920s style restaurant and hotel called the Olympic Club in Centralia, Washington. Visitors assume I work there, some think I am the manager. I direct people to the bathrooms - the urinals in this place are a tourist attraction all by themselves. This is where I write. The chaos and atmosphere prep me for the day, and everyone in town knows if you need to talk to me, just drop by the "Oly Club."

Most don't know I have a master's degree in business, and operated my own technology company for over twenty-five of my last forty working years. I won a national championship on horseback, raced sailboats, wrestled octopus, baby-sat a killer whale, and once was a cook on a salmon purse seiner.

I have led an interesting life - married forty-plus years, have three children, nine grandchildren, and over thirty foster children, some with families of their own. I am now free to pursue my passion for writing - especially about the two great wars of the twentieth century.

So I cherish my role as author-in-residence, or that crazy guy at the table by the urinals - it depends on your perspective.

Made in the USA
Columbia, SC
30 May 2021